THE PLA
&
THE YELLOW LADY

THE PLAYBOY & THE YELLOW LADY

JAMES CARNEY

POOLBEG

A Paperback Original
First published 1986 by
Poolbeg Press Ltd.,
Knocksedan House,
Swords, Co. Dublin, Ireland

© James Carney 1986
ISBN 0 905169 82 4

All rights reserved. No part of this publication may be
reproduced or transmitted in any form or by any means,
electronic or mechanical, including photocopy, recording,
or any information storage or retrieval system, without
permission in writing from the publisher. The book is sold
subject to the condition that it shall not, by way of trade
or otherwise, be lent, re-sold or otherwise circulated
without the publisher's prior consent in any form of binding
or cover other than that in which it is published and
without a similar condition including this condition being
imposed on the subsequent purchaser.

This book is set in 11/12 Plantin

Cover illustration by John Short
Typeset by Computertype Ltd.,
50 Merrion Square, Dublin 2.
Printed by The Guernsey Press Co. Ltd.,
Vale, Guernsey, Channel Islands.

Contents

		Page
	Foreword	vii
	Dramatis Personae	x
I	Achill and Indianapolis	1
II	Lynchehaun's Early Life Brother Paul's *Narrative*	15
III	Lynchehaun's Career in England Brother Paul's *Narrative*	20
IV	Law and Order	29
V	6 October 1894	47
VI	Mary Gallagher Tom	52
VII	At Tailor Gallagher's House	64
VIII	Arrest and Escape	73
IX	The Troglodyte	82
X	Betrayal and Re-arrest	95
XI	Trial at Castlebar: The Prosecution	104
XII	Trial at Castlebar: The Defence	131
XIII	Imprisonment and Escape	148
XIV	On the Run: Maryborough to Glasgow Brother Paul's *Narrative*	157
XV	On the Run: Glasgow to America Brother Paul's *Narrative*	167
XVI	The Authorities Give Chase	175
XVII	Trial in Indianapolis	187
XVIII	The Playboy: *An Buachaill Báire*	204
XIX	The End	219

Foreword

Some nine years ago the accidental discovery of the manuscript of the strange document that I have called Brother Paul's *Narrative* aroused my interest in James Lynchehaun and Agnes MacDonnell. From the first moment I was 'hooked' and the investigation of Lynchehaun's crime, its causes and its consequences, became to me an absorbing spare-time hobby. My own County Mayo origins were not a disincentive, and the thought will inevitably occur to readers that I am a relative of Brother Paul Carney. Relatives in any close sense we are not, but we are doubtless remote, if not genealogically traceable, kinsmen.

The investigation of the intricate affair led to four, sometimes lengthy, visits to the United States, in particular to the Library of Congress, two or three visits to the British Library, and one visit, as delightful as it was hazardous, to the island of Achill, where I met and spoke profitably with many residents of the Valley.

I fear that I owe a debt of gratitude to more people than I can at the moment recall. First I would mention my sister, Mrs Mary Moynahan, until recent years attached to the British Consulate in New York, and my lawyer cousin, Katherine Griffin of San Francisco. Also helpful were John Cleary, formerly of Ballycroy, Co. Mayo, now Professor of Philosophy at Boston College, Massachusetts, Mr Christopher Lavelle of the staff of *The Mayo News,* Professor *emeritus* Lorna Reynolds of University College, Galway, and my old friend Benedict Kiely.

I am indebted to my uncle by marriage, Dudley Solan of Kiltimagh, who died recently at the age of 95 and who once at Castlebar, if only for a brief instant, met the then aged Lynchehaun. I also owe a debt of gratitude to his sons, my cousins, Sergeant Tony Solan of the Gárda Síochana and Dr Gerry Solan of Castlebar.

Others to whom I owe a debt are or were on the staff of the Dublin Institute for Advanced Studies which I have had the privilege of serving as Senior Professor: Mrs Máire Kinsella, Miss Peggy Walsh, the late Miss Cathleen Sheppard, Mrs West (Máire Breatnach) and Mrs Robert Dunne.

I would mention also Dr Nicholas Williams of University College, Dublin, Brother Angelo Holmes of the Franciscan Monastery, Clara, Co. Offaly, and Miss Christine Heuston, until recently on the staff of the Royal Irish Academy.

I must thank the Professor of Folklore at University College, Dublin, Professor Bo Almquist, for permission to use the renowned archives of his department; I am especially indebted to Mr Daithi Ó hÓgáin of the same department for his helpfulness and courtesy.

Mrs Kathleen Fleming of Dublin, formerly of Erris, Co. Mayo, supplied me with a Lynchehaun ballad and my old school-friend Michael O'Connell took a close interest in the project from the beginning. My friend Patrick McEntee SC and my son Paul Carney SC were good enough to read this work in typescript and make useful suggestions.

Many aspects of the story of James Lynchehaun and Agnes MacDonnell need further elucidation. I would be grateful if any reader who has relevant information, documents, letters or photographs would communicate with me at the Dublin Institute for Advanced Studies, 10 Burlington Road, Dublin 4.

James Carney
17 June 1986

Dramatis Personae

Dramatis Personae

ARTHUR, Sergeant, RIC.

BAKER, Francis E., judge of the US Circuit Court in Indianapolis.

BUSH, Mr, a friend of the MacDonnells.

CALVEY, three boys of the name from Innisbeggil.

CALVEY, Tom, a mason from Ballycroy.

CARNEY, Brother Paul, member of the Third Order Regular of St Francis, teacher, friend and biographer of Lynchehaun.

CARR, James, Constable RIC, Dugort.

CARR, T. P., magistrate and Justice of the Peace.

CARR, Edmund, Constable RIC.

CLEARY, Peggy Gallagher, owner of a shebeen.

CONSIDINE, J., District Inspector RIC, Maryborough.

CONWAY, defence witness at extradition trial, Indianapolis.

COONEY, Judy, defence witness at Castlebar trial, a cousin of Lynchehaun.

CORRIGAN, defence witness at extradition trial, Indianapolis.

COSTELLOE, Constable RIC, Achill Sound.

CROLY, Dr Thomas, Dugort.

CRONIN, Sergeant RIC, Cloonacool, Co. Sligo.

CURRAN, John, son-in-law of Patrick Sweeney.

DAVIES, N. M., County Inspector, RIC, Sligo.

DAVITT, Michael, founder of the Land League, resident at Ballybrack, Co. Dublin.

DEASY, Martin, worker on Agnes MacDonnell's estate.

DONEVAN, Sergeant RIC, Mulranny.

DONNELLY, Maurice, manager of Terre Haute Brewing Company, Indianapolis.

DORIS, Mr, editor of *Mayo News*.

DOWETT, Knight and Co., Agnes MacDonnell's solicitors, 3 Lincoln's Inn-fields, London 9.

DUSTING, Joseph, Sergeant RIC, Dugort.

ELLIOT, Leslie, Major British Army, son of Agnes MacDonnell.

FADIAN, John, carpenter.

FAHY, Matthew, foreman of jury at Castlebar trial.

FAIRBANKS, Charles Warren (1852–1918), Vice-President of US, 1905–9.

FALCONER, Dr, counsel for defence at Castlebar trial.

FALLON, Mary, a spinner.

FITZGERALD, J., Head Constable, RIC, Maryborough.

FITZGERALD, Miss, a nurse.

F. J., Mr, an Irish acquaintance of Lynchehaun in Glasgow.

FOX, Charles, of New York, prosecuting counsel at extradition trial, Indianapolis.

GALLAGHER, James, of Sraheens, married to a cousin of Lynchehaun.

GALLAGHER, John (Johnny), Agnes MacDonnell's herd, son of Matthew Gallagher, farmer.

GALLAGHER, Margaret (Maggie), née Carney, originally of Westport, wife of Michael Gallagher, tailor.

GALLAGHER Tom, Mary, a good-looking young spinster, important witness for the prosecution at the Castlebar trial.

GALLAGHER Tom, Mary, senior, mother of preceding.

GALLAGHER Tom, Pat, aged 27, son of preceding.

GALLAGHER, Matthew, farmer, tenant of Agnes MacDonnell, father of Johnny.

GALLAGHER, Michael, tailor, married to Margaret (Maggie).

GIBSON, Right Hon. Mr Justice, judge at Castlebar trial.

GLYNN, Michael, Constable, RIC, Achill Sound.

GREALIS(H), Bridget, see McNeally.

GREALIS, Peter, a tenant of Agnes MacDonnell.

GREY, Lady Jane, Agnes MacDonnell's favourite mare.

GWYNNE, Constable RIC, barrack orderly, Dugort.

HAMSON, Mr, Mayor of Chicago; although Mayor Hamson's office is referred to in the *Chicago American* of 29 November

1902, enquiries in Chicago show nobody of that name holding the office of Mayor at that time.

HICKEY, a jarvey.

HICKS, Head Constable, RIC.

HANNA, Mark (Marcus Alonzo), Republican Senator for Ohio (†1904).

HARDNETT, Sergeant RIC.

HARRIS, Addison C., counsel for defence at extradition trial, Indianapolis.

HARRISON, F., engineer, and Lucy his wife, of London, relatives or friends of Agnes MacDonnell.

HORNE, A. E., Resident Magistrate.

HUNT, Inspector of Chicago police.

HYDE, Douglas, founder and president of the Gaelic League, later President of Ireland.

JACK, the butcher.

JORDAN, Myles J., solicitor for Lynchehaun.

JORDAN, Dr William, *locum tenens* at Castlebar Jail.

KATE, a mare of Agnes MacDonnell.

KEEGAN, Acting-Sergeant, RIC, Castlebar.

KELLY, Malachi J., solicitor for the Crown.

KILCOYNE, owner of a public house near Achill Sound.

LA FOLLETTE, Jesse, counsel for the prosecution at extradition trial, Indianapolis.

LAVELLE, Anthony, smith.

LINDSAY, Mr, of Castlebar, maker of a model of the Valley House; Lindsay is a possible anglicisation of Lynchehaun.

LOUDEN, J. J., Barrister-at-Law, defence counsel at Castlebar.

LYNCH, Thomas J. (originally doubtless a Lynchehaun), 'a reputable citizen of Indianapolis' and former resident of Achill, an important witness at the extradition trial, Indianapolis.

LYNCHEHAUN, Anthony (Tony), Lynchehaun's servant boy.

LYNCHEHAUN, Bridget, née Cafferky, mother of Lynchehaun.

LYNCHEHAUN, Catherine, née Gallagher, wife of Lynchehaun.

LYNCHEHAUN, James, son of Neal Lynchehaun, grocer, rabbit-catcher, land steward, fish merchant, etc., alias Mr Cooney of New York, Jim Dooley, McElwaine, Thomas Walshe.

LYNCHEHAUN Street, James.

LYNCHEHAUN Patt, Mary, a second-cousin of Lynchehaun.

LYNCHEHAUN, Michael, son of Neal and brother of Lynchehaun (the 'Dublin brother').

LYNCHEHAUN, Neal, father of Lynchehaun.

LYNCHEHAUN, Tom, son of Neal and brother of Lynchehaun.

McANDREW, a road worker.

MacDERMOTT, Charles, Barrister-at-law.

MacDERMOTT, The, Attorney General for Ireland, father of preceding.

MacDONNELL, Agnes, of London and the Valley; 'the Yellow lady' (Synge); known in later life as *cailleach a' Valley*, the old woman of the Valley.

MacDONNELL, John Randall, Barrister-at-Law, husband of the preceding.

McDONOGH, a road worker.

McELWAINE, Adam, Inspector of National Schools.

McGINTY, James and Michael, sons of John McGinty, workers on Agnes MacDonnell's estate.

McGOVERN, Dominick, a friend of Lynchehaun.

McHUGH, James, of Cashel, supposed victim of Lynchehaun's violence.

McHUGH, John, an acquaintance of Lynchehaun, informant for Irish Folklore Commission.

McKENNA, Stephen.

McLOUGHLIN, John (Jack), owner of a shebeen.

McLOUGHLIN, Mary, daughter or grand-daughter of preceding.

McLOUGHLIN, Pat, shoemaker, son of John McLoughlin.

McNAMARA, a road worker.

McNAMARA, a defence witness at the extradition trial, Indianapolis.

McNAMARA, a mason.

McNAMARRA, Joe, of Manchester, a friend of Lynchehaun.

McNEALLY (McNeela), Bridget (Biddy), also known by maiden name, Grealis(h).

McNEELA (McNeally), John, husband of preceding.

McNEELA (McNeally), Pat, young son of John and Bridget.

McPADDEN, Edward, acquaintance of Lynchehaun.

McTIGUE, a near relative of Lynchehaun.

MAHONEY, J. P., lecturer, member of Clann na nGaoidheal (Irish revolutionary organisation), member of Lynchehaun Defence Committee, Indianapolis.

MALLEY, Charlie, a resident of the Valley.

MARLEY, Sergeant RIC, Sligo.

MARWOOD, a nickname.

MASTERSON, Mary, a relative of Lynchehaun.

MEAKIN, an ex-British soldier.

METZGER, Sheriff, in charge of the jail, Indianapolis.

MILLING, County Inspector, RIC.

M_____ M_____ a car-owner from Mulranny, whose anonymity is preserved.

MOORES, The Honorable Charles W., US Commissioner in Indiana.

MORRISON, Joseph, Constable RIC, Dugort.

MOYLAN, Seán, Minister for Lands and Minister for Education in the early de Valera Government.

MULDOON, John, Constable, RIC.

NICHOLLS, Bob, a warder at Maryborough Jail.

O'BOYLE, J., from near Newport, Co. Mayo, supposed victim of Lynchehaun's violence.

O'BRIEN, T., 2nd District Inspector, RIC, Tubbercurry, Co. Sligo.

O'CONAÍLE, Pádraig of Druingeen, Cong, Co. Mayo, acquaintance of Lynchehaun in Maryborough Jail about 1902, informant of Irish Folklore Commission.

O'CONNOR, Fr, parish priest, Achill Sound.

O'CONNOR, William L., secretary of the Committee for Defence of Lynchehaun, Indianapolis.

O'DONNELL, Neal, friend of Lynchehaun.

O'SULLIVAN, John, Constable RIC, Dugort.

PATTON (Patten), brother of Bridget Patton.

PATTON (Patten), Bridget (Biddy), Agnes MacDonnell's housekeeper.

PATTON, Connor, of Achill, a supposed victim of Lynchehaun's violence.

PETTIT, Henry C., US Marshal for the District of Indiana.

RAINSFORD, Ross, District Inspector, RIC, Newport, Co. Mayo; transferred at own expense to Thomastown, Co. Kilkenny.

RICHARDS, H. J., Barrister-at-Law, counsel for the prosecution at Castlebar.

ROOSEVELT, Theodore, President of the US 1901–9.

SALT, Josiah, land-agent for Agnes MacDonnell.

SANDERSON, Percy, British Consul-General at New York.

SCULLY, Michael, Sergeant RIC, Achill Sound.

SHIELDS, John A., US Commissioner in Southern District of New York.

SHORT, John, Chief Warder, Castlebar Jail.

SIMMS, Harry, a 'nigger' in fight with Lynchehaun.

SLONE, Sergeant RIC, Castlebar.

SPAAN, Henry N., counsel for defence at extradition trial, Indianapolis.

SWEENEY, Denis, tenant of Agnes MacDonnell.

SWEENEY, Maria, daughter of preceding.

SWEENEY, Michael, son of Denis Sweeney.

SWEENEY, Patrick, contractor for the swivel bridge at Achill Sound, hotel keeper, business man, land agent for Agnes MacDonnell.

SWEENEY, Peter, national teacher at Pulranny.

SYNGE, John Millington, Irish dramatist.

TAYLOR, J., Queen's Counsel, acting for the Crown at Castlebar trial.

TIP, Agnes MacDonnell's fox terrier.

VEREKER, Mr, land-agent for Agnes MacDonnell.

VESEY, defence witness at extradition trial, Indianapolis.

WARD, Patrick, Constable RIC.

WEIR, Tom, tenant of Agnes MacDonnell.

WEISS, E. J. of the Pinkerton Detective Agency.

WINTER, the Honorable Ferdinand, counsel for the defence at the extradition trial, Indianapolis.

CHAPTER I
Achill and Indianapolis

On the sixth of October 1894 there was done in the Island of Achill an act that, though not by reason of restraint on the part of the perpetrator, fell a hair's breadth short of murder.

Judgement in the matter was given in Castlebar, Co. Mayo, in July 1895 and it surely seemed that the whole unpleasant business had reached its just, inevitable and permanent conclusion when the criminal, James Lynchehaun, received a life-sentence.

Seven years passed and there occurred the totally unlikely and unforeseeable event of the escape of the prisoner from Maryborough Jail and his arrival at Indianapolis, the capital of the state of Indiana, in the United States of America.

The British Government demanded extradition and the Irish organised to oppose it. There was a re-trial in Indianapolis, a rejection of the British plea, and finally, as a result of British pressure, an appeal against the Indianapolis decision in the Supreme Court at Washington. The Supreme Court upheld the local decision. James Lynchehaun was now a free man as long as he remained in the States.

The Achill peasant had come a long way in less than a decade. He had come, though briefly, to be compared with the greatest of Irish patriots, Wolfe Tone and Robert Emmet. The final public accolade, attesting though with questionable justice, to his innocence and patriotism was conferred upon him in January 1906: basking in the heady glory of Irish political exile, but ill from rheumatics as a result of his struggle for liberty in two continents, he was visited at his home, 1912 Howard Street, Indianapolis, by Charles W. Fairbanks, Vice-President of the United States.

The 'Great Extradition Case' of Edward VII *versus* James Lynchehaun has continued to affect the American law on extradition up to the present day.

Achill, beautiful, barren, and, for its resources, densely populated, is the largest of the islands surrounding Ireland. It was put on canvas after canvas in the early part of the century by Paul Henry: pale skies, billowing Atlantic clouds, darkly menacing hills reflecting a cold sun, stretches of brown bogland, and everywhere, standing alone or in small clusters, tiny white-washed thatched cottages. Fifteen miles across, the island forms the extreme west of the county of Mayo. It is separated from the mainland by a narrow sound over which a bridge, the Michael Davitt Bridge, was built in 1886, the point of juncture on the island being the village of Achill Sound. In the Circuit Court Room, Indianapolis, Henry N. Spaan, a prominent member of the Indiana bar, and counsel for the defendant, presented Commissioner Moores with an eloquent and moving picture of the island at the time of the crime.

> The conditions in the Isle of Achill were, if anything, worse than they were in the other parts of Ireland. It is a little island away out on the west coast, away from the lines of traffic, away from the lines of so-called civilisation — higher civilisation if you please — but nevertheless, those people felt keenly their condition, and they, too, got together in societies, and banded themselves together to resist the common enemy; even upon that island of mountainside and bog, where the men and the women had to live off the sea moss and the shell-fish — even there the dream of liberty existed; even there men got together and talked about freedom; even there men got together and talked about revolution; even there they cultured the traditions of their race; even there they knew all about Wolfe Tone and Robert Emmet; and they, too, belonged to the Land League, and to the Irish Revolu-

tionary Brotherhood, and they, too, had their own way of carrying on this suppressed revolution, which was in the vitals of that country, and has been for an hundred years.... There were twenty-three hundred people upon that island, seven or eight of whom were landlords; the rest of them tenants.... These seven landlords had so carried themselves that the whole island, the entire tenantry, hated them. Oh, are you going into the school of ethics to determine whether or not they had a right to hate them? That is not the question. The fact remains that it was so. And as described here, they were justified in hating them. Sala once described Russia as 'a despotism tempered by assassination!' The despotism of the Irish landlords was tempered only by their fear of having their houses burned or their cattle put into the sea, or being shot at, or driven out of the country. (*Complete Proceedings, pp. 60-2*).

From Achill Sound there is a road to the right leading to the small town of Dugort. After travelling some miles in this direction over lonely hilly roads, one comes to the Sandy Banks, heaps of sand and clumps of grass and rushes, bordering a shallow inlet of the sea in the northern part of the island; then to a gateway opening into a drive leading to the Valley House, a modest 'Big House' or mansion that, at the fitting distance of a quarter of a mile or so, dominates the scattered clusters of cottages known, rather impressively, in official documents as Tonatanvally.

Nobody living there ever says Tonatanvally. It is always 'the Valley'. But however carefully one looks at the scene, and whatever latitude is allowed in relating the descriptive term to land formation, there is not to be found any coupling of hills that would bring a valley into being. There is, in fact, a linguistic trap, sleight, as it were, of tongue. In Irish, the common language of the island in 1894, the name was *Tóin a' tSeanbhaile*, 'the bottom of the old townland', and the official name, Tonatanvally, is a tolerable effort at representing this name in English spelling. *Tóin* is pronounced tone, not ton, the *s* is silent, *bh* is *v*, and *bhaile* is two syllables (Tone a Tanvalleh). As a result of advancing anglicisation, and doubtless with inspiration from successive landlord owners of the Big House, village consensus drew upon the last element of the name. 'The Valley' meant something, was euphonic, respectable, and at least in rough continuity with the original Gaelic name.

The Valley is not a village in any usual sense: it has no church and no police station. Even if here and there groceries may be got over a small counter fitted into a cottage room there are no shops clearly identifiable as such to the casual driver-by. One comes upon the gate to the driveway of the Valley House quite suddenly, and may pass it without realising that one of the outhouses has been converted, in recent years, into a comfortable lounge bar. Then there is a cluster of cottages, then another and another, all seeming to promise a town or village further on. But finally comes the realisation that there is no more. That was it, the village of Tonatanvally, a promise never quite fulfilled.

James or Jim Lynchehaun, against general usage, pronounced and wrote his surname with -han rather than -haun, a snobbish effort to assimilate the form to common and accepted Irish names like Moynihan, Callaghan and Houlihan, thus accommodating better to the tongue and ears of speakers of Hiberno-English. Lynchehaun was completely bilingual, his first language being Irish; we can assume (since he taught Irish in Indianapolis) that he came to be literate in his first as well as in his second language, a thing rare enough in the west of Ireland in his time: indeed, he was linguistically adventurous, for there is reason to think that he had read enough Latin to appreciate in that language the New Testament and the liturgy of the Church. His effort to affect a 'politer' form of his surname, a symbol of his driving ambition, was not notably successful. Contemporaries, including journalists, used the -han at first, but rapidly fell into the local, and to outside ears more uncouth, usage. The name is virtually confined to the Achill and Corraun areas, and, like some delicate wines, does not travel well. Exported it assumes different guises, but is most likely to appear with the fake label Lynch.

According to a local tradition, which there is no reason to doubt, the Lynchehaun family was introduced into the area, probably from Donegal, by an O'Donnell landlord who used them as land-agents, rent-collectors, and bailiffs. James's father, Neal, a farmer of substance and respectability, lived at Tonregee in Pulranny Lynchehaun, or Pulranny of the Lynchehauns, in the peninsula of Corraun. This was, of course, outside the island, but in such a wild and remote spot that, for those who lived there, Achill Sound was the closest available approach to some kind of urban civilisation. It was the place to which James Lynchehaun, as a young man, would come for an evening's drinking.

James was one of a moderately large family. He was born, it might seem, about 1858, and would thus have been thirty-six or so at the time of the crime. But the assumption that he was born in 1858 appears to be based on the fact that he got the old age pension in 1928. It would be entirely typical of Lynchehaun to get the pension two years previous to the date of proper entitlement, so the other view, that he was born in 1860, may, after all, be more correct. He was a handsome man, about five foot ten inches in height, but, because of his heavy build, looked smaller. His victim, Mrs Agnes MacDonnell, under oath and seemingly near death, stated in court that he was 'a fine, young, strong, dark, animal-looking man'. *The Western People* in 1895 described him as 'soft-featured', intending to indicate that he looked civilised, that the harsh island life had left no tell-tale marks upon his face. *The Mayo News* of Saturday 12 January 1895 carried a competent sketch of him made at the time of his trial in Castlebar. It shows a fine-looking man in his mid-thirties, sporting recently grown side-burns, his total dress and appearance doubtless modelled distantly on that of Bertie, Prince of Wales.

Despite hardship and occasional rheumatics the years were kind to him. Edmund Carroll, member of the Royal Irish Constabulary who arrested him in 1918 stated that he looked less than his supposed sixty years and was 'the finest stump of a man you ever laid your eyes on'. John McHugh, an informant of the Irish Folklore Commission, had known him as a boy; his father had been associated with Lynchehaun in an attempt to exploit Mrs MacDonnell's rabbits that bred and flourished in the Sandy Banks. In 1947, speaking to the Irish Folklore Commission collector, Bríd Ní Mhaolmhuaidh, he gave a not unflattering account of Lynchehaun's appearance, but with hindsight adulterated the description with a pensketch of character, seeing a revelation of his faults in his face. Here and elsewhere he is a highly antagonistic witness.

If Lynchehaun were alive today he would be ninety years of age. He was a tall, well-built dark-haired man. Some people would even say that he was handsome but a peculiar habit of wrinkling his forehead, when talking to people, betrayed his restless nature, and gave him a rather terrifying appearance. Women who knew him were particularly afraid of him. On meeting him anywhere they would draw their shawls closely around their heads and pass by quickly without greeting him. 'He was a very dirty-spoken man,' as one old woman put it, adding 'You would sgunder (fear) to meet him he had such bad language, God rest his soul.' Generally he got on well with men, and in a few cases achieved a certain amount of popularity — at least enough to be of use to him when he needed an accomplice in any of his wild escapades. He was, however, by nature much too treacherous to be trusted by anyone. If he got an idea into his head that any man was better in any way than himself, he thought nothing of waylaying him and beating him up till his victim became unconscious, then leaving him to live or die by the roadside. He would not challenge a man openly to fight as he was coward enough at heart to fear being beaten himself.

It has been suggested time and time again that Lynchehaun was made into a folk-hero in Achill and Ireland generally. T. H. White in *The Once and Future King* (London, 1958) p. 548, puts the matter as follows:

Small flecks in the iris of Mordred's eyes burned with a turquoise light, as bright as the owl's.... He became the invincible Gael, the scion of disparate races more ancient than Arthur's, and more subtle. Now, when he was on fire with his Cause, Arthur's justice seemed *bourgeois* and obtuse beside him. It seemed merely to be dull complacency, beside the savagery and feral wit of the Pict. His maternal ancestors crowded into his face when he was spuming at Arthur — ancestors whose civilisation, like Mordred's, had been matriarchal: who had ridden bareback, charged in chariots, fought by stratagem, and ornamented their grisly strongholds with the heads of enemies.... They were the race, now represented by the Irish Republican Army rather than by the Scots Nationalists, who had always murdered landlords and blamed them for being murdered — the race which could make a national hero out of a man like Lynchehaun....

White's view is far from the truth. When one talks to those few remaining old people who met Lynchehaun or heard accounts of him since childhood, one never encounters admiration. He is condemned for his crime and his name has been used as a bogeyman to frighten children. Brother Paul Carney, who wrote a biography of Lynchehaun, seems to have been devoted to him; but in his book he wrote the chapter on the great crime in red ink to show his abhorrence of the deed. 'This', he said, in case the simple reader would miss the symbolism, 'is the red chapter'. Sometimes charity and indulgence are found in unexpected places. An old Protestant lady from Achill, a friend of Mrs MacDonnell in her old age, stated that Lynchehaun was a good man — the trouble he had with Mrs MacDonnell was caused by people who told her lies about him. However, while his crime was generally condemned, it is true that there was a certain ambivalence, a half-grudging admiration for some of his exploits: a man who many times in his life made the police look foolish, and who was instrumental in humiliating the British Government, cannot have been all bad — there must have been a little of the grace of God there somewhere!

Mrs Agnes MacDonnell, the victim, is a figure of mystery. As she lived on until 1923, one would guess that at the time of the crime, twenty-nine years earlier, she was a well-preserved woman in her middle or late forties. She was at any rate old enough in 1894 for Lynchehaun, not himself in his first youth at that time, to refer to her as 'the old bitch'.

Agnes MacDonnell's husband was John Randall MacDonnell, an Irishman, and, if one can trust local consensus, a Catholic. He practiced at the English bar and at the time of the crime had a house at 19 Belsize Square, London. Belsize Square was part of a middle-class suburb of three-storey over basement terraced houses built about 1860. The district was respectable, but not fashionable, the residents being doctors, lawyers and minor merchants. The degree of its respectability is shown by the boast of the first vicar appointed to the newly-built neighbourhood Anglican church that in the whole new area there was only one family of religion other than Church of England.

Contemporaries call Agnes MacDonnell 'eccentric'; and a Victorian middle-aged lady who lived for the greater part of the year away from her husband, alone in a large mansion, in a wild and inaccessible area, undoubtedly was so. Above all she was tough. Before the crime she was a handsome and, by some accounts, beautiful woman. The old Protestant lady who spoke so charitably of Lynchehaun knew Mrs MacDonnell as a disfigured old woman; she spoke of her beauty in earlier years as evidenced by a photographic portrait of her in what she termed 'court dress'. As a landlord Mrs MacDonnell could probably be called money-grabbing. She exacted the last penny due to her, in labour if cash were not available. She was hard, not greatly moved by the injustices of the system within which she worked, but unkind only when to be so was necessary to maintain her full rights. She never sought to evict any tenant, except Lynchehaun. She was, perhaps genuinely, but at least conventionally, a religious woman, and attended Sunday services regularly at St Thomas's Church in Dugort. John McHugh who reported unfavourably on Lynchehaun has nothing but good to say of Mrs MacDonnell:

> Mrs MacDonnell, who was a daughter of Lord Cavendish, was the local landlord; she was not by any means an unpopular person. She treated her tenants well, and

generally speaking was less open to reproach than the majority of her class at the time. In appearance she was a very handsome women with a fine head of red hair. Her first husband, a Mr Elliot, was, like herself, a Protestant, but when he died she married Mr MacDonnell who was a Catholic, and a barrister by profession. After his death she continued to pay the dues at Christmas and Easter to the Monastery Church at Bunacurry where he used to attend Mass. This action won for her an added esteem among her Catholic neighbours, as at that time the Protestant population of the island was regarded by them as a bigoted and narrow-minded collection of individuals.

John McHugh's evidence must, in some respects, be taken with caution. It has so far proved impossible to discover anything of Mrs MacDonnell's origin. The suggestion that she was a daughter of a Lord Cavendish could only be true if she were illegitimate, and is probably nothing more than a confusion resulting from the fact of her acquiring the Achill property from the estate of the recently deceased Earl of Cavan. His statement that her first husband was a Mr Elliot is probably true, for her son and heir was one Leslie Elliot, who in 1893 was adult and living as a member of the family at 19 Belsize Square. Either Mr Elliot was her first husband or — rather unlikely — her lover.

Agnes MacDonnell had some distant ill-defined marriage connection with the Irish Taafe family, but she can hardly have been closely connected with any aristocratic name. The events of 6 October 1894 were sensational, and widely reported. She is always referred to in court and in press reports, despite the fact that her husband was living, as Mrs Agnes MacDonnell. There is never an addendum to suggest a high social origin or relationship with the great. All that is reasonably sure is that before 1888 she had come into possession of a fair amount of money and had set about acquiring land and property in Ireland and England. Her solicitors, on 9 October 1894, took the strange step of publishing a letter in the English *Times* giving an account of her business acumen, her character, her connections, and, very curiously, details of her landholdings in Achill:

Referring to the cowardly murderous attack on Mrs MacDonnell in Achill Island, on the west coast of Ireland, described in the *Times* of this morning, will you permit us to bear testimony to the fact of Mrs MacDonnell's generosity and justice. The Valley House, the scene of the outrage, is the residence of the Tonatanvally estate, which we sold by instructions of the late Earl of Cavan in 1888 to Mrs MacDonnell. We also sold to her some English properties, and these transactions caused many personal interviews (as she transacted her business matters personally), and her conduct was such as to very strongly impress us that in a remarkable degree she exhibited great firmness of character in the traits of absolute justice tempered by a true generosity. Mrs MacDonnell is an English lady, although connected by marriage with one of the most ancient lineages of Ireland (the Taafe family).

It may be interesting if we add that the Tonatanvally estate comprised:

	Acres	*Roods*	*Perches*
Lands in hand and residence	530	2	21
Lands let in conacre lots	26	2	15
Lands leased to tenants	243	1	20
Turf-fuel land or bog	1,258	2	38
	2,068	1	14

Besides this about 150 acres of the slopes of the Slievemore Mountain were held on lease as a sheep run.

Achill Island comprises 50,000 acres, and has a wild seashore frontage of over 80 miles. The Slievemore Mountain rises to over 2,200 feet.

We are, sir, your obedient servants,
Dowett, Knight and Co.,
3 Lincoln's Inn-fields, London 9

Brother Paul Carney — Paul was not a baptismal name, but a name in religion[1] — in or about 1904 wrote, but never

---

[1] Since writing the above I have discovered that his baptismal name was James!

published, *A Short Sketch of the Life and Actions of the Far-famed James Lynchehaun, the Achill Troglodyte*, a work that may be more conveniently referred to as Brother Paul's *Narrative*.[2] To this he added from time to time some extra chapters, anecdotes and notes which concluded in 1918.

Not merely was Brother Paul Lynchehaun's biographer, but it is not impossible that at times he took an active part in aiding and protecting the criminal. Discretion had to be exercised in writing, for such aid was an act outside the law. Hence, for instance, it will be suggested that Brother Paul hides behind the anonymity of the term 'a sincere friend', one to whom Lynchehaun wrote from Antwerp, having received through him from his father, Neal, the sum of £40 to enable him to escape to America.

Brother Paul's *Narrative* consists largely of anecdotes of cunning, violence, and adventure. Lynchehaun, Brother Paul says more than once, was a mixture of good and evil. But little of the good is recounted there, and, on the writer's own admission, much of the moral evil is suppressed to avoid polluting youthful ears. Perhaps the most positive evidence of 'goodness' in James Lynchehaun's character lies in Brother Paul's devotion to him.

Brother Paul was born in 1844 in Co. Mayo, precisely at Ballindrihid, near Ballyhaunis, on the road to Knock. To understand the involvement of this gentle monk with Achill and James Lynchehaun we must go back to events that preceded his birth by about a decade.

In the early 1830s one Mr Edward Nangle, a clergyman belonging to the Church of Ireland, embarked on a mission to the papish and Irish-speaking Island of Achill. His mission, which was eventually to founder, had, nevertheless, some enduring successes. It led to a number of conversions, the publication over a period of a journal called *The Achill Herald*, the coming to the island of Protestant immigrants who founded the Colony, a village not far from Dugort, some improvement in local agricultural and building methods, and, although this was hardly amongst his fore-

---

[2] All substantial quotations from Brother Paul's *Narrative* are given in smaller type. Brother Paul's spelling is corrected and occasional words, dropped in writing, are supplied.

seen objectives, the development of the island as a popular centre of tourism. But as regards Mr Nangle's primary mission, the original inhabitants of the island, with a few exceptions, remained stubbornly and perversely Roman.

On the chessboard where was played out the game of pre-ecumenical rivalry, the invasion of the outer extremity of the largely Roman Catholic diocese of Tuam by the Reforming forces called for a smart counter-move. The play lay in the hands of John McHale who had become Archbishop in 1834. McHale was a vigorous man. He had been christened 'The Lion of St Jarlath's' by Daniel O'Connell, and in the future was to fight hard against the doctrine of papal infallibility, yielding with a dramatic '*Credo*' when his position was irretrievably lost. Unusual for a cleric at that time, he was devoted to the Irish language — the common language of his diocese — and he later translated into Irish six books of Homer's *Iliad*, and the popular *Irish Melodies* of Tom Moore.

The Archbishop's move in this situation was to send to Achill a group of monks of the Third Order Regular of St Francis, a mediaeval order revived in the West of Ireland about 1820. In 1852 this group was commissioned to found a school, church and monastery at Bunacurry, not far from the Valley. They were to maintain the faith, give a Roman Catholic education to the boys of Achill and generally counter the machinations of Mr Nangle and his cohorts.

In 1869, at the age of twenty-four, Paul Carney, baker's boy in Ballyhaunis, speaker of Irish, bearing the marks of an indifferent education in English which he would never quite lose, entered the religious and teaching life at the monastery in Bunacurry. Despite his disadvantages he was to become a beloved and successful teacher, as well as filling the offices of bursar and master of novices.

Brother Paul taught in Achill for twenty-six years, that is, until 1895, and spent a brief period in Dublin for special training in 1877. He taught the young James Lynchehaun, and was in Achill for his arrest and trial in 1895. In that year he was transferred to Errew, another house of the Order. Eighteen months later, in 1896, he was sent by the Archbishop of Tuam to the United States to collect funds for a new Church in Castlebar, and thereafter, for a number of years, he travelled to and fro between Ireland and America. He was present in the courtroom in Indianapolis in 1903 when the 'Great Case' of Edward VII versus his ex-pupil was heard.

In a curious way Brother Paul re-created and re-lived the life of an early Irish monastic figure. In Ireland, in the eighth and ninth centuries, monks wrote chronicles of events, and sagas of princes and great men. They had, in a sense, abandoned the world as the domain of the devil, but remained, nevertheless, compulsive observers of it. Brother Paul wrote a chronicle recording the outstanding events in Achill during his time and then turned his hand to saga in telling the exciting story of James Lynchehaun.

The story of Lynchehaun passed orally from house to house of the Third Order Regular, for Brother Paul was not the only monk interested in the matter. Here fictitious names, Brother Gabriel and Brother Austin, will be used for two of the monks.

Brother Gabriel as a young man had listened in the monastery of Clifden to tales of Lynchehaun told by the old monk, Brother Austin, who had formerly been in Achill. Brother Gabriel was busy and bored and did not appreciate the value of old Brother Austin's anecdotes. But in the mid-forties he visited the monastery of Bunacurry, and, while there, read Brother Paul's *Narrative*. He was particularly interested in the American portion of the work, because this had not been touched on by Brother Austin.

Ten years or so later, in 1955, Brother Gabriel was appointed superior of the Bunacurry community, a position he held until 1961. While there he discovered that the *Narrative* was lost. He searched every likely place but failed to find it. In other words the book had disappeared from Bunacurry between 1945 and 1955.

There was a certain amount of talk in the Valley about the disappearance of the book, and popular opinion laid the blame on a local doctor who for some strange reason was the only person outside the monastery privileged to hold a key to the bookcase in which the manuscript was kept.

The manuscript had, in fact, made its way to Dublin, but

how this happened must for the moment remain hidden. Suffice it to say that the doctor who was the prime suspect was entirely innocent.

CHAPTER II

Lynchehaun's Early Life
Brother Paul's Narrative

James Lynchehaun, the subject of the following lines, was born about the year 1860 in the townland of Pulranny, one mile from Achill Sound, Co. Mayo, Ireland. His parents were of the farming class, honest and industrious. His father's name was Neal Lynchehaun and his mother's Bridget Cafferky. Some of his maternal uncles were demented.

Most of Jim's early days were spent herding his father's stock on the elevated mountains near his paternal home. Although the goats and mountain sheep were pretty wild, they were not as mischievous as their young herd, for while they often browsed quietly on the mountainside he occupied his time skipping from cliff to cliff in search of sea-birds' nests and quarrelling with his comrade boys, and so often returned in the evenings with black eyes, bruises and scars to get more from his father for his bad behaviour.

The mountains where he herded his father's stock were about 2,000 feet in height and formed the peninsula known as Curraun, located between Clew and Blacksod Bays. From these elevated mountains the view of nature is very picturesque: Clew Bay with its 300 islands and the placid waters reflecting the shadow of Croagh Patrick, while Blacksod Bay received the surging billows of the wild Atlantic. Jim, though wild, had an observant turn of mind, and when alone, would often muse on the stories he had heard from his parents and grandparents about the Penal Laws and especially of the deeds done in Ireland in 1798. The one which made the deepest impression on his young mind was the story about Father Manus Sweeney's arrest and execution without trial, judge, or jury. It is as follows.

When the French landed at Killala in 1798 they travelled on towards Newport on their way to Castlebar. Father Manus

15

Sweeney was seen talking to one of the French officers. A spy conveyed the news to Sir Richard O'Donnell of Newport, who sent a band of yeomen in pursuit of the priest. After a few days searching they found him concealed in a flax-loft in a small house in the Valley, Achill.

They took him to Newport where he was hanged on the market crane by orders of Sir Richard O'Donnell.[1] On the priest's way to execution he felt very dry and requested someone in the crowd to bring him a drink. A man named Murphy brought some water, but, as the priest was in the act of raising it to his mouth, a trooper dashed it from his hand. Murphy brought another drink and, when the priest had taken it, he blessed Murphy and wished him a long and happy life, then, turning towards the trooper, predicted that the hand which spilled the drink would cause the owner's death. Both predictions were verified. Murphy lived to be about ninety years of age and the trooper's hand got diseased and so caused the owner's death. Thus the good was rewarded and the wicked punished.

While the priest was suspended on the market crane, another ruffian trooper, named Lightle, said scoffingly 'Priest's meat is high to-day'.

A few weeks later this Lightle's dead body was found on the mountain, near Newport, about 1,800 feet high and was taken down piecemeal by dogs and devoured by them. So his flesh was more elevated, but not so venerated, as Father Sweeney's.[2]

Thus ended a few of the scoffers of the Lord's anointed. 'Oh,' said Jim Lynchehaun to the writer, 'if I were then in my manhood how many of those cruel ruffians I would have hewn down. I think the blood boiled in my veins whenever I heard my father telling the story. Ah, my country! Wolfe Tone, Emmet and Lord Edward did well to try for freedom.'

The portion of Jim's time not occupied in herding was spent at the village school. Being naturally talented he made rapid progress, was appointed monitor at the age of fourteen. After his monitorial term being ended, he stood an examination for classification as teacher but failed. Although he failed, he was not foiled; 'Try again' was his motto. He went to another teacher to

[1] *Brother Paul's Note:* The O'Donnell family became extinct in Newport about 90 years after Father Sweeney's death, Sir George being the last member of the family, who died about 1888 without issue.

[2] *Brother Paul's Note:* Father Manus Sweeney was born in the village of Dookennella, Achill, and captured in a house in the Valley, Achill, and hanged on the market crane at Newport in 1798. His crime was, to talk to a French officer who was on his way from Killala to Castlebar.

prepare for a second trial but was unsuccessful as before. But like Robert Bruce he resolved to make a final effort; so he did, and succeeded. Shortly after his classification he got charge of a small school near Achill Sound.

In the above trials patience and perseverance showed the determined will Lynchehaun had even in his school-boy days. This will grew stronger with his years....

After his appointment to the Belfarsad National School at Achill Sound, his transactions there may be curtly explained in his own words, as under:

> During my short term in charge of the Belfarsad National School my average was small and as a large portion of my income depended, during the Results System, on my average I was determined to increase it by names of pupils yet unborn. I mustered up a large roll. The device seemed to work well for a few months. But to my grief, I found that honesty is the best policy; for though long the fox runs he gets caught at last; so was Jim.
>
> The then District Inspector was a pug-nosed fellow with a grog-blossomed face, a Presbyterian by profession and McElwaine by name, a real detective who delighted to catch a teacher in a trap. He was hated by all the teachers in his district owing to his numerous mean acts, such as disguising himself when approaching a school, jumping off the car and running round the outside of the school to make a sortie on the pupils. When he entered the stampede was general, they feared him so much. When examining the pupils he held a pencil between his teeth to cause his northern accent to be more unintelligible and puzzling to the children, and to deprive the teacher of his results. As the pupils did not understand his mumbling questions they usually gave wrong answers and thus deprived the teacher of his hard-earned Results' Fees, along with degrading his school by bad reports.
>
> This detective inspector was very searching for defects or falsifications in the school accounts. If he found them he would smile with joy. If he found none he would grin with anger.
>
> In one of his visits he found me truly guilty of falsification. He smiled, drew my attention to the matter, asked me so many irritating questions that he aroused my ire. So in the heat of the passion I did give him some short answers and said 'What is it to you if I did falsify? You lose nothing by it.' He looked fierce and said, 'I am a government official whose business is to detect such frauds and report the offender.' When leaving the school I

accompanied him to the boat which was about 200 yards away, but he never exchanged a word with me. Seeing by his dark, sulky countenance that he was determined to injure me, a thought crossed my mind to give him the 'hand and foot' and dive his corpulent body in the briny waters to keep it from putrefaction. And certainly I would have done so if I foreknew that his vindictive report would be the cause of my dismissal.

A few days after the Inspector's visit to my school the manager got a copy of his damaging report and ordering my immediate dismissal or they would withdraw the grant from the school.

So I had to discontinue or to teach gratuitously and this would not pay for food and clothing for Jim.

On resigning the school I returned, like the prodigal, to my father's house, there to meditate on my next move. Days weighed heavily upon me. I felt somewhat despondent yet I did not despair. I read the daily papers and *The Teachers' Weekly Journal*. Finally I saw to my great joy an advertisement for a teacher in Roundstone, Co. Galway.

You may guess I did not delay in forwarding my application to the manager who received me courteously and granted my request. Never did hare run to cover, nor fox to den, more anxiously than I did to the little school in Connemara, resolving to be a better and more cautious boy now than before. But how vain were all my resolutions while I carried my corrupt nature and violent passions! The change of place did not change vicious habits. Being now removed from the influence of my good father my passions grew stronger with my years as the sequel will show.

I got the school and the good old manager notified the Commissioners of my appointment. They sent him a large sheet of inquiries, told him give an account of my antecedents and asked was I the James Lynchehaun lately dismissed from Achill Sound School. I told the manager a plausible story; so he wrote to the Commissioners that he knew nothing about my antecedents, but that I appeared to be a good young man; and if they would not sanction him he should close the school and the responsibility would be on them. So after a large number of correspondence they sanctioned me on condition that I would be good for the future.

After my being sanctioned my chief policy was to get ingratiated into my old manager's good graces; so I did, and we were like two old comrades and lived in very friendly terms. All seemed to go smoothly for a year or so. After this my former fears began to abate. Money, the source of evil, began to get flush with me. I got into company and spent more freely, but, to my sorrow, when wine is in wit is out with me.

About this time I got into a serious trouble by assaulting a native who attempted to pick my pocket which contained my quarter's salary.

This would-be robber had a bottle of whiskey, and while putting it in a seemingly friendly manner to my mouth with one hand, he was manipulating my pocket with the other. But he suffered for the attempt, for I danced on his body, although I had to pay the piper afterwards. This man's friends pursued me in order of getting even with me, so I had to act the fugitive and desert the school and parish. After hiding for a few days I was discovered and arrested, brought before a Justice of the Peace, confined in the bridewell in Clifden to await my trial in Galway at next sessions.

Two influential friends took compassion on me and bailed me to stand my trial. When I got out I gave them 'leg bail' and left them to settle their accounts with the law authorities.

So much according to Jim's own version. Others state that he broke a policeman's spinal cord and caused a school inspector who left him a bad report to go on his knees and promise to cancel it or he would shoot him.

On leaving the bridewell at Clifden he marched towards Westport. On his way he entered a country school, examined as an inspector, found faults, and wrote a very unfavourable report, and so terrified the poor teacher that he feared his dismissal would follow.

When about to leave, the would-be inspector put his hands into his pockets, as if to search for something, then exclaimed 'Oh! By the by, I forgot my purse with my valise in the hotel. I say, teacher, would you lend me a few pounds till I return?'

The poor, simple, trembling teacher, glad to be able to oblige him, in order of getting ingratiated into his favour, ran to his boarding-house, brought him the sum demanded, hoping to get it back with interest. They parted, never to see again. So the simple teacher lost his foe and cash and had to enter it on the debit side of profit and loss account.

CHAPTER III

Lynchehaun's Career in England
Brother Paul's Narrative

When Jim was out on bail and while his trial was pending in Galway he visited his friends in Achill, picked up a few pounds and made off to England to try his luck there. On his arrival at Birkenhead he hired a cab and ordered the driver bring him to the Temple in Dale Street where there was a merchant with whom his father used to deal and through whose influence he hoped to get some situation. When the cabby brought Jim to his destination Jim handed a shilling to the driver and demanded sixpence change. The jarvey grew saucy and refused to give change. Jim told him he would get straight with him and so he did.

After taking some refreshment, and thinking it too early to retire, he set out for a stroll to see some more of the city. On his return he missed his direct way to the Temple and got somewhat mixed up, and forgetting the name of the street and number of the house where he left his trunk, he knew not what to do. But his fertile mind soon supplied him with a plan to surmount his difficulty. As his boarding-house was near Dale Street he guessed that by getting to the latter he would soon find the former. Being only a few hours in the city, and not knowing the streets or lanes, and thinking he might be misdirected and robbed by corner-boys, he made towards a cab-stand. And whom did he espy amongst the jarveys but his former driver whom he employed to drive him to the Temple in Dale Street. When there bold Jim jumped off, told the jarvey return to the cab-stand, that he paid him on the double before. Jarvey got noisy, shouted for a bobby to arrest Irish Paddy. But none being at hand Jim turned the corners while jarvey was in search of bobby. So Pat outwitted Bill this time.

Next morning James Lynchehaun sought for employment in a tram-car office. Being asked from whence he came, how long he was over, etc., Jim answered 'From Ireland, only yesterday'.

'If that be so,' said the official in uniform, 'You know not the streets and we cannot employ you.'

Although refused he got not confused but resolved to make use of the old maxim 'Try again'.

He had recourse to his fruitful brains for plans, set his fingers to work, drew a number of bogy[1] references and recommendations, called to office next day, presented them and said the manager told him to call with his deposit of £2.6.8 as an entrance fee. All appeared satisfactory so Jim was sent to learn on a trail-car that evening. His progress was so rapid that, after a few days practice, the conductor reported that his new pupil was master of his business and therefore capable of conducting a car himself.

Next day Lynchehaun was appointed conductor with a nigger driver. White Pat and black Sam got on fairly well for a time until the following episode occurred and dissolved their friendship and partnership. It happened thus. The darky had a long familiar conversation one night with two ladies who rode on the car he drove. Jim asked the cause of such intimacy. 'Oh!,' said Sam, 'I am about to marry one of them.' 'Poor is her taste,' said Jim, 'to marry a nigger like you.'

That was enough to rouse the ire of Blacky, and proved to be a proclamation of war between Black and White. The rebuke piqued Darkey's vanity so much as to vow vengeance on Jim, and give him so much trouble as to make him resign that car and apply for another.

If a man's life on earth is a warfare it has been truly verified in Jim's, for he is scarcely out of one trouble when he gets into another, as from the frying pan into the fire.

His next driver was an Orangeman who was no less vindictive than the nigger. The Orange and Green lodged in the same house. They seemed to agree during the week-days. But when Sunday arrived each hoisted his own colour and got different newspapers. Lynchehaun got *United Irishman* and the Orange boy got *Belfast News*. So the papers and readers were as antagonistic as the Orange and Green. The readers got into loggerheads about politics and religion. From words fists came to be used. The landlord, failing to make peace, threatened to evict both. After tongues and hands being tired there was a lull for a few days. But it proved to be a deceptive calm which precedes a gathering storm. Hostilities were resumed with greater violence than before, so much so as to cause a dissolution of Orange and Green as well as of the Black and White.

[1]=bogus.

After spending about eighteen months in the service of the Tramcar Company he resigned, or had to do, owing to his altercations with drivers and passengers, etc.

He next sought for an easier and more lucrative employment which he found in the city Police Force, although this idle strolling life sowed the seeds of his ruin in after life as he himself acknowledged. He saw and learned too much evil during his nocturnal patrols.

Shortly after his resignation of, or dismissal from, the tramcars he sought for admission to the Metropolitan Police Force in Manchester. On making his application at headquarters he was asked his reason for applying. Jim answered 'Because the situation suits my taste.' Being an able-bodied man he was soon admitted.

Being told to apply next day and produce his credentials, certificates of birth, character, etc., Jim set his mind thinking and his pen writing these requirements for himself. Lynchehaun appeared at the Metropolitan Police Station with the required certificates and credentials, all autographs. This was outwitting the lawyers. All appeared satisfactory and he was ushered into a waiting-room where there was a number of English and Scotch recruits awaiting examination like himself. As an Irishman feels not happy when idle, Jim sought for something to occupy his time. He soon espied a map of Europe suspended on the wall. He looked at it for a time. The thought of his schooldays flashed through his mind and how he could marshal and interrogate a fifth class around such a map. Irish Pat (Lynchehaun) wished to test the Johnnies and the canny Scotch that he was superior to them. So he marshalled them into class form, interrogated them on topography and geography, but finding them to be a lot of ignorant gawks he domineered over them in such a noisy way as to attract some of the higher officials from the next compartment who inquired into the cause of so much noise. Bill and Scotch threw the blame on poor Patch (Lynchehaun). 'Aye, Pat', said the officer, 'which did you come here, to teach or to be taught?'

'To do both, sir', answered Pat. 'I found these young recruits so deficient in the requirements of geographical knowledge that I considered it an act of kindness to help them on'.

'Now, Pat,' said the officer, 'Come here till I see what you know.'

So Pat, or rather Jim, went into the examination hall, got through his oral and written examinations in splendid style, was declared fit for entering the Royal Force, got the black uniform with turban hat and sword, baton and revolver. Being thus fitted out he scarcely knew himself, and somewhat resembled a pragmatical jackdaw in borrowed feathers.

Lynchehaun declared to a friend that this situation was to him the forerunner of his ruin: 'For instead of being an officer of peace I became an officer of mischief. Shortly after learning the topography of the city my next lesson was to learn how to turn the corners into a public house and get a pint.'

As the publicans would give him all the drink he wanted free of charge, hoping he would not report them for transgressing the licence laws, Jim was often drunk while he should be on duty. Many other evil deeds Jim Lynchehaun learned while on night-duty which would not be good for young readers to have narrated here.

However, the following story which was told to the writer by an ex-policeman is worth relating on account of the amusement which it caused to the lookers-on.

One day as Jim was on duty in Manchester, he saw a crowd of people who blocked the thoroughfare. An Italian was playing a street-organ, and a number of foolish drunken women dancing around it with a crowd looking on. The bobby, thinking it his duty to disperse them, he approached the mob and ordered them to remove. One of the dancing dames took hold of him, twirled him around and asked would he dance a jig with her. The crowd laughed at seeing the bobby in the hands of the foolish dame. She clung to him like a leech. Not being able to extricate himself from her grasp he whistled for his comrade in the next beat who ran to aid a friend in danger. Both, seeing they were unable to restore order, had to signal for more men. Next came a sergeant with four men who took the most violent of the drunken women prisoner. She refused to go, threw herself on the ground, screamed, cursed, bit, kicked, and acted more like a tigress than a human being. So four men had to take her hands and feet, partly carry, partly drag her like a sack. The sergeant cleared the way with his baton and rebuked the men for not marching quicker with their burden, while they complained of her kicks and bites. The fifth bobby brought the Italian, and the Italian brought his monkey and organ. As the laughable procession moved along the crowd increased. Some of the corner-boys twisted the handle of the street-organ and played the marching tune. Some of the passers-by asked what was being enacted in the procession. Some answered 'A comedy', others 'A tragedy' while others rebuked them and said it was a 'laughable farce'.

As the procession neared the depot the crowd and noise

increased. Laughing, shouting and booing got so boisterous that the police were glad to get inside doors with their charges which they locked up in irons in revenge for all the shame and trouble they caused them.

Such scenes as these gave Jim a dislike to police duties and he grew careless in the observance and discharge of them.

In a few months after the above episode Jim's drinking habits brought himself into trouble. The sergeant of his division while going on his round of beats to see was each man at his post found Jim under the influence of drink and neglecting his duty. He ordered him to the rear of the division and so marched him to the police station, then brought him under the notice of the Head Constable.

Jim Lynchehaun was well tested, questioned and cross-questioned. The officers had a long hesitation and consultation before pronouncing sentence. The outcome was that Jim was declared to be under the influence of drink while on duty, was given in charge to a fellow policeman to be conducted home to his lodging.

While on his way and a short distance from the barrack Jim saw a cabman, beckoned at him, and ordered the jarvey drive him to his lodging. When Jim Lynchehaun got into cab his brother bobby thought to get in also to see his charge safely at home. Jim Lynchehaun resisted and evicted the saucy intruder. As the bobby made a second attempt to enter cab Jim Lynchehaun resisted and used threats of violence. And to give effect to his words he took off his night-duty belt and belted the would-be intruder.

On Jim's reappearance in barrack next day he was arraigned before the Head Constable, told to give an account of his late transactions and why he hired a cab. Jim Lynchehaun answered 'To avoid observation, sir'.

The Head Constable seemed pleased with Jim's prudence. Still he fined him ten shillings with a severe caution.

As custom is like a second nature, and as this nature is prone to evil from youth, Jim was unable to overcome it when temptation approached. And as the publicans gave him plenty of the mountain dew free of charge, and Bacchus tempting his votary and saying, though unseen:

'Drink,' said the demon, 'drink your fill.'
  'Drink of these waters mellow.
They'll turn your eyeballs sear and dull
  and make your white skin yellow'.

'They'll fill your home with care and grief,
   and clothe your back with tatters.
They'll fill your hearts with evil thoughts,
   but don't mind what it matters.'

'Be merry for to-day,
   what care you for to-morrow...'

Apparently Jim took Bacchus' advice, drank copiously of the mellow waters, for he was arrested while in the act of raising a beaker to his mouth. He was marched again before his superior officers, accused of insubordination, of being drinking when he should be on duty, and therefore neglecting the duty he was paid for. This being the second or third time he was charged before his superior officers, he was now ordered to send in his resignation. This was a polite way for dismissing a public servant.

So Jim Lynchehaun left or had to leave. For he was stripped of his borrowed garb like the pragmatical jackdaw and ordered not to associate with his former companions as a peace officer ought not to be a disturber and an officer of the law ought not to be a transgressor thereof.

During Lynchehaun's short term of eighteen months in the Metropolitan Police Force in Manchester he got a warrant for his own arrest for the deeds he did in Connemara and for his absconding while his trial was pending in Galway. Jim must have assumed a new name while serving in the Police Force. Otherwise he would have been arrested, as a copy of said warrant was in each barrack.

Shortly after severing his connection with the Police Force an English newspaper reported that grave suspicions arose that he had been acting in collusion with certain notorious forgers.

    And from time to time he went from place to place assuming different names and various characters, amongst others that of a clergyman. In this guise he posed as having been a Roman Catholic priest who was converted to Protestantism and actually occupied several pulpits in the north of England, eloquently denouncing the church he was supposed to have left. His acts on the stage of life are many, daring, and mischievous. And most likely they are not ended as he is yet a young man in prime of life with a fruitful mind and a determined will. The state may be nurturing a vicious animal so the sooner he would be encaged the better.

About a year after his being dismissed from the Police Force in England bold Jim returned to Ireland, and like the Prodigal Son made for his father's house. Paternal affection touched the father's heart at seeing the son he thought lost return safely home. He ordered a feast to be made ready and all the family make merry over the recovery of the long lost treasure. Not that alone but he bought a house and established him in a little shop business.

Jim observed the proverb 'Never marry till you're sure of a house wherein to tarry'. Now, having his house, his next thoughts were about marriage. His choice fell on a respectable girl named Catherine Gallagher who had a fair fortune and a good tact for business. They got on well for a few years, Jim being such a go-ahead venturesome fellow that if one trade failed he would try various others, so that in the space of four years he had a dozen of occupations, viz. grocer, eggler, usurer, fish-monger, lobster, cockle, and periwinkle dealer, rabbit-catcher, road-contractor, land-steward, etc, etc.

Jim showed an aptitude for business in various ways and that he retained some of the detective tactives[2] which he learned while in the Metropolitan Police Force may be shown by the following instance.

While he dealt with a merchant in Manchester to whom he sent lobsters, cockles etc. he suspected the merchant was not giving a fair market price for them. He went over unaware and in disguise, entered the Fishmarket in Manchester, went from stall to stall asking prices and pretending to be bargaining for to purchase, and even went to the very merchant to whom he sent the fish etc. They knew not each other except by name and address. By this stratagem Lynchehaun found he was cheating him in price.

While Jim Lynchehaun minded his business and the prudent counsels of his wife he prospered. But prosperity brings luxury, and luxury brings negligence, and both are followed by ruin and so it was with Jim. Fortune and misfortune were both ruinous to him as they caused pride or depression in his mind. In both circumstances he would indulge heavily in intoxicants, and when wine was in wit was out and Jim was up for violence as the three following instances will show.

First, as Jim Lynchehaun was returning home from the town of Newport, Co. Mayo, an elderly man named J. O'Boyle, who was trudging along the road, accosted him. Lynchehaun, who had a horse and cart, told the old man to sit on the cart and give ease to his feet. The old man complied and thanked him for his kindness.

[2]=tactics.

They chatted along in a social manner till the old man was about alighting near his own house. When leaving the cart he sought for his walking stick and merely asked Lynchehaun did he take it. Lynchehaun got so irritated that he took the old man and pitched him from the cart into a dirty dyke on the road-side, then gave him a few blows of the stick which he found under straw on which they were sitting on the cart. After this deed Jim drove off and left the old man to swim or sink, to live or die. It happened that some neighbours who were passing the way soon afterwards found the old man in an exhausted state, took him home, put him to bed where his wife nourished and revived him. Lynchehaun was arrested for the deed and got a month on hard labour in the County Jail.

Second case was concerning a man named Connor Patton who went to buy tobacco in Lynchehaun's store. In the course of a conversation Patton asked Lynchehaun how was his Mrs. Jim drew false meaning from the simple question, asked Patton what he had to say or do with his wife, and immediately, acting like the wolf in the fable towards the lamb, seized Patton, tumbled and kicked him out of the shop, and continued doing so till he left him about forty yards from it. Another man interfered and so saved the life of Patton. The latter struggled home, took to his bed, complained of his ribs being broken, was under doctor's care about three months. Patton, being poor, was unable to take law proceedings against him. So Lynchehaun got over this case by paying the doctor's fees and giving a little compensation to Patton for his lost time, but nothing for his broken ribs.

Third and worst assault was that administered to a strong young man named James McHugh who was drinking with Lynchehaun at Achill Sound, it being late at night when they left the Sound, both being pretty beery, having two horses, and both having to travel same road home. They jogged and chatted along till they came about midway on their journey where a by-road crossed a bog, when McHugh said to Lynchehaun 'Of late years I never pass this spot at night but I think the hairs stand on my head and I shudder with fear. It's here I gave the beating to McTigue of which he died. May God forgive me!'

This McTigue was a near relative of Lynchehaun's although McHugh did not know it. Therefore Lynchehaun's ire got excited at hearing McHugh confess the crime, and he said to McHugh 'Whatever God gives you, I give you this', drawing his loaded whip, striking McHugh on the head, tumbled him off his horse and left him weltering in his blood.

McHugh, seeing his life in danger at the hands of this violent man, went on his knees and begged for mercy for the sake of his wife and children. Lynchehaun, whose hand was raised to strike another blow, hearing McHugh's pitiable appeal, had compassion, as he did not wish to leave his wife a widow and his children orphans. So he raised him up, ordered him get behind him on the horse, as McHugh's horse made off during the row, keep his tongue silent, not tell who struck him, say it was the horse threw him. These were Lynchehaun's instructions to McHugh. When they travelled about an English Mile farther they reached a village named Cashell where McHugh's father-in-law kept a public house. So the two Jims, McHugh and Lynchehaun, entered to wash themselves on the outșide with water and inside with whiskey.

McHugh, true to his promise, told his father-in-law that a wild horse threw him and then made off. After satisfying their thirst with bad drink Lynchehaun left McHugh in safe keeping in his father-in-law's and made off to his domicile in the famous Valley in mid-Achill, there to brood or dream over his night's work.

CHAPTER IV

Law and Order

The relationship between Lynchehaun and Mrs Mac-Donnell in the six years between 1888 and the sixth of October, 1894, is obscure in many details, but above all in one, the reason for their venomous quarrel. The date of the falling out was, in all probability, the autumn of 1891. Was the quarrel caused by rabbits, as first suggested by the reporter for *The Morning Post,* writing on 9 October 1894? Was it on account of bent — a stiff-stemmed grass of some economic value? Was it because she dubbed him 'grocer' when he wished to be called 'agent', thus putting him down socially and economically, for she would have him at her beck and call for £15 a year, a very much smaller sum than she would pay had she conceded him the agency?

That Mrs MacDonnell felt some physical attraction for Lynchehaun seems not unlikely, for, when seemingly near death on 11 October, she stated on oath that 'Said James Lynchehaun is a fine, young, strong, dark, animal-looking man.' Might there have been some sexual incident, an unfitting overture on his part, perhaps a momentary yielding on hers, something of which she was immediately ashamed, and which turned the attraction she felt into hatred and fear, giving rise to a determination to have him out of her sight for ever? Rabbits, bent, social and economic ambition on his part: doubtless all had a part in the developing situation. But the very intensity of their mutual hatred, the evasiveness in court of Mrs MacDonnell and of The MacDermott, the Crown prosecutor, together with some bizarre aspects of the crime, might seem to point to some sexual situation being at the root of the breach. A local tradition come upon by Professor Lorna Reynolds 'many years' before 1976, and deriving at one remove from a person present as a child at the tragedy would seem to give some support to this.

Mrs MacDonnell bought the estate out of her own money in 1888. Her first agent, whom she probably acquired with the property, was Josiah Salt, and she became rapidly disenchanted with him. Her second, Patrick Sweeney, was a local, a man of substance, the contractor for the swivel bridge which had been built over Achill Sound in 1886; Lynchehaun intrigued against him, and was possibly the cause of his dismissal.

At the end of 1888, according to Mrs MacDonnell's statement in court, she first employed Lynchehaun. She handed in a document in his writing, an agreement by which he was to serve her 'in various capacities':

> He entered into my service under that agreement. I paid him a quarter's salary and discharged him; *there was no quarrel or hostility between us.* He held a small holding called the Scraw and two cottages united. In one he carried on a business as a general shopkeeper. He wished to be called my agent. I declined to recognise that and called him a 'grocer'. He was a yearly tenant of the two cottages. I served notice to quit as regards these. I held my part of the notices, which were burned on the night of the sixth of October (1894). There were four notices to quit served, three by myself personally.
> [All italics in this chapter are the author's.]

His Lordship intervened: 'All for the cottages?'

'For the Scraw and the cottages, two each.'

Then turning to The MacDermott, she said: 'The last notice came to an end on 29 September 1894.'

The MacDermott, in his opening address for the Crown, was either ignorant of the original reason for the breach or chooses not to reveal it. His words imply that the cause of the quarrel was not the description of Lynchehaun as a 'grocer' but some more serious matter:

When she first got this property her agent was a Mr Salt; next she had a gentleman named Sweeney; and she thirdly had as agent for a period of three months, or so, or rather as steward, the prisoner, James Lynchehaun. In addition to being in her employment for a short time he had also a power of attorney, which was not signed, describing the terms under which he was to be in charge of the lady's property, and he was set out in that document as 'James Lynchehaun, grocer'. It appears he held two small houses from her, in one of which he carried on the grocery business, and with some success; and beside that he had a small farm of land which he purchased from a man named Burke with her consent and which was known as the Scraw. When he became her agent, or under-bailiff, he was receiving from her an annual salary of £15 a year. *Now for some reason or another he did not give her satisfaction,* and at the end of the three months she dismissed him from her service. *Further owing to the dislike she entertained to him, either from his misconduct or whatever may have been the cause of it,* she served him with a notice to quit of the premises where he carried on the grocery business, and she also sought to determine his tenancy in the holding called the Scraw.

Mrs MacDonnell stated in court that she had Lynchehaun in her employment for three months, and that this period began 'at the end of 1888'; hence, one would gather, his employment began at latest in December 1888, was terminated in March 1889, and after that there was no relationship between them, apart from the distant and in this case uncomfortable one of landlord and tenant.

There is something very wrong here. Three letters survive which were sent to Mrs MacDonnell by Lynchehaun during her frequent periods of residence in London. These letters are well outside the period when, according to her apparent testimony, she had discharged him. Either Mrs MacDonnell made a slip of the tongue in court, saying 1888 when she meant 1889, or this error somehow crept into reports of the proceedings. The letters cover the ten months between 1889 and March 1890, and apart from Mrs

MacDonnell's probable error of a year, they show a continuous relationship enduring for ten months as against the three months of employment which her statement would suggest. At the time of the first letter Lynchehaun may not yet be in her employment, but if perhaps only as grocer and tenant, has already had dealings with her, gaining her attention and respect; he feels that he can discredit and hopefully replace her then agent, Patrick Sweeney. At the time of his final letter his employment with her has perhaps ceased, but he is still in communication with her and has some hope of reinstatement. The three months that he served her must lie somewhere within those ten, most likely from early December 1889 until late February 1890. In his last letter he protests strongly that her herd, Johnny Gallagher, and her then housekeeper, Biddy Patton, were persecuting and maligning him. It is clear that there had been intense jealousy and a struggle for power and influence between the servitors of the frequently absent landlady. The letters are those of what for that time and place may be regarded as a very well educated man and the only fault in his English, if fault it be, is that he occasionally lets himself be influenced by Gaelic idiom. The first is dated 30th May, 1889.

Mrs A. MacDonnell,

You will be surprised to hear from *me*, but when you will be aware of my object in writing. I hope you will not consider it an unworthy motive. It is to give you a little idea of how your business is being transacted in your absence. I know but very little of what is transacted for you, and of that little I can see plainly intention to defraud you. By whom? By your agent Patrick Sweeney. The first item to make you aware of is the ten or eleven sheep he has bought for you. And from whom has he bought these sheep? From his son-in-law, Mr John Curran, and the price of them (the sheep) like the cow he sold for you, will be well in advance of the present times.[1]

---

[1] The letter was, of course, read out in court. On 18 July 1895 the following appeared in *The Mayo News:* Dear Sir — Will you allow me to say that there was no truth in a letter read in the case of the Queen *v* Lynchehaun that I ever sold sheep or cattle to Mr Patrick Sweeney in his capacity as agent for Mrs Agnes MacDonnell. The statement was absolutely without foundation, Yours faithfully, John Curran.

Certainly they will be good-looking and well improved when you may see them, as their pasture around the Valley House is excellent. Secondly, every time he comes to the Valley House he must see to have his horse fed on Mrs MacDonnell's oats, and I am informed on good authority that, notwithstanding to feed the horse, he must have another feed brought with him. (My authority is Biddy Patton and John Fadian, carpenter, who accidentally mentioned the cleverness of Mr Sweeney). Thirdly, he is reporting that Mrs A. MacDonnell is in Co. with his fishing transactions. He has begun to fish in Achill Head, and is to begin here on the Valley shores next week. He has engaged a crew at present. He will be hauling on the Valley Strand. I need not mention to you that you, as Landlord, will be liable to pay extra rates for fishing on your property. I mention this in order that you may not be a loser at the expense of Mr Sweeney's cleverness. Of course, if you and he are joined in the fishing, as he distinctly says, that matter of fishing is all right.

He has visited the Valley three or four times since you left, and on any of these occasions I know him to be *on his own business,* that is, in connection with this fishing. Also in order to have the freight of the materials ordered for the repairs of the Big House, he ordered all those things for his own hooker which caused considerable delay in delivery and besides left John Fadian, carpenter, almost, I believe, wholly idle, at least I heard Fadian say so.

The 'cleverness' of this agent is not yet known to you. I cannot call it 'cleverness', but I dare say it will convey to you a meaning. I am sure at the time of his appointment you did not know his history, not yet is it known to you, but had you been in the country a few years ago you should certainly learn something interesting from those very reverend gentlemen who now look upon P. Sweeney as an infallible man of business and intellect, etc.

I am, Mrs A. MacDonnell,
Yours most respectfully,
James Lynchehaun

Granting, as it seems we must, that Mrs MacDonnell was at worst guilty of a slip of the tongue when she said 1888 instead of 1889, her evidence was nevertheless evasive. In his second letter Lynchehaun speaks as a trusted agent, uniting himself with her, not merely in the first person plural pronoun, but in taking a common stand against a difficult tenantry. There is an unclear reference to 'a lot of gossip that will soon die down', but which, perhaps, refers to the mutterings of the tenantry, the type of talk that he has told Bridget Patton, the housekeeper, to ignore. His manner of writing is surprisingly imperative for one whom she regarded, or claims to have regarded, as of inferior social rank; and while he writes with the conventional courtesies he never admits that he is anything but Mrs MacDonnell's equal.

Some years later in a letter to Ross C. Rainsford, the District Inspector for the Royal Irish Constabulary, Newport, Co. Mayo, Lynchehaun will accuse Dr Croly of attempting to bring about Mrs MacDonnell's death, thereby banishing him (Lynchehaun) for life and, through her death, getting an opportunity to purchase the estate for himself. This accusation may give a clue to Lynchehaun's thinking, and to his assumption of landlord attitudes. He had a hope or a dream, that in some way in the future Mrs MacDonnell's Achill estate would come into his hands.

Friday, 11th October, '89

Mrs Agnes MacDonnell,

I beg to inform you that Tom Weir who was processed for two years' rent has settled as follows:

Amount of process	£2:5:0.
27¾ days labour 1/6d	£2:1:7½
By cash paid £0:3:4½	£2:5:0.

His rent has been fixed by the Commissioners and does therefore not admit of any increase or decrease. He produced the document from the Commissioners confirming his statement — the annual judicial rent fixed for the sum of £1:2:6.

I hold his process. The others who have been processed assume an air of independence, and appear not to take notice of the position in which they stand. I presume they are being taught to adopt their present course of indifference and independence. I anxiously await your final instruction in these cases as the time is running out fast. Those who hold processes would, I am sure, come to a settlement by paying as much as they could, promising the balances in a short time. In that case one or two are exceptions, as they can very well pay, such as Denis Sweeney. I cannot find out as yet what steps are about being taken by them, but I know from what accidentally slipped from one of them 'that their cases are in good hands, namely in that of your solicitors'. We are to infer from that that Mr Kelly will take the matter as easy as he possibly can, and give his opponent brother lawyer room to work. You will also please direct to have a complete list of rents of *all* your tenants sent me. The present lists I hold do not contain the name of *all* tenants. You will also please to give me any instructions you deem necessary in Peter Grealis's present process case. He may come to settle the process business, as I hear he is not combining with this other lot. In coming to a conclusion about these cases you must dismiss from your mind any weakness or doubt regarding the effectual result of the decision given in these cases. The law will be carried out. Those times have left, thank God, when law and order were not respected. On the other hand I would suggest anything I could think of to have peace and quietness among your tenants but unfortunately it was too much petting that was given them and shown them on your first coming among them and, now, you see their black ingratitude. But it is not themselves *entirely* who are to blame in this matter; they are worked up to the highest pitch of dishonour.

As I write a few workmen (the day being good) are to work at the hayricks, which shall be finished today. I have been two days at cutting the bent, and I do not intend to have any more cut. The bent affair has turned out as we predicted, namely that no one has courage or honesty to buy it. Intimidation in that line has already been used. But you may rely upon it that there will be no more of it stolen. I have vowed not to rest until someone is caught stealing it. I have posted notices about it, a copy of which I enclose. The price fixed per barth[2] is 1/1d. and to defray expenses and to leave you a small price for your bent is the basis on which I have fixed this nominal sum. In order to induce people to buy, in spite of intimidators, I have made it as low as possible. Still, we have received no order for any of it. You must not feel any way unhappy about the matter as we are bound to win in the long run — honesty will, and our line of action is honesty and justice.

I do not seem to notice that I am in any way put about through this illegal interference. I have not even let Bridget know much about this affair lest it may annoy her in any way. I always encourage her and tell her to take no heed of what she hears.

Jack, the butcher, and the woman from whom you bought the calves, have been paid by me for them. They are very restless and one of them is not feeding satisfactorily. John McNamara, mason, has finished up, and has put the black bottle on top of wall. Everything is going on all right as yet except a lot of gossip that will soon die out. Bridget's brother is with us yet. He feels timid to go out at night and I did not therefore press him. I go by myself. The Sandy Bank is actually infested with dogs at night. One has fell a victim and is well buried. You will not forget, I hope, sending me a few pills for these dogs. The owners of these dogs feel happy at the annoyance they give us.

I have written to my father today asking him to change the cow for us. She will be at home with *him*. There is another thing I want to bring before your notice, and that is those cattle which are to graze from November till March. If you remember there was some trouble about the same affair last year. You were not represented there by anyone except Jack McLoughlin. The magistrate decided in the tenants' favour because Father O'Connor swore that *all* the tenants' cattle were, by agreement,

[2]=Irish *beart*, 'bundle'.

allowed to go on the Banks for payment of 1/- per head.

Your instructions to me are 'not to allow any tenants' cattle on except those who have paid up', and your instructions will be carried out to the very letter, unless you order otherwise. But I anticipate some trouble from those who have not paid up, and their trouble in that line, by their forcing the cattle on to the Banks, will be only play to me. I am a match for their devilment.

Bridget has told me that you would send bran meal, salt, oats, etc. from Westport. I was to order it, and if you had had no time to do so when you were in Westport, may I supply the order?

Again I have to ask you not to be in the least troubled about this place. Your stock, hay, bent, etc., will be better taken care of than if you were on the spot yourself. Trespassers have already been put a stop to. Everything will settle down quietly after a bit. The only question you have now carefully to consider is this process affair. Your instructions now to me are to be final as the time is short. A complete list of *all* the tenants is now necessary. Dugort tenants are likely to be the first to pay their rents, and I have not all these tenants' names. In Peter Grealis' case, as he now stands on the conacre list given me by Mr Leslie, he is represented only to owe one year's rent. Last year, your agent, Mr Sweeney, refused to accept any money from this man. If he comes in to settle am I to take his rents, and to give him a receipt? Full instructions in this particular case are required.

Hoping that you, Mr Leslie and Mr Bush reached home all right.

I am,
Yours most respectfully,
James Lynchehaun.

Mrs Agnes MacDonnell,
19, Belsize Square,
London, W.

Jack McLoughlin has neither collected money due, nor has he delivered locks or marking irons. Neither has he come to work.

From Lynchehaun's third letter of 10 March 1890 it seems clear that he has not been dismissed, nor is he out of favour; he has recently had some instructions from Mrs MacDonnell which he handed on to John Gallagher, the herd, and Bridget Patton, apparently much to their surprise and little to their gratification. Not merely has Mrs MacDonnell not yet taken steps to evict him, but he hopes to extend his holding and rent more land from her. He also makes bold to criticise her latest agent Mr Vereker whom he obviously hopes to supplant.

> The Valley,
> Dugort, P.O.,
> Achill, Co. Mayo,
> 10th March, '90

Mrs Agnes MacDonnell,

The piece of land (soil) next the lake, for which you paid me £2, is still in the same unprepared state for sowing any corn this year in it. The fences are levelled to the ground and the whole place is an exercise field for the pigs of the village. From its present appearance I have come to the conclusion that probably you do not intend to sow anything this year in it, and if you did not itself it would be as cheap for you, as it would be almost impossible to save any crops put into it. In case you think it more profitable to have it rented, I will now give you £4 fine, and £1 yearly for rent. The rent to date from this 25th March, '90. You told me that if ever you should re-let the piece that I should have the preference of it, and my bid now is one which will be far more profitable to you than to begin sowing it yourself.

I told the herd that you confirmed the order about the potatoes and not a word have they (herd and Biddy Patton) spoken about them since. They seemed thunderstruck to have any communication from you at all.

Mr Vereker has been to the Valley as you are probably aware by this time and he has given liberal terms in the way of settlement, at Mrs MacDonnell's expense, but I presume by her permission.

Your herd reported me to the police 'for discharging a

gun on the public road' for which I was fined 2/6d. and costs. Isn't that hard enough in trying to calumniate me? It would be far better for him to turn his attention to bent cutters, timber thieves, and house-breakers, etc., than trying to trump up charges against me. But it is not him entirely, it is the famous inventor, Biddy Patton.

Wishing to hear from you soon about the proposal.

I am yours most respectfully,
James Lynchehaun.

Brother Paul did not create his *Narrative* exclusively or immediately from reliable documentary sources. He behaved in some ways like a bearer of oral tradition, a teller of tales. Documents such as letters and newspaper cuttings he indeed had, but the bulk of his sources consisted of talk, local gossip, yarns and anecdotes, some told by Lynchehaun himself. He may also have had some autobiographical notes of Lynchehaun for it was supposed in local tradition that Lynchehaun was writing a book. What he has to tell us about rabbits, bent, and unstamped receipts are, in a general way, true. But these are incidents in the war that was being waged, perhaps from as early as a number of months after Lynchehaun's dismissal[3] but certainly from March 1892: this was the date of the reporting by Lynchehaun to the Inland Revenue of Mrs MacDonnell's reluctance to waste penny stamps in legalising receipts. Brother Paul's time sequence is completely wrong. Apparently in order to achieve an eventual dramatic effect, the unpleasantness over rabbits, bent, and unstamped receipts is made to precede Mrs MacDonnell's employment of Lynchehaun; and his period as 'agent' is made to follow rather than to precede the agency of Harry Vereker. Thus the final tragedy is made to follow rather shortly on Lynchehaun's dismissal and there is no dramatically uncomfortable lapse of three and a half years to account for. Brother Paul shows little sympathy for

---

[3] In his letter to the *Chicago American* (see p. 183) Lynchehaun states that Mrs MacDonnell's efforts to evict him began three years before the assault, in other words, about October 1891. There is no reason to disbelieve him in this matter.

the 'eccentric lady'. He entitles this chapter 'His Transactions with Mrs Agnes MacDonnell'.

About the time that James Lynchehaun established a little shop business in the Valley, Achill, an English lady named Mrs MacDonnell became Landlady of said townland. Some of the poor tenants left their houses and went to America on the Emigration scheme. It is in one of the vacated houses James Lynchehaun established business; there was another vacant house convenient which he utilised as a store; there was some land to which he also laid claim, without getting possession of these from the landlady.

He promised to pay rent, and she strove to evict him as he did not get legal possession of them. Litigation ensued. Lynchehaun, learning law while in Police Force, was able to dodge her, so he used to get the case adjourned from court to court and from quarter to quarter, still having the use of the land and houses. He also considered that for every shilling he would lose by law-costs she would lose a pound and by this means she might discontinue the law-suit.

He also annoyed her in various other ways. She had large sand-banks on which bent was sown to prevent the sea-sand from being blown over the sheep pasture. She forbade her tenants to cut said bent.

James Lynchehaun despised said commands, cut bent by night, thatched his house with same, putting a little straw on the outside.

She had a warren on the Sandy Banks which she made well of for a time by setting to a rabbit-catcher in winter. James Lynchehaun, thinking it was a lucrative trade, made an offer for it which was accepted for one season. But learning that he trapped in and out of season until he had the rabbits nearly extinct in the warren she refused to sell it to him for the future. But James Lynchehaun, who was as tricky as a fox, was not going to be foiled. He gave the cash to another man to buy it in his name; when the bargain was closed and the cash paid, this man employed Lynchehaun, as it were, to trap them. The Landlady got furious and vowed vengeance. In her next sale of the warren she made sure to insert a clause in the agreement that James Lynchehaun would have no part in catching the rabbits. Still he used to poach by night.

So much for the rabbits. The following is another [example] of Lynchehaun's vicious cleverness. Mrs MacDonnell sold some sea-weed to neighbouring tenants. She gave them a written agreement which was not stamped. Sometime afterwards James Lynchehaun saw the agreement with one of the tenants, asked leave to read it, saw the defect, sent it to Dublin to the Revenue Office and stated that Mrs MacDonnell was cheating the Revenue in not stamping her agreements. After a long correspondence between the parties concerned I was informed that the want of the Revenue penny stamp on the little agreement paper cost Mrs Agnes MacDonnell £10.

The Landlady was much blamed for some of the trouble brought upon her, as she was very exacting and eccentric in her ways, as the following instances will serve to show.

When she got possession of this little property there was an Englishman named Josiah Salt as agent, by his being employed by her predecessor. She continued him in office for about one year, then found fault with him by saying he was too partial to the tenants, and appropriated some of her household furniture to his own use. For these real or imaginary faults, she dismissed him from her service.

Her second agent was Mr Patrick Sweeney, contractor of the swivel bridge at Achill Sound. This man was cool and polished, thought to get greatly ingratiated into her favour. But he soon learned the frailty of this woman's favours, that they were as fickle as a vane, and the sequel proved his learning true in this case. For she soon got suspicious of him, and soon discarded him for self-aggrandizement and embezzlement, and said that the tallest tree in the forest was not high enough to hang this unfaithful agent on for feathering his nest with her feathers. But she soon plucked them from him and sent him off deprived of his borrowed garb.

Her third agent was Harry Vereker. This man was agent for some fourteen or fifteen other Landlords, so he thought himself well able to manage business for this eccentric lady and her one townland of tenants, but he was soon deceived and discarded. She seemed pleased with him for a short time as he screwed the rents from the tenants pretty well. But finding he fed his horse on her hay and oats, she charged him with same. An altercation ensued which dissolved partnership and friendship. So she gave him his poundage and the road.

She was now mistress of all the situations in her townland property. She tried to act the parts of landlord, agent, bailiff, land-steward, etc., but seeing things growing worse, and finding herself unable to bear such a strain of anxiety, she again resolved to share the burden with someone more capable of bearing such a strain. She thought, looked around, made enquiries, and asked the opinion of some of those she had some confidence in, where she could get a reliable agent, or even one who would act as land-steward for the time being. Some of her advisors advised her to appoint Lynchehaun, even as land-steward, that he was young and energetic and would advance her business, being living in the townland, always ready at her call. That he would also cease troubling her with lawsuits. She considered the matter, agreed to appoint him steward, but reserved the agency for herself. So the fourth agent (or steward) in four years was brave Lynchehaun of whose transactions much will be recorded in the following chapters. James Lynchehaun gladly accepted the stewardship as a stepping-stone to the agency, and hoping to make a friend of his landlord foe.

About three months after the appointment to the stewardship Jim's ambitious spirit prompted him to aspire higher; applied for the agency which was scornfully refused, said she would not entrust the collection of her rents to such a man. He also made various other demands which were steadfastly refused. He got so pressing and persistent in his various demands that she considered him a source of annoyance rather than a help to ease her burden. So she treated him like his predecessors in office, deprived him even of his stewardship and sent him back to his little shop again.

Lynchehaun, seeing himself degraded instead of being promoted, revenge was rekindled in his ambitious breast; he promised to get straight with her. Hostilities were again renewed with vigour. She got determined to evict this troublesome man from her estate, and get him served with notices to quit.

This inflamed Lynchehaun the more and he vowed vengeance and said 'If she leave me houseless, so I will leave her.'

Litigation followed. Jim defeated her by some technical point in law. After this victory James Lynchehaun grew more insolent towards her. So much so that the landlady's anger was up to boiling point. More notices to quit were served and special lawyers employed.

At learning this Lynchehaun took a more serious view of the affair and said 'Though long the fox runs he gets caught. So I fear my doom is sealed this time.' He brooded over the matter, planned his schemes of resistance or vengeance. While the trial was pending in Castlebar he had some men employed repairing a road of which he had the contract. Although he was bodily with the men his mind and thoughts were centered on the lawsuit.

For two weeks previous to the trial he drank to excess of bad whiskey which he got in shebeen shops. He thought this would drown his troubles but it's how they fanned the flames of passion and incited him to put his evil designs into execution....

There is no evidence as to the relations between Lynchehaun and Agnes MacDonnell between the date of his third letter to her (10 March 1890) and 2 March 1892, the date of a letter of his to the Collector of Excise in Galway (not, as Brother Paul would have it, the 'Revenue Office' in Dublin). At this later date his vindictive persecution of her had started. It will be implied in The MacDermott's opening address to the jury, as quoted below, that Mrs MacDonnell set about evicting Lynchehaun and his wife and child immediately after his dismissal from her service.

The evidence of John Gallagher, the herd and general manager, who was on bad terms with Lynchehaun, suggests (quite wrongly) that eviction proceedings were begun as late as September 1893. On 26 January 1895 he deposed as follows: 'I know that the Defendant, James Lynchehaun, and Mrs MacDonnell were not good friends. I saw him a few times when she met him on the road, and I used to be with her and he would not speak to her. I was present when Mrs MacDonnell served James Lynchehaun with a paper. It was about twelve months ago last September. I was present twice when she served him with a paper but I cannot say what date. The second time we came it was to get possession of the house and Scraw, and he said he would give no possession until she would compensate him for the bogland about the house he broke in.'

There is thus a very incomplete picture of the relationship of this strange couple, but it would appear that the period of intense hatred began about October 1891, five months before the episode of the unstamped receipts.

Some time in 1893, according to Mrs MacDonnell's evidence in court, Lynchehaun made a pathetic move towards reconciliation and reinstatement. She was sitting at a table in her house, holding a rent office, while her tenants waited on her, and in turn came forward to pay their rent. Amongst them came Lynchehaun.

'I suppose,' said she, 'you have come to give possession of the houses and the Scraw.'

Lynchehaun asked to be allowed to remain in the cottages for two months until he had another house prepared.

'He then came round the table and offered to assist me but I declined it. He then paid his rent and went away. I told him that if he did not give possession of the houses at the time he stated I would charge him treble rent for them. He was then very pleasant and agreeable. I never saw him from that time till I saw him at the kitchen door on the night of the 6th October.'

Some years before 1976 Dr Lorna Reynolds and a friend, Kate O'Brien, the well-known novelist, visited the Valley and heard a 'folktale' of Mrs MacDonnell and Lynchehaun. This tale is true in many circumstantial details, such as the name of Mrs MacDonnell's favourite mare, Lady Jane, and her opening the door to Lynchehaun while dressed only in her night attire. In this account the name MacDonnell has been changed to Ellis, not unreasonably, for her son and heir was Leslie Elliot, and this name is often called Ellis on the Island. The name MacDonnell has been restored here but otherwise Dr Reynolds' words are given *verbatim*. The tale has many of the inaccuracies that one expects in an oral tale of historic events.

Many years ago I spent the summer in Dugort on the Island of Achill, and on one occasion walked to the village called the Valley. On the way back there was a large house obviously in process of being turned into an hotel. I and the friend who was with me turned into the avenue and decided to see if we could get tea. Our request caused some anxiety but we were shown through the dining room into a smaller room beyond, which would have been used, I thought, as the morning room or smoking room of the original house.[4] This room looked onto a small paddock.

We had to wait for a considerable time and as we waited I was invaded by a strange unease which grew into an overwhelming sense of depression and claustrophobia. My instinct was to get up and run away as quickly as possible. But I controlled myself and sat in silence until

[4] It was, in fact, the room in which Mrs MacDonnell slept.

after what seemed a long time tea was carried in. It was hastily swallowed and we left without delay.

That evening, talking to the owner of one of the hotels in Dugort, I asked her if she knew anything about the Valley and the house. She looked at me for a second in silence and then said 'But don't you know about it?'

I said 'No, what is there to know?'

Whereupon she recounted the following story, the central events of which she had heard from someone who was a child at the time described.

The new hotel had once been a fine house belonging to a Mr and Mrs MacDonnell who were English and very wealthy. Mr MacDonnell did not like Ireland and was seldom in Achill but Mrs MacDonnell loved the country, and spent most of her time there. She walked and rode around the island, keeping several horses and employing a groom called Lynchehaun. Mrs MacDonnell was a very beautiful woman and Lynchehaun, it was clear to everyone, soon developed a passion for her and followed her around like a faithful dog. This went on for some months and nobody knew whether Mrs MacDonnell was aware of her servant's feelings and encouraged them in any way or simply took his unusual devotion for granted. One day Lynchehaun lost control and declared his passion, only to be repulsed and rebuffed in a way that maddened him. He left the Valley, went over to Dugort and got roaring drunk. Late that night he returned to the house in the Valley, set fire to the stables and then hammered on the door, calling out to Mrs MacDonnell that the stables were on fire and that her favourite mare, Lady Jane Grey, was in danger. Mrs MacDonnell came down in her night clothes and dressing gown and opened the door. Lynchehaun fell on her, bit off her nose and practically flayed her alive. He then flung her behind some bushes and decamped. The fire naturally brought the villagers around and the child who originally told the story said that she had been with her mother and had said to her that she heard something whimpering in the bushes. But her mother told her 'to whist up and be quiet'.

I was not told how Mrs MacDonnell was discovered,

but she was rescued and taken to hospital where she recovered from her terrible injuries. She came back to Achill and lived in the house and used to walk invisible along the roads with her face behind a thick veil.

Lynchehaun was hidden by one of the people who dug a hole in the earthen floor beneath a dresser. There was a warrant out for his arrest. He escaped from Ireland to America, where he joined the police force under an assumed name. After some time he went to England and joined the police force there and under his assumed name was walking around with a warrant for his arrest under his true name of Lynchehaun.

The child who was present at the time of the assault on Mrs MacDonnell and who eventually told the story to Professor Reynolds' informant also appears in the account of the incident in the narrative of John McHugh:

No sooner was the alarm given that the Valley House was on fire than all the tenants on the estate, and many other neighbours living some distance away, collected to the place and worked hard till the fire was under control. Lynchehaun himself was one of the best workers and nobody among the crowd suspected that he was really responsible for the blaze. However, a story is told in this connection. Apparently while the people were still working at the fire a child ran up to its mother and said 'Mammy, I hear something crying in the bushes', or words to that effect (The whin bush into which Lynchehaun had thrown Mrs MacDonnell was fairly close at hand). The mother looked sternly at the child and said 'Hush, that's none of our business'. Whether she suspected foul play on Lynchehaun's part or not would be hard to tell but one thing is certain, that no man who knew him, and certainly no woman, would run the risk of falling into Lynchehaun's disfavour. So rather than find out who was crying the woman remained where she was.

CHAPTER V
6 October 1894

There were two entrances to the Valley House, the front door and the massive sliding 'wagon' door opening into the yard and to the back door of the house. The wagon door stood to the right-hand side of the front door as one approached the house. In the wagon door there was a wicket gate, and when door and gate were barred and bolted, there was no entrance to the yard from the outside other than by the daring and illegal act of scaling the great surrounding wall, which was covered with broken pieces of black glass. Immediately inside the wagon door to the right was the carriage house; then came the boat house and the stable that on the night of 6 October housed a horse, and, in a loose box, the mare Kate and her foal. Continuous with these were other stables, facing the kitchen door, some housing a number of sheep.

It was still dark at 5 o'clock on the morning of 6 October when the lady of the manor rose to set about her normal day's work. Biddy McNeally, wife of John McNeally, better known by her maiden name of Grealish, was the only indoor servant but she slept at her home nearby. She had only been in service at the Valley House for the previous six weeks when she replaced Biddy Patton who had died shortly before. Biddy arrived as usual, at about 6 o'clock, accompanied by her 'little boy' Pat McNeally, a youth in his early teens at most. Pat worked with the men in the yard and about the place; he could earn a trifle, get his meals, and his mother would have him under her eye.

As well as young Pat there were six working men, for Mrs MacDonnell, as well as being an extensive farmer, was constantly improving and rebuilding. First and most important was Johnny Gallagher, her herd and general manager. Whatever the nature of Lynchehaun's original contract, it is certain that he was put in a position superior to Johnny, for Mrs MacDonnell, always anxious to insist that she had never employed Lynchehaun as her agent, described him in one of her depositions as 'instructor to my herd'. Ironically, in later years in the court in Indianapolis, when it would not suit Lynchehaun to claim to have been Mrs MacDonnell's agent, an office that he had sorely coveted, a gentle mutation of her phrase turned him into her veterinary surgeon, a humanitarian office that gave him no hand in her 'iniquities'. Johnny, not unnaturally, had an intense dislike of Lynchehaun, and this feeling was reciprocated in full measure. Johnny's father, Matthew Gallagher, a farmer, also worked at the Valley House on that day. On this day Johnny, who in the morning was occupied in the kitchen garden, felt unwell, and Mrs MacDonnell told him to go home. He left before nine o'clock and spent the day in his own house.

The McGinty brothers, James and Michael, worked for Mrs MacDonnell as agricultural and general labourers. Tom Calvey, a young mason from Tallagh in Ballycroy on the mainland, was engaged in building a wall. He lodged with Matthew Gallagher, that is, he would eat his meals at Matthew's house but he slept at Johnny's. Since the Gallaghers were father and son he didn't think it mattered at which house he slept and he doubtless preferred the younger and livelier company. Finally there was Martin Deasy, about whom nothing more is known than that he worked for Mrs MacDonnell on that fateful day.

The McGinty brothers stopped work that evening between 6.30 and 7 o'clock and left the yard by the wicket gate. At seven Matthew Gallagher, Tom Calvey, Biddy McNeally, and young Pat, felt that they could call it a day. Biddy and her son had now worked continuously for thirteen hours. Tom had brought a lantern from the kitchen to the stables, and the McGintys fed the horses by its light as the last chore of the day; when they took their departure, the lantern was left with Matthew and Tom.

Tom locked the stable door and the door of the carriage house. Then, as he, Biddy and Pat, passed through the wicket gate, he handed the keys to Mrs MacDonnell who bade them 'goodnight', and carefully locked up after them. She was now alone, except for her lively little terrier Tip. She had worked hard all day and the fires had been let go out. The night was chilly so she went to bed immediately, forgoing her usual cup of tea. No hint here of gracious or luxurious living. On the contrary, there emerges a stale odour of miserliness which is not lessened by the presence of a carefully counted £83 in sovereigns, golden fruits of industry, frugality and self-denial, stored safely in a bag in a drawer, but destined, before the night was over, to be melted into an indistinguishable mass.

In contrast to Mrs MacDonnell's lonely evening, her peasant workforce enjoyed a brief period of companionship, relaxation, and, for them, extravagance, before going to bed. The McGinty brothers, on their way home, called in for a drink at John McLoughlin's shebeen. John was there as host together with his son Pat, the shoemaker, and a little girl, possibly John's daughter or grand-daughter, Mary McLoughlin. About seven o'clock Lynchehaun came in, holding a light boot in his hand. He spoke to Pat: 'Would you put a few stitches in that for me?'.

'I will'.

Lynchehaun took no drink; he had to go to Anthony Lavelle's, the smith's. He had just come from home on a couple of essential errands, the end of his day's work. He wore his strong working boots, was without coat or jacket but he sported a broad-brimmed beaver hat with the rim turned up. Meanwhile Matthew Gallagher and Tom Calvey left the Valley House, walked down the road together and turned into Peggy Cleary's shebeen for the ritual evening drink. Peggy, as was to be elicited in court by a typically light-hearted and unnecessary judicial intervention, sold whiskey at one and four-pence a half pint, two-pence less than the daily wage of an unskilled male worker. At about 7.15 Lynchehaun, his errand at Lavelle's done, came in with three men whom he had working at a contract job on the road: Ned McNamara, Tom McDonagh, and a man named McAndrew, perhaps the very one of that name who was later to marry the pretty spinster, Mary Gallagher Tom. Since he was boss of the three, and economically the most comfortable person present, Lynchehaun called for drinks all round. The scene was merry — nobody would appear to have spoken of weighty matters, nor was there any sense of impending tragedy. When Lynchehaun's drink was downed Tom Calvey, at the same time asserting a proud tradesman status and demonstrating his generosity and good-fellowship, bought a half-pint of whiskey for the company. After about seven or eight minutes Lynchehaun imperiously sent his workmen on their way — they would have to work the next morning — while he and the rest waited some two or three minutes longer.

'Come on home', said Matthew to Tom who showed signs of lingering.

'Jim'll be with us,' answered Tom, anxious for Lynchehaun's company.

'No, I want to go to the shoemaker for a boot I left in,' said Lynchehaun, going out the door before them and heading in the direction of John McLoughlin's.

The McGinty brothers were still drinking there at about 7.30 when Lynchehaun joined them for the second time that night.

'Is my boot finished?', he asked.

'It is,' said Pat. If he was a person for unnecessary words none of them were ever recorded.

Lynchehaun took his boot and left without having a drink. It was now just turned 7.30. He had drunk moderately and was on his way home. He had no coat or jacket and wore the same hat and boots that he had when he first came to McLoughlin's. When he was seen not much later that night, after the tragedy, by the McGinty brothers, Tom Calvey, Johnny Gallagher, and others, he had a cap instead of his beaver, but was in his stockinged feet.

The McGinty brothers stayed on drinking at McLoughlin's for another three quarters of an hour. They had been drinking, one assumes steadily, since 7 o'clock and when they finally left it was close upon 8.15. There was a watch in the McGinty house — a luxury not to be taken for granted — and James looked at it as he came in. It showed exactly 8.15. He went to bed immediately but Michael and their father stayed up a while. Then Michael, too, set about going to bed. As he was about to burrow down into the bedclothes their father rushed into the room crying out, 'The Big House is on fire'. The brothers jumped out of bed, dressed hastily, and ran in the direction of the fire. As they approached they could see the newly white-washed outhouses of the Valley House all lit up, for the October night had already been dark since long before 7.30.

As they ran, they gave the alarm to others. They took a route across a field and came towards the whin bushes and the hayrick that stood about thirty yards from the Valley House. Here they heard Biddy McNeally keening and olagoning and shouting at them, and about half a dozen women with her.

James deposed:

> They were beside the hedge. They called us as we were passing and we ran towards where the women were. I saw Mrs MacDonnell lying on the ground when we went over. Biddy McNeally was the first one I seen. She had her two hands round Mrs MacDonnell's neck and she had her sitting up.... Mrs MacDonnell had nothing on but her nightdress and, seeing her in her nightdress, I ran towards the fire....

James's modesty was commendable, for, bachelor that he was, the sight of a women in her nightdress must have been as scary as it was unusual. Even to the women the sight of Mrs MacDonnell was strange, for they handed on in tradition the image of the near-murdered woman as she lay there between the hayrick and the whin bushes: she looked like nothing so much as 'a scalded seal'.

CHAPTER VI
Mary Gallagher Tom

It was clear to the authorities that, even if the attempted murder of Mrs MacDonnell was a brutal and completely unjustifiable attack on a lady, it would be looked upon over the whole of Ireland, particularly in the west, as an agrarian crime. What with the tense state of the country, and the activities of the Land League, led by the western hero Michael Davitt, it would be difficult, if not impossible, to get independent witnesses against the accused. As the event turned out, all such witnesses were either officials, or employees of Mrs MacDonnell; all, that is, except one, the pretty and independent-minded girl, Mary Gallagher Tom. To follow her part in the affair, it is necessary to return to the point when the fire first broke out. At this time Mary sat talking after dark in the house of her next-door neighbour and friend, Peggy Gallagher Cleary. Their chat was sensationally interrupted by the sudden appearance at the door of Mary's mother, Mary Gallagher Tom, Senior. 'The Big House is on fire,' she cried.

Mary lost no time. She was up and out in a flash, running off in the direction of the blaze. The whole village was now in the grip of excitement. As she ran there were men and women before her and others after her; but she alone was to have the courage to intervene in the unfolding drama.

Approaching the wagon gate she could hear a voice inside; she recognised it as that of James Lynchehaun, but could not hear his words. The crowd, mostly women, who had arrived before her, held back, but Mary entered the yard through the wicket gate. Many of the outhouses were ablaze, and she saw Lynchehaun and Mrs MacDonnell standing there facing the fire. She deposed:

> As I was going over I saw James Lynchehaun catching a hold of her round the waist with his two hands; she had nothing on but her nightdress. When he caught Mrs MacDonnell she called to him in a loud voice to let her out,[1] and she said this more than once but I cannot say how often. She was wanting to pull herself away from him. Lynchehaun said he would not let her out until Johnny would come — that he would be here in a few minutes. Mrs MacDonnell had, at that time, a herd called Johnny Gallagher. Lynchehaun had a hold of her and they went very near to the fire, and he brought her very close to the fire. I don't know whether she went with him to the fire. He had hold of her, and with the struggling that was going on I don't know whether he pushed her into the stable or whether she fell into it. She got inside the stable door; when she got inside the stable door she fell; her head was turned out towards the door. Lynchehaun was inside her in the stable door. When I saw Mrs MacDonnell fall I ran over to take her out. I said to James Lynchehaun, 'Keep away, you murderer you'.
>
> James Lynchehaun looked at me with a cross look. I caught hold of Mrs MacDonnell and lifted her and took her out of the stable — that was the stable which was one side the one that the flames were going through the roof of. I don't know whether the flames had reached that stable at the time. When I was taking Mrs MacDonnell out of the stable she said to me, 'Oh, woman, take me out from this scoundrel'; she said this more than once. She appeared excited at that time. I took her into the yard. When I took Mrs MacDonnell into the yard she put up her hand and said, 'Remember that, James Lynchehaun'. She said this more than once. Before that she said to Lynchehaun, 'You'll pay for that, James Lynchehaun'. She told me to keep her. Before she said that to James

[1] =go.

Lynchehaun I said to her, 'Do you know me, my lady?' and she made no answer. After she made that observation to Lynchehaun she told me to let her out.

She went to the back door, and I went over after her. When I reached the back door it was closed and Mrs MacDonnell was inside. I was speaking to Mrs MacDonnell from the outside but I cannot say if James Lynchehaun heard what I was saying. I did not see James Lynchehaun at that time. When I was speaking to Mrs MacDonnell at the back door James Lynchehaun was standing at the corner of the house in the yard. He told me to come out of that before I would get burnt. I told him I would not. I told himself to go out. There was no sign of fire in the Big House at the time. The fire was beyond at the stables, facing the back door. I felt Mrs MacDonnell going away from the back door. She was going into the house. When I was standing at the back door and heard Mrs MacDonnell going away from the back door I did not see anyone in the yard. When I was going to go out on the yard door I saw Maggie Gallagher standing inside in the yard at the corner of the house.... When I got outside the little gate I saw a good deal of people standing outside. I did not see Mrs MacDonnell there. I did not see her until I saw her coming out through the little yard gate; that was immediately after I had passed out through it. She had the little dog in her arms with her.

When she came out she stood at all the people, and stood alongside me. She had another black coat on her. It was a cloak. She had only her nightdress and that on her. I knew a number of the people that were there. I saw James Lynchehaun, the defendant, there at that time. He was standing out facing the front door — the hall door of the Big House. Mrs MacDonnell put up her hand and said, 'Remember that, James Lynchehaun — you'll pay for that'.

But the exacting of vengeance would have to wait a little longer while Mrs MacDonnell dealt with her immediate problem. The men who had now arrived came into the yard at her behest and set about containing the fire; and the women were sent to fetch buckets of water. Everything was being done that could be done and Mrs MacDonnell wandered off with her terrier Tip towards the hayrick that stood thirty yards from the house.

Mary Gallagher Tom waited a while and then ran to her house for a bucket. She was soon back and looked into the yard for a moment to watch the men fighting the fire and did not notice Lynchehaun amongst them. She then joined another girl, Maria Sweeney, Denis's daughter, and they went together towards the lake:

> As we were going there we saw Mrs MacDonnell's little dog. He came out before us. We went coaxing him. I then heard noise — it was between sighing and crying. The noise was coming from beyond at the ditch. That was between the hayrick and the Big House. The little dog came over from that place.... I recollect coming back from the lake with the water. I heard noise as I was coming back. I heard sighing and crying coming from the same place that I heard it before....

Mary and Maria then went back to the yard. The fire was still blazing and Lynchehaun was not there 'unless he was in the stables'. Again they went for water, and on the way back Mary heard one of the windows in the Big House breaking. She looked in at the yard but saw no sign of Lynchehaun. Then she heard commotion and shouting at the gate and together with many of the people in the yard she ran out. She saw Matthew Gallagher, Bridget McNeally and others. They were at the ditch from where she had heard the sighing and crying and they were carrying the body of Mrs MacDonnell towards the house of Michael Gallagher, the tailor. Mary followed, and when she entered the house Mrs MacDonnell lay stretched on the floor near the fire....

Following her deposition, Mary was subjected to a gruelling cross-examination by Mr J. J. Louden, BL, acting for Lynchehaun. Her evidence was of such importance that it was necessary for the defence to cast as much doubt upon it as possible. Mr Louden tried to suggest that Mrs MacDonnell's injuries were caused by Mary, or by her brother

Pat, or by both acting together. Indeed, he had made a curious suggestion while cross-examining Doctor Croly: 'Are you aware that the biting of the nose and lip is a common occurrence amongst women through jealousy?' The Doctor replied drily, 'I am not aware of it personally.'

Mr Louden tried to suggest that Mary was part of a police conspiracy, perhaps even that a police officer had offered to marry her in return for evidence that would incriminate the prisoner. Mary could not be browbeaten or intimidated and her answers were pert and self-confident.

- Q. Who helped you to make that long statement that you made to the police?
- A. Myself.
- Q. Who helped you?
- A. *No answer.*
- Q. Was there any person helping you to make that statement, on your oath?
- A. No one helped me.
- Q. Can you read and write?
- A. Yes, sir.
- Q. Did you make that statement in writing or was it written for you?
- A. It was written for me.
- Q. Who wrote it?
- A. Mr Rainsford and Mr Horne.
- Q. Mr Horne took your information and no more?
- A. Yes.
- Q. Has any policeman promised to marry you lately?
- A. No, sir.
- Q. On the night of the burning, your mother said something to you when you were in Peggy Gallagher Cleary's house, what was it?
- A. She told me to come out, that the Big House was on fire.
- Q. What age is your brother called Pat?
- A. About 27 years.
- Q. Your father is alive?
- A. No, sir.
- Q. Where was your brother that night?

A. He was in his own house.
Q. Did he any time that night leave his own house and go to the burning?
A. He did, sir.
Q. Was he up before the Big House was set fire to?
A. Yes, he was.
Q. Was he up before the stables were set fire to?
A. No.
Q. How long were you in Peggy Gallagher Cleary's house before your mother came in and told you the stables were on fire?
A. I was about twenty minutes.
Q. When your mother told you the house was on fire did you go straight up then to see what was the matter with it?
A. I did.
Q. When at the fire did you see your brother first?
A. I seen him when I came up with the first bucket of water from the lake.
Q. Where did you get that bucket?
A. In my own house.
Q. Now is it not a fact that when you went down for the bucket your brother was in his own house?
A. He was not.
Q. Where was he?
A. I don't know.
Q. Now was not your brother in your own house when you went to Peggy Gallagher Cleary's?
A. Yes, he was.
Q. And after leaving him in your own house the first place you saw him was when you were coming up with the first bucket of water?
A. Yes.
Q. Now can you offer any explanation as to where your brother was during the twenty minutes you were in Peggy Gallagher's house?
A. I cannot. I don't know.
Q. So that he may have been at the stables which were set fire to, for all you know?
A. I don't know.

Q. Mrs MacDonnell I understand summoned your family to Petty Sessions for trespass on her land?
A. She did, sir.
Q. When were they summoned last?
A. I don't know.
Q. Is your mother one of the conacre tenants that Mrs MacDonnell served notice to quit upon to give up the land?
A. No, sir.
Q. Who accompanied you up to the burning?
A. Myself.
Q. You were a courageous young woman?
A. Well, there were people before me and people after me.
Q. Who were the people before you?
A. Well, I don't know, sir.
Q. Were they men and women?
A. Yes.
Q. Going to the fire like yourself?
A. Yes, sir.
Q. Would you say there were eight or twelve before you, to the best of your belief?
A. I don't know.
Q. Were there men and women behind you too?
A. There were men and women.
Q. The people who were after you would arrive at the burning nearly as soon as yourself?
A. Yes, they could, sir.
Q. And the people who were before you would get there before you?
A. Yes.
Q. The fire was in the yard?
A. It was in the stables in the yard.
Q. When you entered by the wicket where were all these people?
A. I don't know. It was not at them I was looking.
Q. What were you looking at?
A. I was looking at the fire.
Q. You told us of Lynchehaun having his arms round Mrs MacDonnell's waist. What clothes had she on

her at the time?
- *A.* Her nightdress.
- *Q.* Where were the horses then?
- *A.* I don't know, sir.
- *Q.* Were you present when the keys were asked for?
- *A.* No.
- *Q.* Were you present when Lynchehaun let the horses out?
- *A.* No, sir.
- *Q.* Did you hear he let them out?
- *A.* Well, I heard it passing.
- *Q.* Who told you?
- *A.* I don't know.
- *Q.* You saw James Lynchehaun having a hold of Mrs MacDonnell round the waist?
- *A.* I seen him catching a hold of her.
- *Q.* If Mrs MacDonnell swore she was dazed and stunned on the occasion and that she could — (*question objected to and withdrawn by Mr Louden*).
- *Q.* Did you observe anything queer about Mrs MacDonnell?
- *A.* Well, she seemed frightened.
- *Q.* Did you remark anything else about her except that she seemed frightened?
- *A.* No, sir.
- *Q.* Upon that occasion Lynchehaun did not commit any violence upon Mrs MacDonnell except to hold her round the waist?
- *A.* Well, he had hold of her and he brought her very close to the fire.
- *Q.* How long had he hold of her round the waist altogether?
- *A.* Well, I don't know.
- *Q. Question repeated.*
- *A.* About twenty minutes.
- *Q.* And did you and the crowd of people who went there not say a word during those twenty minutes?
- *A.* Yes, sir; I told him to let her out.
- *Q.* It was in the stable you said that, was it not?
- *A.* Yes, and outside, sir.

Q. And during those twenty minutes what were you and the people in the yard doing?

A. I don't know what the people in the yard were doing, my back was turned to them. I was standing looking at them.

Q. From where you saw them standing first how far were they from the stable where she fell — was it as far as the board where the gentleman is writing?

A. Yes, about that [about three feet]. Witness added 'I am not quite sure'.

Q. Now during the whole twenty minutes, what were they doing at that spot?

A. Well, he had a hold of her, and she was trying to pull herself away.

Q. Do you mean to say that that strong man could not push the woman into the fire if he liked during those twenty minutes?

A. Well, I don't know, sir.

Q. Would it not be easier to push her into the fire than keep her standing there for twenty minutes in the same place?

A. But she wasn't in the same place, sir.

Q. But nearly in the same place?

A. Well, I don't know, sir.

Q. It was not into the burning stable she went?

A. No, sir.

Q. After she came out of that stable with you was her chemise scorched in any way?

A. I don't know, sir.

Q. You saw no marks of burning on the lady's chemise?

A. Well, no sir, I did not look.

Q. There was a barrel of tar or petroleum on fire that night?

A. I don't know, sir.

Q. Well, did you hear it?

A. Well, I heard there was.

Q. Were sheets of flame passing over the yard that night?

A. Yes, sir, and passing over the stables.

Q. Mrs MacDonnell walked quietly with you from the

stable to her own house?
A. She did not.
Q. Didn't you say you took her out of the stable?
A. I did but I didn't go to the house door with her.
Q. But she walked quietly from where you stood with her in the yard to her own house door?
A. She did.
Q. From the time she left the stable with you up to the time she reached her own house did Lynchehaun attempt to molest her?
A. No, sir.
Q. You are aware that the stables were fired on that night and later on the Big House was burned?
A. I was not there when the Big House was burned.
Q. What were you doing there without a friend or relation on that night?
A. I was there trying to save as well as every other one.
Q. After Mrs MacDonnell went into her house didn't you follow her up to the door?
A. Yes, sir.
Q. And when she was inside you had your ear to the keyhole outside, hadn't you?
A. No sir, I had not, I was standing outside.
Q. Had you your ear close enough to the keyhole to hear her going upstairs?
A. Well, I could feel[2] her, sir, but I hadn't my ear to the keyhole.
Q. Was it not with your ears you felt her moving about inside?
A. Yes, sir, it was.
Q. So you were listening.
A. I was not listening.
Q. What brought you up to that door after the woman that night?
A. Well, I followed her. I thought that she was frightened.
Q. Why after she closed the door did you stop listening outside?

[2]=notice, perceive.

A. Well, I did not, but I was telling her to come out to me.

Q. What? — 'I was telling her to come out.' What did you want her out for, and she in her nightdress?

A. Well, because I thought she was frightened when she seen the way the stables was being burned, and I seen the way she was talking to James Lynchehaun.

Q. Can you now give me the names of the people who were in the yard this long time?

A. I don't know but I knew them when I went in.

Q. Well, who were they when you went in?

A. James Lynchehaun, Pat McLoughlin, Jack McLoughlin; there was a lot of little children, boys and girls, but I cannot tell you who they were.

Q. From the time you were at the back door when Mrs MacDonnell went in how long was it until you went out the wicket?

A. Well, about three or four minutes.

Q. Did you not state on that table that you did not know anybody there except Lynchehaun and Mrs MacDonnell? (*Question objected to and withdrawn*). When you went out the wicket there were people outside?

A. Yes.

Q. How many women were there outside?

A. Well, I don't know, sir.

Q. How long were you outside until Mrs MacDonnell came out?

A. Well, I was only outside when she was out after me.

Q. When you were at the kitchen door didn't you ask her to come out?

A. Yes, sir.

Q. And when she did come out the wicket door what did you do to her?

A. Nothing, sir.

Q. When she came out the wicket then did you speak to her?

A. No, sir.

Q. Having asked her to come out of her house why did you not speak to her when she came out?

A. Well, sir, she was at the people then and I thought she

was all right.
- *Q.* Who were the people?
- *A.* Well, there was a good deal of people but all I knew was Denis Sweeney, Anthony Lavelle (Smith), Pat McLoughlin and James Lynchehaun Street and Charlie Malley.
- *Q.* Was James Lynchehaun, the prisoner, there amongst that crowd?
- *A.* Yes sir, he was.
- *Q.* Why didn't you mention his name until I mentioned it?
- *A.* Because I wasn't asked.
- *Q.* Where did you go to from the crowd at the gate?
- *A.* I went home, sir.
- *Q.* And I take it you did not see James Lynchehaun, the defendant, from then until you saw him in your own house that night?
- *A.* No, sir....

Mary Gallagher Tom gave evidence in court against James Lynchehaun, and then retired gracefully from history, marrying a man called McAndrew and living to a ripe old age.

CHAPTER VII

At Tailor Gallagher's House

As Mrs MacDonnell lay on a feather bed on the floor of Michael Gallagher's house the men in the yard continued to fight the fire; no one was any longer conscious of time and its passing so that in retrospect an event that might have otherwise gone unchronicled was used to mark a point in an hour of horror. This was the appearance at the wicket of a group of women, 'the cursing women', three of whom were named, one being Judy Cooney: she would later appear as a witness for the defence. A kind of Greek, or rather Gaelic, chorus, they warned of evils to come, 'cursing' the men out of the yard or all would be arrested. They symbolised dramatically the Irish peasant fear of the Landlord and his power.

Many of the stables were nearly burnt out, and James and Michael McGinty, John Gallagher and Tom Calvey set about knocking down the galvanised roof of one of the sheds to prevent the fire spreading. At this moment, according to their evidence, Lynchehaun appeared, wild-looking, apparently somewhat intoxicated, a stone in each hand. They all stopped to look at him.

'What's up?,' he asked.

'The stables are on fire,' answered James McGinty.

'What's on you,' said Michael. 'You're cut. Where's your cap and your boots?'

'I fell two or three times since leaving home, and I fell coming in the yard door.' He threw down the stones, pulled a cap out of his waistcoat and put it on. 'I hadn't time to put on the boots when I was called.'

James looked at him closely. 'There was a small bit of blood on his left cheek. I observed his trousers. The legs of his trousers down here at the front of the thighs were wet or dirty.'

Lynchehaun now joined with the rest in fighting the fire but after a short time became tired. 'To hell with the old sheds,' he said.

It was now about 11 o'clock. There was as yet no fire in the Big House, and no apparent danger, for the wind was south-west, blowing from the direction of the house, and towards the sheds. The men abandoned the remains of the fire and went off towards Tailor Gallagher's.

Mary Gallagher Tom, after leaving the fire some time before, had first gone to the tailor's house, but as it was very near her own she soon left and went home. But there might still be some excitement left in the night so instead of going to bed she stood at the door of her house. She saw Lynchehaun approaching and retreated inside, standing beside the fire with the widow Gallagher, her mother, and her brother Pat, aged twenty-seven. In a moment Lynchehaun appeared in the kitchen and addressed Mary, probably in Irish, for the short but pregnant conversation has a flavour of translation.

'You are the only one that can free me.'

'I can't free you. I'm the only one that can guilty you.'

'For your life don't speak. I am not afraid of anyone but you.'

'Don't speak of me, and I won't speak of you.'

'I will not speak.'

'Be off with you to your own house,' said Mary's mother, bustling him out of the door.

Lynchehaun left and went back to the tailor's house.

After leaving the fire and separating from Lynchehaun, the rest of the men were approaching the tailor's house when they met Denis Sweeney emerging from it. He was in a state of anxiety and after a hurried conversation it was decided that Michael McGinty and Ned Grealish should go to Dugort — about a mile and a half away — to fetch Dr Croly.

Meanwhile Matthew Gallagher, still up at the Big House,

had also decided to go to Dugort to fetch the doctor and the police. First, he must get a horse. The mare, Lady Jane, was in the waste garden behind the yard, closed up, and there were three or four other horses with her. Six other horses were down on the Sandy Banks. When he found the two horses that Lynchehaun had released from the stables he saw that they had both been stabbed in the flank. He gave up, went off to his own house, got his own horse and set off with young Pat McNeally.

After an hour and a half they had all returned with the doctor and the police, the latter consisting of Sergeant Joseph Dusting, and two constables, Morrison and O'Sullivan, both of whom could speak Irish. All gathered in Michael Gallagher's kitchen, together with a sizeable percentage of the population of the Valley. It was now 12.10 on the morning of 7 October.

The first thing the doctor ordered for the patient was a drink of whiskey. There was no whiskey in the house. Lynchehaun jumped up, went off and after some time came back with a jugful.

'Does anyone know how it happened her?' asked the doctor of the company as he started to examine the patient.

'It was letting out the horses,' volunteered Lynchehaun. 'They threw her sky high, and she would insist on letting them out in spite of my advice. There were twenty more that saw it as well as myself. It was Lady Jane that rose over her. Isn't it easy knowing it was the mare that kicked her!'

'What are the names of the others that saw it?' interposed the Sergeant.

Lynchehaun ignored the question and the doctor commented 'She was a foolish woman to risk her life for a horse.'

The doctor was now dressing the patient's head. 'Look at her mouth and see if she has any teeth broken,' ordered Lynchehaun.

No broken teeth were found. 'I would like her removed to the upper room to examine her to see are there any more injuries on her body.'

'Examine her from her hole to her poll!' said Lynchehaun.

'Fie, James, you ought not to make use of such language,'

said the doctor, but he could not afterwards remember clearly whether he said 'Fie' or 'Shame'. He was under oath and had a tender conscience.

Lynchehaun now came over and sat at Sergeant Dusting's left and gave him a light kick on the shin to attract his attention. 'Arrest Matthew Gallagher, John Gallagher and Tom Calvey,' he whispered. 'They threw the new wall on her.'

He now moved to a stool on the Sergeant's right. 'That's Calvey,' he said, 'That's the mason,' pointing to where Tom Calvey stood at Mrs MacDonnell's head.

The Sergeant looked, then turned to stare intently at Lynchehaun. There was only a faint light, but he could see that the bottoms of Lynchehaun's trousers were wet. Noticing the Sergeant's interest, Lynchehaun pulled his feet back under the stool.

Mrs MacDonnell was now brought to the upper room and placed in a bed the bottom of which touched the head of another. Constable Morrison stayed a while in the kitchen, following the Sergeant's orders to keep Lynchehaun under observation. After a while he said 'It's as good for you and I, James, to go up to the bedroom to see what is going on.'

They went up together and Lynchehaun threw himself on the second bed. 'The most the bloody old bitch can do is to live until morning.' With that he either fell asleep or feigned sleep. Meanwhile the patient said nothing except to repeat 'I'm cold, I'm cold'.

The Sergeant now approached Mrs MacDonnell. 'I am the Sergeant of the police in Dugort. Can you tell me who done this to you or who injured you?'

She was now fully conscious but could as yet only remember the incident in the yard. 'James Lynchehaun threw me into the burning building and tried to strangle me. I screamed so loud he let me go. He forced me down on the ground and tried to strangle me.'

'There are two James Lynchehauns. Which of them?'

'James Lynchehaun, grocer', but with her English habit of diphthongising vowels most of the listeners, including the doctor, heard her say 'grouser'.

It was now about 12.35 a.m. Constables Morrison and

O'Sullivan were put in charge of Mrs MacDonnell and Lynchehaun, and from now on the latter was under constant surveillance. He was snoring while the doctor continued his ministrations. The results of his examination were given in a deposition made at Westport on 19 January 1895.

When I first saw her she was in an almost lifeless condition. Her hair and nightdress were saturated with blood. I examined her, and found her pulse weak and trembling and scarcely perceptible. Her breathing was very weak and stertorous. The body was almost cold. I examined her head. I found three wounds on the head. The first wound was almost on the crown of the head, reaching over to the left parietal bone. It was about three inches long. It went to the bone. It was a lacerated contused wound. The skull was not fractured there. That wound would likely be caused by some blunt instrument. A stick would cause it, or a bar, or a long stone. The second wound I found was on the left parietal bone. A similar wound to the last, but not so long. There was no fracture corresponding with this wound. It was a lacerated and contused wound. The third wound was over the left temporal. It was a lacerated and contused wound also. This wound seemed to me to have its origin over the angle of the frontal, and extended over the left temporal. The temporal bone was fractured. It was a starred fracture. The wound was about two inches and a half in length. I was of opinion that this wound was caused by a blow of a stone. The second wound I spoke of would be likely to be caused by any blunt instrument. A kick of a boot would cause it. There was some parts of her hair very thin, but none of the scalp was torn. The whole of the cartilage of the nose was gone and the nasal bone exposed. I was of the opinion that it was bitten off. There was a deep wound underneath the left eye. The left eye itself was swollen and tumefied. The eye itself was not torn. There was a semi-circular wound passing through the right eye completely crushing it, making bits of it in pulp. This eye was very much swollen and tumefied. In my opinion the wound underneath the left eye was caused by some blunt instrument. It could be caused by a kick. The wound on the right eye looked like as if it was caused by the kick of the toe of a boot. There was a complete gap in the upper lip, it was deeper in the inside, getting narrower at the edge, and that piece was completely removed. I thought it was taken off at the same time as the cartilage of the nose, that it was bitten off and the lip was averted at the time. It corresponded with a gap in the ullea or wing of the nose. The right jaw bone was greatly inflamed, which would be likely to be caused by some blow or crush. The crush of a boot would cause it. The larynx was inflamed and congested. There were four distinct marks on one side, and one on the other, as if four fingers and a thumb had been pressed on it. It would require considerable pressure to produce the appearances I saw. I examined the body. There was a large contusion over the two lower ribs of the right side, about the centre of them. That would be caused by a kick, the lower lobe of the right lung was inflamed and the upper portion of the liver was congested, corresponding with external contusion. Immediately over the navel between the lower margin of the stomach and the navel there was a semi-circular contusion. In my opinion it was caused by the heel of a boot being pressed upon it. There was a corresponding contusion over the region of the bladder, under the navel, and in my opinion that was caused in the same manner. The bladder itself was inflamed and the urethra was torn. For eleven days she suffered from retention of urine. In my opinion the urethra was ruptured by a kick. The vagina was torn, the right side of it was lacerated and torn, I thought it was caused by kicks, I applied poultices, stupes, and healing lotions to that part. On the third day I found pieces of whin bushes embedded deeply down in the tissues of the vagina, and I removed them. Until then she complained of intense soreness, but this relieved her very much. In my opinion the whins were forced in by the kick which lacerated the vagina. There was a deep, lacerated wound in the perineum, caused, in my opinion by a kick. The buttocks were all contused and black. I formed the opinion that this was caused by kicks and blows. The right knee was slightly lacerated and contused, and the whole of the inner portion of the leg, from the knee to the ankle, was slightly burned. I could not tell how the injury to the knee was caused. One of the toes of the right foot was bruised and swollen. There was also a toe on the left foot and part of the instep contused; and in my opinion this was produced by violence of some kind.

Under cross-examination by Mr M. J. Kelly, Crown Solicitor, Dr Croly said: 'I will not take it upon myself to swear, as the result of my examination, that this lady was outraged; she may or may not.'

When the doctor had done all he could, he decided to return to Dugort, and Sergeant Dusting, having left Morrison and O'Sullivan in charge, was to accompany him. But on opening the kitchen door they stepped back, shocked for a moment into immobility: the Big House was ablaze. When they pulled themselves together, the doctor, realising that his part in the affair was finished, took his leave. He had spent nearly an hour and a half with the patient, and it was now 1.30 a.m. The Sergeant, very curiously, reckoned that it was past 2.30, but the doctor was probably right.

The Sergeant gathered together Mrs MacDonnell's employees, Mathew Gallagher, John Gallagher, Tom Calvey and young Pat McNeally, and they ran up to the Big House.

As the Sergeant tells it in his deposition:

> We broke in the hall door first and found one room on the basement storey, to the right of the hall door as you go in, on fire and also the room over it. The flames were bursting through the roof. We could not at that time see any trace of fire in the room on the ground floor to the left of the hall door, but we got fire in the room above it when we were removing the furniture. We broke in the window to the left of the hall door where there was no fire and we removed the furniture. We afterwards broke in the window of the upper room on the left. I did not enter that room. John Gallagher did, and he handed out the furni-

ture. I observed that two chair cushions, that is the seats of two chairs, were burning when handed out, and I stamped them out. The wood-work was not injured. A sofa was partly burned too in the seat of it, but the wood-work was not injured. Shortly after we had removed the furniture out of the two rooms the roof fell in, in fact it was partly falling in while we were removing it. The wind was about south-west at that time. It was blowing from the house towards the stables. I returned to Michael Gallagher [tailor's].

Subsequently the Sergeant discovered that the pantry window, facing on to the yard, had been broken and the lower part of the sash was broken off. The opening was large enough to admit a person and the Sergeant himself proved this by entering it himself. There were blood marks on the shelf resting inside the window and in other places too. He carefully removed all blood marks and brought the bloody stuff so removed to the barracks.

It was now accepted by the police that Lynchehaun had scaled the wall and set fire to the sheds and stables, that he had attacked Mrs MacDonnell and later set fire to her house. But the evidence for arson, especially with regard to the Big House, was not strong. Supposing, however, that Lynchehaun really did set fire to Mrs MacDonnell's house, when did he do it? The fire was seen at earliest at 1.30 a.m. and Lynchehaun had been under close observation since 12.10, except, of course, during that period of unspecified duration when he went on his errand of mercy to get a jugful of whiskey for Mrs MacDonnell. When he came back he was not asked where he got it but it was probably assumed that he had gone to one of the local shebeens, Peggy Cleary's or McLoughlin's, and bought out of his own pocket a half a pint for one and four pence. But, however unlikely, it would seem at least possible that when he went for the whiskey he broke into the Big House through the pantry window, started a fire in one of the rooms, using a little oil that he got in the kitchen. He got a jug, went to the dining room or wherever the whiskey was kept and returned quickly with the reviving draught, thus appearing creditably anxious for the health and quick recovery of the patient. He went out through the front door, leaving the fire slowly smouldering.

Mrs MacDonnell was to remain in Michael Gallagher's for many weeks until she could travel to London. Meanwhile a nurse, Miss Fitzgerald, had already been engaged to look after her on the night of the fire. A relative of Michael Gallagher's wife, Margaret Gallagher née Carney, has a graphic detail as to her care and diet, preserved up to the present day in family tradition. 'She didn't get the food she ordered, she got what was going. One thing she loved and couldn't get enough of, *sleamhcán*.'

Sleamhcán, or sloke, is a jelly made from sea-weed, eaten by itself or served with roast mutton. Mrs MacDonnell found it comforting to her injured throat.

CHAPTER VIII
Arrest and Escape

At 7.30 a.m. in tailor Gallagher's house Constable Morrison, the senior police officer present, cautioned Lynchehaun, and then arrested him on charges of murderously assaulting Mrs MacDonnell and burning the Valley House and its outhouses.

'There should be more fellows arrested than me,' said Lynchehaun. He was still as he had been all night, attired in dirty blood-stained trousers and a cap, but wearing no boots. In this condition, he was hand-cuffed and brought to Dugort police station by Constables Phillip Carrigan and John O'Sullivan.

As they were passing his house Lynchehaun asked permission to go in to change his clothes but was refused. He was allowed, however, to go to the door and he spoke to his servant boy in Irish. Constable O'Sullivan understood and heard him tell the boy to bring his clothes and shoes after him to the barracks. The boy said he would.

The servant boy — his name is not given in official documents — was Tony Lynchehaun, then aged about fourteen. He was related to Lynchehaun on his mother's side, and more distantly on his father's. His function was to make himself generally useful and to serve in the shop. He was a close friend of Brother Paul — who gives no hint of this friendship in the *Narrative* — and they used to go hunting together. Tony lived on until 1965, unmarried, increasingly unwilling to speak of Lynchehaun, or of his own part in the affair; he remained a good and honest servant boy to the end of his days.

The party arrived at the barracks at about 8.15 and Lynchehaun made a statement which O'Sullivan wrote down: 'It was my own simplicity. But for myself this would not happen to me. It would be easier for me to come to Dugort and give a night in the barracks for drunkenness. I wish to God she died, and that she may never recover!'

He also remarked that it was the horses that had kicked Mrs MacDonnell in the stables but no note was made of this. O'Sullivan then handed him over to Constable Gwynne, the barracks orderly.

Shortly afterwards the servant boy was seen outside the barracks on a horse; he carried a bundle of clothes and in the bundle a pair of light shoes without any nails, one of which was probably the very one which Lynchehaun had had mended the night before by Pat McLoughlin. Gwynne took the bundle and gave it to Lynchehaun who straight away changed his clothes there in the day room, but kept his incriminating and blood-stained waistcoat, apparently for no better reason than that the boy had not brought him a clean one. Gwynne took the dirty clothes — trousers, drawers, shirt and stockings — rolled them in a bundle, and threw them in a corner of the room.

Lynchehaun tried to get Gwynne to leave the room, first asking that he should go over to Dr Croly to find out how Mrs MacDonnell was doing, then that he should go to the kitchen to light Lynchehaun's pipe. 'I cannot leave you while I'm in charge of you', said Gwynne.

At about 9 o'clock Gwynne was relieved by Constable O'Sullivan. The bundle of clothes was in the corner when he left and the window of the room was open. Five minutes or so later O'Sullivan went out of the room for a few moments, all the time keeping an eye on the front door so that nobody could gain access to the prisoner unknown to him. When he came back he noticed that the bundle of clothes was gone. He immediately realised that Lynchehaun, in his brief absence, had handed the bundle through the window to the servant boy. He hurriedly called Gwynne and asked him to relieve him, then set off in pursuit. He overtook the boy at about two miles' distance but the bundle of clothes had vanished. Tony came back to barracks with O'Sullivan and was brought into the day room. 'Did you see the clothes?' said Lynchehaun, speaking in English. 'No,' said Tony.

Then Lynchehaun changed to Irish. 'If they're below in the house bring them up,' but he may have given some private negative sign.

'I will.' Tony then went off and did not return. That night, according to a newspaper report, quoted below, Lynchehaun's house was ransacked by the police, but no trace was found of the clothes. But the next day O'Sullivan paid a call on Mrs Lynchehaun, whom he knew. She handed him the shirt, trousers, drawers and stockings, all of which were hanging on a line near the fire, clean and newly washed.

Over half a century later, the reticent Tony cleared up, at least to some extent, what had happened to the clothes.

On his way home to the Valley, in the neighbourhood of Glacca, he became conscious of police pursuit. He walked his horse in off the road, threw down the bundle, and had the horse trample it into the wet bog. If he were seen and questioned he would say that he was giving the horse a drink. A woman saw him and shortly afterwards retrieved the bundle, which, in due course, found its way to Mrs Lynchehaun.

Knowing the persons involved and the sequence of events in this episode affords us an opportunity of observing Brother Paul's technique, or that of his informants, and evaluating the historic worth of the *Narrative*.

His story has reduced three constables — Carrigan, Gwynne and O'Sullivan — to one, Carrigan being chosen to bear all the ignominy of the affair. Such a simplification does not interfere seriously with the historicity of the *Narrative* — it is a sound and permissible story-telling device and saves the reader or listener from being wearied by unnecessary detail. The barrack orderly, it is implied, knew no Irish. This is strictly untrue, but makes a better story. Lynchehaun's retiring to a closet (by which is meant a toilet) to change his clothes, and the substitution of an air-vent for an open window, are unimportant embellishments: Lynchehaun is shown as planning the action carefully and exactly, instead of quick-wittedly taking advantage of a momentary lapse on the part of his custodian, a situation that he had tried to bring about, but without success. The questioning of a female servant, for which there is no evidence in official sources, would appear to be Brother Paul's addition; some such thing, he would have thought, must have happened. As to the rest, Brother Paul, writing in the second decade of this century, would have had an account of the whole affair from Tony, at that time in his early or mid-twenties and perhaps not so reticent with his friend as he later became. However, it would appear that Brother Paul or Tony exaggerated somewhat the part that the latter played; for once Lynchehaun has been upstaged in his constant and dramatic battle with the police.

As Lynchehaun was being conveyed to barrack he passed by his own house, and shouted to his wife (in Irish) to send his clean clothes after him, which she did. When the clothes arrived he asked permission of the barrack orderly to retire to the closet while getting them on, a request which was granted. On his retiring he told his servant boy, whose name was Tony Lynchehaun, and who brought the clean clothes to him, not to go for a while, and to stand outside the closet where there was a small air-hole (he addressed him in Irish). The servant being nearly as clever as his master took the hint. And as Jim was divesting himself inside of the blood-stained clothes, he shoved them out the air-hole to Tony who bundled them up on the outside, then mounted on his horse and rode off with them. In order to give plenty of time to the boy to escape, Jim delayed longer in the closet than was needed for the mere change of clothes. The barrack orderly would shout occasionally, 'Have you done there yet?' Jim would answer, 'What great hurry are you in with me? Have patience.'

On his return the barrack orderly asked him where were the soiled clothes. Jim said they were thrown in a corner of the closet. It was searched but no clothes found there. He next stated that the barrack servant may have taken them. She was asked but knew nothing about them. So the blood-stained clothes, which would be the greatest evidence of his guilt, had disappeared.

The barrack orderly named Carrigan, being a married man, fearing to lose his belt and jacket, or at least be heavily fined and removed over it, reported the matter to Sergeant Dusting who sent a policeman in haste after Lynchehaun's servant who was about a half mile away at this time.

A man who was digging potatoes on a hill-side saw the policeman coming in haste, told the boy of it, who threw the bundle in a sequestered place, and walked leisurely till the policeman overtook him and demanded the soiled clothes.

'I have none,' said Tony.

'Come, come,' said the bobby, 'get off this horse and get the clothes for me or I will arrest you also.'

'Where is your warrant for arresting me?' said Tony, the boy.

The blustering bobby, in order of frightening Tony into compliance, ordered 'Dismount, let the horse go,' clapped a pair of handcuffs on him and marched him off to barrack.

Tony, being nearly as clever as his master, Jim, said to the bobby 'You have arrested me illegally and if anything happens to the horse you shall be accountable for it.'

The bobby said 'You are drunk'.

Tony answered 'I will let you know I am not.'

So as they neared the barrack Tony refused to enter until he would see the doctor. So the doctor examined him and declared him sober. He went next to see the Magistrate, who was close by, and declared that he had neither taken food or drink that morning, and still this policeman had illegally arrested him under the false charge of being drunk.

'I see no sign of drink on you,' said the Magistrate, 'nor does the doctor either. You have outstepped the bounds of your duty. Release the boy.'

The bobby had to unlock the manacles, set Tony free. So the boy outwitted the bobby.

At 7.20 a.m. Constable James Carr had arrived at the Valley and began a search of the land between the Big House and the haystacks. At 3.30 p.m. Ross C. Rainsford, District Inspector of the RIC, arrived from Newport to take charge of the case. At 5 p.m. the prisoner was brought to Tailor Gallagher's to be present at the taking of a deposition by Mrs MacDonnell before Mr. T. P. Carr JP. Lynchehaun was remanded in custody and lodged for the night in the barracks at Dugort. The next morning he was taken to Mulranny on his way to Castlebar Jail. At Mulranny he was handed over to Sergeant Michael Scully of Achill Sound, who was accompanied by Constable Costello. At the Railway Station in Castlebar Scully made a note of statements that the prisoner had made during the journey:

Is not this an extraordinary business. I was called out of my own house by Judy Cooney. I was just going to bed at the time, and had my boots off. When I went out I saw the blaze, and I ran down and saw her in the middle of the flames. I rushed in at her and shoved her out, and she fell. When she got up I asked the keys of the stable of her, and she gave them to me, and I ran and let out the mare and foal, and I saw no more of her until I saw her in Michael Gallagher's house. The poor woman is destroyed right enough; the way her head is she must have fallen again, or struck against something, or the galvanised roof might have fallen on her, as the whole roof was galvanised, or when she went down where she was found, the horses might have walked on her, or kicked her. I was a bloody fool anyway that did not remain in my own house, and laugh at the whole thing; but sure if I was in London she would say that it was I that done it, but I don't know what they arrested me for, as when the magistrate, Mr Carr, asked her where she was, she said she was in her own house. You won't be long at home until you are coming this way again with more.

On arrival at Castlebar Jail, Scully handed him over to John Short, the Chief Warder, who took his waistcoat as evidential material and gave it to Acting-Sergeant Keegan.

Owing to Mrs MacDonnell's natural confusion she had to make in all four successive depositions as her strength gradually returned, one on 7 October, two on 11 October, and her final one on 20 October. The defendant had to be present at every deposition and this meant, as well as journeys by rail, trips in custody on that most insecure of vehicles, the Irish jaunting car, from Mulranny to the Valley and back. The way from the Valley lay through Achill Sound, past Pulranny, James' early home, and still that of his father, Neal.

On 20 October A. E. Horne, the Resident Magistrate, having heard the final deposition of Mrs MacDonnell issued a warrant remanding Lynchehaun in custody pending his appearance at the Petty Sessions to be held in Castlebar on 24 October at 11.30. He was put in charge of

Constables Ward and Muldoon, and all set off in the jaunting car at about half-past six. Constable Ward took the seat beside the handcuffed prisoner and Constable Muldoon sat on the other side of the car. When, at about 8.30, they were close to Neal Lynchehaun's house the prisoner jumped off the car and sped into the darkness of the night. The London *Daily News* had the following account:

ESCAPE OF THE ACHILL PRISONER

> The escape of the Achill prisoner has many elements of romance as it is understood on the Adelphi stage. The island of Achill is the fitting scene for it, for it is gloomy and lonely to the last degree, and no small part of its surface is bog. The prisoner was charged with the attempted murder of a lady who lives in one of its valleys.[1] He was manacled after arrest and was being taken to the gaol at night when his brother stopped the escort and asked leave to provide him with an overcoat. The police consented, a manacle was removed to allow the man to slip his arm into the coat, and in the slight confusion the prisoner managed to slip away in the darkness. Four hundred police are looking for him in the bogs and mountains. He is probably in hiding in some gloomy retreat known only to himself and the few others to the manner born.

Brother Paul gives a vivid, and no doubt substantially accurate account of the escape, identifying Lynchehaun's brother who had been mentioned in the *Daily News*.

Lynchehaun was handcuffed and placed on an outside jaunting car, given in charge to two burly policemen named Ward and Muldoon with a jarvey on deck. The peelers had long guns and long overcoats, as the night was cold. They left Mrs MacDonnell's about 7 p.m. and constable Ward, who sat beside the prisoner, had his hand in the prisoner's pocket for fear of his jumping off. This precaution Lynchehaun did not seem to notice, although he was meditating on how to get rid of it.

When they reached the police station at Achill Sound both

---

[1] The *Daily News* of course, made this false deduction from the name of the village.

guards and prisoner alighted and entered the barrack where prisoner was supplied with refreshments from his sister's shop close by. After an hour's delay the escort and prisoner remount the jaunting car, it being about 9.30 p.m., and fairly dark as moon was not visible. As they advanced on their journey Lynchehaun's brother, Michael, trotted after them on horseback, going towards his own house. He proffered an overcoat to prisoner as night was cold. Prisoner refused the coat as he wished to be light for the run. As prisoner's brother kept trotting pretty fast close to the car prisoner ordered him 'Go easy with the horse'. As he heeded not the first orders they were repeated with more force which had the desired effect. His reason for giving the order was that by his going slowly the car-boy would do likewise as the prisoner was nearing the place where he wished to make the dash for freedom.

It being now about 10 p.m. and prisoner nearing his father's house where he knew the highways and byways, the hills and hollows, the holes and corners as well as a rabbit in a warren, Lynchehaun shook his shoulders and said he was cold, and said to policeman Ward who still held his hand in prisoner's pocket for precaution sake, and which unwelcomed thing prisoner wished to get rid of, 'Please take the pipe out of my pocket and light it and give me a smoke to warm me.'

At this place there was a little rise in the road and the car went slow, so the bobby took out the pipe, and with the pipe he took out the precautious hand out of prisoner's pocket as he wanted the use of both hands in lighting the pipe. While the policeman was searching for the pipe prisoner was removing the rug with his manacled hands to have all ready for a spring when the silly bobby would have both hands engaged in lighting the pipe. So now the eventful moment arrived as car was going easy, rug removed, and both of bobby's hands engaged in kindling the pipe. At this moment Lynchehaun, being near his father's house, he bounced off the car like a hare, ran up the byway.

Policeman Ward shouted to his comrade, Muldoon, who sat on the opposite side of the car, 'By gob, he's off.'

The pursuit commenced, and a close one too, as prisoner declared he thought he felt their breath at times they were so close to him. Although the night was dark prisoner knew where and how to avoid the dangerous pits, which the police did not, being strangers to the place. So when they were very close to prisoner he passed by a sandpit into which they fell. While they were extricating themselves prisoner advanced ahead of them and as he was passing his father's house he shouted in Irish to them who were in to be out, in order to confuse the police the more, thinking they would not know who was who in the dark.

An old lady in Achill, telling of this incident in recent years, changed dramatically from English to Irish when she came to repeat what Lynchehaun called out, as he ran towards his father's house, '*Bígí amuich*', 'Let ye be out' — an interesting corroboration, in one detail, of the accuracy of the *Narrative*.

So he succeeded in his plans of escape for the time being. Although he was manacled he still had three advantages, in knowing the place in the dark, in being without an overcoat, and in being in the midst of his friends, while the police were strangers to the place, loaded with guns and coats, and having no friends to direct them. So after a fruitless pursuit they gave it up, returned to the barrack at Achill Sound, told of their mishap, pursuit, and loss of their quarry.

After James Lynchehaun's escape from the police he went to his uncle's house, it being now about twelve at night, doors being shut; when Jim knocked he was refused admission until he spoke in Irish and said '*Leig a stagh me*[2]'. Knowing the voice they opened the door, then their hands[3], and embraced him, asked how he escaped, lighted a fire, prepared a good supper, bathed his feet, gave him clean stockings and some under-clothes, broke the handcuffs into bits, and thus prepared him for another run.

So he retraced his steps that night, went towards the shore, got a little boat, crossed about a mile of a channel, entered Achill Island, and took up his abode in a friend's[4] house, named James Gallagher, Sraheens, within about half a mile distant from the barrack at Achill Sound.

In this house he made or got made a burrow or hiding place under a boarded floor in the little room. In this he placed a layer of turf to prevent dampness and over it a pallet, where he could stretch in time of danger. The entrance to this was covered with an old box into which clothes were carelessly thrown.

[2]='Let me in'.
[3]=arms (*lámha*).
[4]=friend=relative.

CHAPTER IX
The Troglodyte

Official Ireland was shocked and outraged at the escape of Lynchehaun. But the generality took him, not perhaps to their hearts, but to wherever is the seat of the feeling of malicious pleasure at another's discomfiture. The escape from Constables Ward and Muldoon on the night of Saturday 20 October 1894, was the beginning of the Lynchehaun legend.

Brother Paul revels in the difficulties experienced by the police, their grave loss of face, the consequent demotions.

Now to return to the police who lost their charge, these men knew that by losing their prey they would lose their pay, and their jackets to boot. So they were anxious to recover that which was lost. So on the night they lost their prisoner messengers were sent to the other barracks in the neighbourhood and a telegram to Dublin Castle early next morning.

Lynchehaun's escape was gazetted, and all the available police in the County Mayo ordered to rendezvous in Achill and search for the scapegoat.[1]

So constables, officers, and magistrates, to the number of about 300 in all, came to the island, searched houses, mountains, valleys and caves, for the space of about three months. Still the fox evaded their grasp, he being shut up snugly in his den, while they traversed the mountains and shores night and day, amidst wind and rain, snow and hail.

[1]=escapee.

The winter of this year being very severe the constables suffered so much hardship that some got paralysed and others insane. It won't be wondered at if the way they were treated be taken into consideration. The major portion of the constables had only one suit of clothes each. When they would come in from their day or night's patrol, drenched from head to foot, they had neither a fire to warm themselves nor an article of dry clothing to put on, nor yet a bed to lie on. Their only comfort was some ill-cooked food, a shakedown of straw thrown like cattle litter in a cold courthouse, or go to Sweeney's public house to drown their sorrows with bad drink.

While the imported police were thus treated, some of those stationed in the island were being courtmartialled for their neglect of duty. Some high officials from Dublin Castle came to Dugort, Achill, held an investigation there during six days. The men charged with neglect of duty were the District Inspector Patterson,[2] the sergeant in charge, Dusting; the barrack orderly, Carrigan; and Muldoon and Ward from whom the culprit went. The result of the investigation was as follows. The District Inspector was removed to another district at his own expense; the barrack orderly, who allowed the blood-stained clothes to be taken away, was fined £3 and removed to another county at his own cost; those who allowed the prisoner to escape were stripped of their uniform and told to earn their bread some other way. So Lynchehaun brought trouble to many a family as well as his own and all not over yet.

The *Freeman's Journal* reported at length on Monday 22 October the happenings of that Saturday night and Sunday morning.

THE ACHILL OUTRAGE
ESCAPE OF THE ACCUSED MAN
EXCITING CHASE OVER THE MOUNTAIN

Westport, Sunday

At eight o'clock last evening James Lynchehaun, the man charged with the attempted murder of Mrs MacDonnell, the Valley, Achill, and with the burning of the Valley

---

[2] There is no Patterson in the case. The District Inspector intended is Ross C. Rainsford.

House, escaped from the police at his father's house, near Achill Sound. The announcement of his escape caused considerable excitement throughout the district and from midnight last night cars laden with police are pouring into the Island of Achill. Lynchehaun was removed from Castlebar Jail yesterday and conveyed to Mulranny by the 10 a.m. train. He was present in the cabin at the Valley where poor Mrs MacDonnell lay when Mr Horne RM, took a further deposition from the unfortunate lady. The prisoner was sent from the Dugort Police Station in charge of two constables, Muldoon and Ward, to be relodged in Castlebar Jail. Lynchehaun's father lives about a mile from Achill Sound *en route* from Dugort, and at this point, the constables state, Lynchehaun, who was handcuffed, leaped off the car and ran up a passage in the direction of his father's house. The night was very dark, but from the light in the doorway the constables are positive Lynchehaun never entered the house but passed round the end of the gable and this is the last was seen of him. There are several houses close by, but the police have failed so far to find the slightest clue to his whereabouts. The escape took place in the wildest part of the Corraun mountains on the shores of Blacksod Bay. The police now crowd all over the mountains, and from Castlebar, Westport, Newport, and every part of the country they continue to arrive on the spot to search for the fugitive. The constabulary in the Belmullet and Connemara districts are on the watch for the arrival of Lynchehaun by hooker on either side of Clew Bay or Blacksod Bay. Lynchehaun was a man of considerable strength. Some time after Lynchehaun's arrest on Sunday morning his friends sent him his Sunday clothes and boots which he proceeded to put on in the day room of the Dugort police barrack previous to his removal to Castlebar Jail. The constable in charge of him left the day room while the prisoner was getting on his better clothes. On the return of the constable Lynchehaun was dressed in the clothes sent in by his friends but the old clothes had mysteriously disappeared and have not since been found. When inquiry was made as to what became of them the prisoner informed his custodians that he would hold them responsible for the missing garments. The prisoner's house was ransacked and all the clothing belonging to him seized, but the constables state that the clothes worn by Lynchehaun on the night of the occurrence have not yet been discovered ...

The reporter, writing on Sunday evening, had not heard of Mrs Lynchehaun's breach of the Sabbath, of her unusual Sunday wash, which was later retrieved by Constable Sullivan. The same reporter was still at work next day, and his account made the Tuesday edition.

LYNCHEHAUN STILL AT LARGE

The search for the prisoner Lynchehaun was continued all night and to-day but not a trace of him has been found. Fifty-six additional constables proceed to Mulranny by train this afternoon to join in the search and the country for many miles around is overrun with constables. The prevailing impression is that Lynchehaun will evade capture, at all events for a considerable time. The two constables, who composed the escort, were armed with rifles and revolvers, but the rifles were not loaded. The islands of Clew Bay have been searched by constables and coastguards, as it is thought not unlikely that the prisoner took to the sea by one of the small boats easily available along the coast.

Some few ballads were made concerning Lynchehaun, and surviving fragments will be quoted later. The first of this *genre,* but not quite a ballad, and sung to the air of 'The Minstrel Boy', was published in a newspaper, and is quoted by Brother Paul. The government had offered £100 for the capture of the fugitive, rapidly raised it to £200, and Mr MacDonnell had brought the total up to £300. The parody mocks the avidity of the police for the reward, and Brother Paul, never one to let such a chance pass, introduces it with relish!

This proferred reward and hopes of promotion set the police almost frantic, and caused them run hither and thither like bloodhounds in search of their prey.

Lynchehaun — Where Is He?

I

Our peeler boys on the trail have gone,
O'er hill and dale you'll find them,
Their bayonets bright they have girded on,
And their rifles slung behind them.
'Dreams of fame', says each constable grim,
'That long have ceased to craze me,
My heart doth swell with hopes again,
Bold Jim, I swear I'll find thee.'

II

'I feel as a bloodhound loosed from his chain,
I'm fierce as the rolling thunder;
Now, now, the reward of my genius to gain,
Too long hath its light lain under.'
They speak and strut with martial strain,
'Aye! proud of our force are we.'
Their helmets gleam by mountain and stream,
But Lynchehaun — where is he?

Lynchehaun could not, of course, return to Achill in the ordinary way by crossing the bridge at Achill Sound. Brother Paul shows him crossing over in a small boat. But it is more likely that he crossed, not to Achill, but to the tiny island of Achill Beg, situated at its southern tip, and lying directly opposite the Corraun district. Then there took place the incident on Achill Beg, which the *Narrative*, awkwardly and unconvincingly, places later, showing Lynchehaun as venturing out from his hiding place in Achill, and taking for a second time to his boat, for no other purpose than to break the monotony of his troglodyte existence. The islands were the first places to be searched by police, and the incident may be regarded as happening on the night of Sunday 4 November.[3]

---

[3] "On Sunday Achillbeg was closely searched by a party of police, information having been received that he was in hiding there." *Mayo News*, Saturday, 10 November.

One night, as he was concealed in a cave in a little island named Achill Beg, he heard an unknown voice which cried 'Na fan fad in shin', i.e. 'Don't stop long there'. Taking this as a friendly admonition, he left the cave and climbed to the top of a cliff hard by, where he concealed himself on the sheltery side. He was not long there when he observed with the light of the moon a boat approaching the island, and the men who were in it, on landing, walking towards the very cave he left. After searching different places they had to return to the mainland without their quarry, while James Lynchehaun looked down from his high cliff with scornful glee on the poor deluded bobbies.

Fact or fiction? And if the latter is Brother Paul the author? Brother Paul sometimes embellishes, helps a limping story on with a little art or dramatic cunning. But rarely, probably never, does he appear to create out of nothing, or present the acts of others as those of Lynchehaun. The nub of the anecdote is the mysterious, and (significantly) Irish-speaking voice — without this, in fact, there is no story. The most obvious interpretation is probably the true one. This is an account of an experience undergone by Lynchehaun and communicated by him to Brother Paul. That tired, hungry, shivering in a cave on a remote Atlantic island, on a miserable morning in early November, the imaginative fugitive should hear a warning voice — with what definition, with what clarity? — is not beyond expectation in a Gaelic atmosphere. There the fey or supernatural mixes easily and naturally with harsh, or even commonplace, reality. Indeed, this mixture of the commonplace and the supernatural, strange in the English scene, is almost definitional of the Irish, present as well in the eighth century *Cattle Raid of Cooley* as in contemporary folk anecdote, and no less in all the literature that emerges from the centuries in between.

The voice speaks in Irish, not in English, because Irish was Lynchehaun's first language, that of everyday prayer, the *Our Father*, the *Hail Mary* and the *Rosary*. But the voice that comes from the sky or the air is not of God, of the Devil, of saint or of fairy, but has some of the mystery of all, and hearing it is essentially a religious experience. It is a voice that warns, threatens, comforts, is neither good nor evil, simply true and infallible, the voice of immutable Destiny.

That Lynchehaun should hear it, that it should speak to him, implies that he is chosen, destined for great things, and is not to be taken by the police, at least not yet.

The earliest of many instances of the voice of Destiny is in an eighth or ninth century tale of a lady known as Mór of Munster. She constantly heard a voice in the sky that always spoke the same words: 'Woe to you, Mór'. One day she spoke back saying: 'I would rather it were given to me than constantly promised.'

'Will it be in the beginning or the end?' asked the voice.

'In the beginning,' said Mór.

As a result she wandered throughout Ireland, dirty, clothed in rags, miserable and insane. Finally she came to the house of the king of Cashel. The king's wife taunted him and dared him to take Mór to bed. He did so, and, as happens elsewhere in Irish literature, sexual intercourse was therapeutic and her sanity was restored. The king put away his wife, married Mór, and she became legendary for her happiness.

After (as we assume) the incident on Achill Beg, Lynchehaun made for Achill, seeking out as his place of refuge the house of James Gallagher of Sraheens near Achill Sound. James Gallagher had a holding of land, could read and write, and held an 'important position' with the railways, earning, when he worked, thirty shillings a week. Comfortable and well placed, with a wife and two children, it was his misfortune that his wife was a first cousin of James Lynchehaun. His counsel, Mr Louden, would eventually plead, in extenuation of his criminal harbouring of Lynchehaun, that when the latter came to the house James Gallagher was not at home but was working on relief works at Pulranny; Lynchehaun was admitted by his wife.

At that time Mary Masterson, a niece of Mrs Gallagher was visiting at the house; her surname is not, as it might seem, English, but a translation of the Irish name Mac-Mháistir. She was eighteen years of age, in very delicate health, and was a survivor of a terrible boating disaster that had taken place near Westport Quay the previous summer. She slept in a room with the Gallaghers' two children, and this room, with its full company, was the only place available to Lynchehaun.

Lynchehaun, according to Mr Louden, dug a hole near the wall of the room but he may have had some help from Mrs Gallagher and Mary. At any rate, there was much sweat. It was about three feet deep, two feet square at the surface, and underneath it extended to about seven. At the bottom there was water and a little hay. In times of danger the fugitive would get into the hole; two planks would be put over it, then a coating of earth, some bags and bottles, and all would be hidden by a large box or chest which was moved into place. There was no way of letting in air; it was cold and wet, and during the periods that he had to stay underground he was virtually buried alive.

Brother Paul shows a number of women associated in a helpful way with Lynchehaun in the two periods he was on the run, some in Achill, one in Dublin, and one in New York. He treads carefully, making no overt suggestion of romantic involvement — he is, after all, a Catholic puritan, writing about a married man and explicitly for young readers amongst others. Nevertheless, each of the unnamed ladies in Dublin and New York bears the ambiguous title 'lady-friend'; if challenged, Brother Paul could say that they were 'old flames', who had an altogether creditable concern for the fugitive. Mary Masterson, whose association with her cousin Lynchehaun was doubtless quite innocent, is shown as 'a faithful girl' who watches during the night, and is only named later in the context of her arrest.

There was a bed beside the den in which he used to sleep at night, and a faithful girl watched and if danger approached she gave the alarm; he jumped from the bed into the den, she covered its entrance with the old box, then went to the door and opened it for the police. Finding her fully dressed, still a delay in opening the door, and the bed quite warm, caused their suspicion. They asked who slept in the bed; she said it was herself. However, they searched the house, but did not find the fox this time.

It is beyond belief that Lynchehaun had an underground lair and a 'young lady' cousin to watch over him in more than one house. In the following tall story, full of rustic humour, and probably told to Brother Paul by Lynchehaun, the den, in an outhouse with calves and chickens, is necessarily given a different location. Brother Paul's use of 'friend' is generally ambiguous, and, as used by him normally, as here, means 'cousin', one of many Gaelicisms in the *Narrative*. There need be no doubt that the anecdote is based on the situation in James Gallagher's house, and that Mary Masterson is the original of 'the faithful cousin'.

At another time he lay concealed for weeks in a friend's house where he had his lair covered with a trap-door under the bed of a few young calves. The police often visited this house and searched it minutely, even amongst the calves. And one of the constables rubbed his hand on the very calf under whose side Jim was lying in his lair. The constable was about making a very minute search, and while doing so, said, rubbing the calf, 'Oh, poor calf!'. The hens' roost was directly over the calves' bed and Jim's lair. The young lady of the house, seeing the danger her friend Jim was in, used a stratagem to draw the constable from the den. 'Oh! sir,' said she, 'as the hens are over you, their droppings may spoil you.'

The exclamation was scarcely uttered when one of the fowls let a cannonade down on his tunic, and he ran off to clean it. 'Oh! sir, I am sorry but these dirty fowls have no regard for cleanliness. May I help you to clean your uniform.'

'No, thanks to you. I shall do the servile work myself.'

After this event the sergeant left the constable in the kitchen cleaning his garment while he got the young lady to light him upstairs to make a search there. After a fruitless search, he addressed the lady in flattering terms, even proposed marriage to her if she would become an informer. Still she remained firm and faithful to her cousin. She did not wish to sell his life for doubtful promises made by a peeler who wanted to get promotion and reward money for capturing her friend.

Another incident involving the 'young lady' is related by Brother Paul in Lynchehaun's own words.

'Being crippled so long in my lair my limbs were getting stiff, so I resolved to go out by night and exercise them in a field near the house. The night was fine and I had one on the watch. When I was in the act of opening the door to go out I heard a gentle knock. As one of the inmates went out shortly before I thought it was she that was on the return. However, a forethought saved me as I sent the young lady of the house to question the incomer. On the girl asking 'Who is there?' the answer from the outside was 'All right, Open.' These simple words warned me that an enemy was at the door, so, like a fox I ran to my den. To give me time to hide, the lady slowly opened the door. Police entered, a search was made, but Reynard not found.'

Passages like this, in the first person, raise the question as to whether Brother Paul had access to any autobiographical notes made by Lynchehaun. It is not unlikely that, keen letter-writer that he was, Lynchehaun, as local tradition held, was writing a book on his own life. If so, the soliloquy reported in the *Narrative* might have been a part of it, although the confession to the crime of arson would seem to be against historic fact and was, in later life, firmly denied by the criminal.

Jim was there ever a troglodyte in Achill before you? Yes. My father told me there was one McHugh who was pursued in famine time (1845) for stealing sheep. But his was a less crime than mine. Hunger caused him to do the deed, while envy caused me. He shed the blood of sheep, I that of my landlady. He injured no houses, while I burned them to the ground. So it's no wonder he fared better than I am, for he got off to Australia where he breathed the air of freedom, while I am confined to this barren isle, like a Robinson Crusoe in the Isle of Juan Fernandez, even worse, because he had liberty to roam over the island, no bloodhounds guarding him, while I have 250 in Achill alone, besides all the ports in Ireland are watched for fear of my escape. In McHugh's time there were only a few yeomen, there were neither trains nor bicycles, telegraph nor telephones, while Ireland is like a network of them now. So it's hard for Jim to escape. However, while there is life there is hope.

As Lynchehaun had a host of relatives, says Brother Paul, whom he visited from time to time he fared better than other refugees would. One of them, nicknamed Marwood, traced him to his den and thereafter 'acted the part of a jackal to a lion by providing him with food.' There are brief references to other anecdotes.

Notwithstanding all Jim's friends he had many narrow escapes, even while he was in the den-house. On one occasion he went out to exercise his limbs he saw police approaching the end house, and as he had not time to get into his den, he took an old bag, wrapped it round his shoulders, and a basket on his back, and walked toward the bog for turf, while the police were at a short distance from him.

At another time he was in a namesake's house. The housekeeper saw police approaching. She asked Lynchehaun what to do. He told her to fling the doors open and go sweeping the floor, while he went behind a tent bed, stood on a small box to raise his feet from view. Police entered, looked and searched, yet found not their desired quarry.

Bríd Ní Mhaolmhuaidh records an anecdote referring to this period:

> One day while he was on the run in Achill, he was walking along the road near the village of Dugort when he spotted two policemen in the distance. Knowing that they were on the look-out for him, and that he wouldn't have time to make an escape, he hunched himself up like an old man, picked up a shovel that by chance happened to be lying nearby and started to clean away the grass from the side of the road. The policeman came up to him. 'You didn't see Lynchehaun passing this way?' they asked him.
>
> 'I wouldn't be sure,' said he, assuming a rather feeble old man's voice, 'but I think it was like him I saw going by there a while ago.'
>
> 'This direction,' said they, pointing the way they were going.
>
> 'Yes,' said he, so they continued on their wild goose chase.

J. M. Synge, as will be seen, referred inaccurately to Lynchehaun as a murderer. Curiously, Brother Paul almost does the same by comparing him with Cain, and, to emphasise the point, as he has done before, writes the accusatory passage in red ink.

In many of his nocturnal rambles he visited his wife and child. As the little boy of ten happened to be always asleep when his father came the latter would kiss him and be off.

Even in these short nocturnal visits he experienced many narrow escapes. Even when there was no danger near his guilty conscience feared, like that of Cain's after killing his brother Abel. He thought everything was in pursuit of him, and that his blood cried for vengeance.

Lynchehaun, as time went on, must have felt that, with the heavy police presence in Achill and the neighbouring parts of Co. Mayo, and the watch on the ports, escape would be very difficult indeed. He sought therefore to convince the authorities that he had already escaped from Ireland. Brother Paul tells us that Mr Horne, the Resident Magistrate, was getting telegrams from England and Paris asking how was Mrs MacDonnell getting on, and signed James Lynchehaun. 'This', said Brother Paul, 'was a clever ruse to make them think that he had escaped from Ireland.' One such communication survives, a letter from Lancashire, post-marked *Kirkham, Dec. 1*, to the District Inspector in Newport, Ross C. Rainsford. The letter is a skilled piece of work, even down to the sympathy for constables Ward and Muldoon and the affected generosity in trying to save them from the consequences of their negligence. That from his den in Sraheens he could have contact not only with the north of England, but probably also with Paris, is indeed impressive.

Sir,
I beg to inform you that I have managed to get this far. My object in writing to you is to let you know that I will attend my trial in March next or at any time that you name. You can do this by putting a notice in any of the Dublin papers (*Freeman* or *Times*). I also wish to point out to you that if you wish Mrs MacDonnell to live you will get some other medical man besides Croly. He will put her to death surely for two reasons, (1) to banish me for life, (2) to have an opportunity to buy the Valley estate himself. On this subject I will write to her husband. The

wonder is why the poor lady has survived Croly's devilment so long. If you make inquiries you will find that Croly was death on me. It may be interesting for you to know how I managed to get here. Well it was this, I got to Ballycroy, that night crossed into Doohoma, thence to Blacksod into Iniskea, and boarded the first steamer passing. You need not put yourself to any trouble looking for me here. I am something like Mr Balfour in writing and dating his letters. My reason for escaping was I did not like to be such a long time awaiting trial in prison and you need not blame the constables that were with me. Until that moment Ward never lifted hand out of my overcoat pocket and even if he had the hand there that minute I had intended to make the plunge. If there were 100 police there at the time I'd go as the night was extremely dark and I knew every nook and turn in the place. Lest you should have any doubt about this letter being genuine as coming from me, let me remind you that one day in September you were coming out by Mr Hickey's car ['on the Dugort mail' *crossed out*], and that I asked you 'how you were' after your illness. I am not sure now as to exact words but it was something like what I state, or 'I hope you are all right, sir.' I was road-making that day. I also wish to add that when my trial time comes that I will deliver myself up to Constables Ward and Muldoon but to no others. They did their best to capture me and Muldoon is nothing but a good runner.

> I am, Sir,
> Yours respectfully,
> Jas Lynchehaun.

CHAPTER X

Betrayal and Re-arrest

The police were treated with suspicion in Achill as in many parts of Ireland: they were the agents of an authority that was not regarded as altogether legitimate, and the gap between them and the people was accentuated by the agrarian troubles of the period. The great majority of the police were Catholic and of the people. But they stood apart from the community during the week, re-entering the tribe for a short time on Sunday mornings.

On one such Sunday, which was New Year's Day, Constable Michael Glynn of Achill Sound met James Gallagher at Sraheens, and together they walked towards Kildownet to hear Mass. Inevitably they talked about Lynchehaun.

'Ye're killed looking for him,' said Gallagher. 'Ye're out day and night. But it's not as bad for you as for the rest of them — you were away for a while.'

They continued talking, or, at least, Gallagher talked and Glynn, for the most part, listened.

'Ye'll never catch him. He's left the country by now. If he committed that crime, no one should let him into his house, and it'll do a lot of harm to the people of Achill.'

But James' efforts to put the police off the scent were unavailing, and few days were to pass before information was given that would lead to Lynchehaun's re-arrest and bring calamity down upon the Gallagher household.

On 5 January at 2 a.m., a group of police, including the County Inspector, Mr Milling, District Inspector Ross C. Rainsford, and Sergeant Michael Scully, noiselessly approached James Gallagher's house and surrounded it.

With nice social discrimination all the force except Milling and Rainsford took their boots off and approached in stockinged feet. Sergeant Scully knocked. Minutes passed and the knock was not answered. They shouted out that they were police, that the door would be broken down if it were not opened immediately. The point was emphasised by a few kicks from a policeman.

The door opened, and James Gallagher appeared, apologising for the delay.

'Have you him there, James?'

'You are welcome, gentlemen. There is no one here.'

They searched the kitchen and then went into Lynchehaun's bedroom. Mary Masterson was there in one of the beds with the two young Gallagher boys. Sergeant Scully ignored all three, went over to the chest, caught hold of the near end and pulled it out. James Gallagher fell to his knees, caught hold of Scully by the hand and squeezed it. Scully looked down at him. 'Is he there, James?'

Gallagher said nothing but shook his head.

Scully pulled the chest out onto the floor. Gallagher seized his hand and squeezed it a second time, as if it were possible to restrain him. 'Is he there, James?' asked Scully again.

'He's there, Sergeant,' said Gallagher, defeated.

Rainsford approached with a candle, and peered down at the spot. Sergeants Scully and Hardnett removed the bags and bottles, the loose earth and the planks and Sergeant Hardnett called upon Lynchehaun to come out. He emerged, dirty, half-naked, wearing nothing but a shirt, and the police, for decency sake, helped him to put on his clothes which were hanging up in the room.

Rainsford searched the clothes. He found a little bag with £5 in gold, a half crown in silver, a copy of the New Testament, a manuscript copy of the first chapter of St John's gospel in Latin, a Moore's Almanack for 1895, a map of England, and some other articles. All these, including the money, the religious material, and the newly published Almanack Lynchehaun had acquired since he went on the run.

There was an alarm-clock in the room, and it went off while the police were there, at 3 a.m.

Lynchehaun was now formally re-arrested, Gallagher arrested, and the two were handcuffed together. Mrs Gallagher pleaded hysterically with the police 'Don't take James away from me. It was all my fault.'

'It was my fault,' said Gallagher, 'for letting him into my house at all.'

'Hold your tongue, you bloody fool,' shouted Lynchehaun, 'your house is your castle. What can they do to you?'

Rainsford now turned to Mary Masterson who had got out of her bed. 'You don't live in this house. What brought you here?'

Mary, terrified, could only answer 'I don't know', and Rainsford arrested her.

It became known immediately that the police had received information as to Lynchehaun's hiding place. *The Freeman's Journal* reported:

> The house was on several occasions previously closely searched without effect but the police got information that Lynchehaun was concealed in a hole under Gallagher's bedroom. Gallagher, the owner of the house, and Mary Masterson, a cousin of Lynchehaun were arrested.... Lynchehaun appears to be in good health, but is altered somewhat in appearance. He has grown long side-whiskers.

There are a number of accounts of Lynchehaun's betrayal to the police that, while not totally irreconcilable, differ in some essential matters such as the intentions and identity of the betrayers.

Brother Paul gives what may be called the exculpatory account in second place, briefly and without endorsement. The betrayers who are 'friends', that is cousins, of Lynchehaun have only good intentions at first, but one later succumbs to greed.

It has been stated that he eventually allowed himself to be taken so that two needy friends might secure the offered reward of £200.

One of the friends fled off to England with his share while the other acted more faithfully as he spent it in defending him at the Castlebar assizes.

As Lynchehaun had lost hopes of getting out of Ireland while the stations, ports, and docks were so well watched, he considered it better that his own friends would get the reward and expend it in defending him than that strangers may get it. However, such money goes badly.

The second exculpatory account is that related for the records of the Irish Folklore Commission about 1947 by John McHugh. This indulges in a literary economy by making Lynchehaun's brother, rather than 'a friend' or brother-in-law, his betrayer. The help that this brother either gave, or was thought to have given, in later years in Lynchehaun's escape from Maryborough jail can then be shown as remorse for the act of betrayal.

Although not named, the brother referred to in McHugh's account is undoubtedly Michael. At the time of the escape from Maryborough jail Michael, who was known to the police as 'the Dublin brother', was suspected of complicity. That he should be engaged in the fish trade, as McHugh says, is probably true, and would be in accordance with family tradition. The Lynchehaun family was a tightly knit and mutually supportive group; that any brother of James's should betray him is highly unlikely.

An even more serious 'economy' in McHugh's account is that he ignores Lynchehaun's trial in Castlebar and telescopes eight years of his life in jail.

> For some time nobody even considered betraying him. He was fixed up very comfortably in a cottage near Achill Sound belonging to a man named Gallagher who had a job on the railway. There was a hole dug in the mud floor of the kitchen where he could disappear if ever there was any danger of the police visiting the house and there was a cupboard just large enough to cover the hole, and nobody would suspect on looking at the harmless array of mugs and platters which this cupboard held that underneath it lay a dangerous criminal. Lynchehaun, of course, retired

to this hole only when there was grave danger that he might be spotted by the police. At night he played cards with the lads who came rambling to the house and there was a bed available in the room for him to sleep on. Rumour has it also that he occasionally dropped into the parish priest at the Sound for a chat.

As time went by, however, his brother who was chiefly responsible for his safety from the fact that he had to keep him informed about the activities of the police, and the likelihood of a surprise attack on his hiding place, began to tire of this rather thankless job. Sooner or later he surmised Lynchehaun would be captured so he decided to avail himself of the reward. He went to the police barracks, told the Sergeant that he would bring him to his brother's hiding place, and arranged the time at which he was to accompany him.

Lynchehaun duly got word about what was to happen — who told him it would be hard to tell — but evidently, considering that there wasn't any better hiding place to be found, he decided to remain on in the cottage. He went to bed, intending to have a few hours sleep before the police would arrive, and in order to make sure that he would not oversleep he set an alarm clock, and placed it near his bed. The alarm clock went off, however, just as the police were nearing the house. He jumped out of his bed and retired to his hiding place but not quite quickly enough to avoid being detected. A policeman pointed his revolver at him and ordered him out of the hole, and seeing no means of escape Lynchehaun allowed himself to be arrested and handcuffed again. He was taken to Maryborough gaol and detained there while awaiting his trial, which this time was to be held in Dublin.

Seeing that matters were not looking too bright for Lynchehaun, and that there was very little chance of his escaping from the gaol, the brother began to experience a certain amount of remorse on account of having betrayed him so he set about to do what he could to have him released again. He got a job as a fish agent in Dublin, and he used the hundred pounds, together with any money which he could earn, in bribing the warders in the gaol so that they would be agreeable to help him in whatever plan he decided upon for Lynchehaun's escape. Luck favoured him....

McHugh's account of Lynchehaun's betrayal shows some of the weakness of oral tradition when used as a historical source. In a continuous mental process, somewhere below conscious level, a number of individuals hand on, one to the other successively, an account of an historic event, gradually moulding and simplifying, rejecting complexity of action or motivation. The final state of the tale should be smooth, with no loose ends, nothing unexplained, a somewhat impressionistic picture of the original historic event. The alarm clock in McHugh's tale is historical. It went off at 3 a.m. during the police raid, and why it was set for such an early hour can only be a matter for speculation. Oral tradition does not like complicated speculation. The alarm clock must be rejected or given a simple and easily appreciated function: thus it becomes the alarm that was set too late, an error that proved the undoing of the hero.

There are two other versions of the betrayal of Lynchehaun that, though in a strict sense oral narration, have minimally short and independent pedigrees, a high degree of congruence, and are thus vastly superior in character to the anecdotes just related. They lead back, if not to things as they veritably were, at least to the truth as James Lynchehaun saw or chose to see it no later than the year 1902.

In 1939 one Pádraig Ó Conaíle from Druingeen near Cong, Co. Mayo, a man of 87 years, related to Mícheál Ó Hoibicín, collector for the Irish Folklore Commission, the story of Lynchehaun's escape and betrayal. He had heard the story 37 years before in Maryborough jail from Lynchehaun himself, and though he had doubtless confused some details, he had never forgotten it.

Druingeen is a considerable distance from the Valley, somewhat over fifty miles as the crow flies. Survival of tradition often seems to be best well away from the scene of the main action. Manifold conflicting interests often cause distortion at the centre so that, for instance, as a noted Dutch scholar maintains, the genuine tradition of St.

Teresa, the Little Flower, is to be found, not at Lisieux, but at more distant outlying convents of the Carmelite order. The story told to Ó Conaíle by Lynchehaun corresponds in two important details with the version to which Brother Paul gives pride of place, and which he reports in the first person, in Lynchehaun's own words: the betrayer was a shop-keeper and a bottle of whiskey played an important part in the betrayal. But let Ó Conaíle speak for himself:

> He was in charge of two police going to Castlebar jail when he made his most daring escape from them. The police failed to trace him and he, being a very nimble young man, he went to a neighbour's house and was very welcome when they heard of his escape. This man was a very wealthy farmer and he owned a lot of horses. He had a big oats' bin in the house, and he dug a hole under it and Lynchehaun was made very comfortable for a month, but his freedom did not last long.
>
> A reward was put on him, dead or alive. A young shop-keeper near the place was very keen on getting the reward, and one day a daughter of this farmer went to town for groceries. And when she was about to leave the shop he took down a bottle of whiskey from one of the shelves and said, 'If you have any idea where poor Lynchehaun is, give him this.' The girl took the bottle and that was enough for the shopkeeper. He told the police about it and Lynchehaun was arrested that evening and lodged in Castlebar jail.

Brother Paul, in what he clearly regards as the more authoritative version, compares the betrayal of Lynchehaun by his 'friend' with that of Christ by Judas, a comparison that Lynchehaun also is shown as making when the story is put in his mouth.

Though long the fox runs he gets caught at last. The £300 reward proferred for his arrest, or information leading thereto, tempted the cupidity of a couple of mean men who were in the know. These, like Judas of old, sold their friend for gold, which soon went, like the traitors, to destruction without buying even a potter's field for it. Thus ends blood money. Although he did a bad deed it was very mean of his relatives to sell him for a bribe. Lynchehaun stated that the chief of these informers was his own brother-in-law who picked the secret from his wife and then betrayed her confidence.

> James Gallagher, Sraheens, in whose house I had my den, was accustomed to call at my sister's shop. My deceitful brother-in-law asked him would he bring me a pint of good malt as he heard I had a cold. Gallagher said he would, and give it to me within the hour. This ready compliance confirmed him in the opinion that I was concealed in Gallagher's house.
>
> Knowing all this the traitor went privately to the session at Castlebar on the 3rd of January 1895 and from thence to Ballina to see the County Inspector Milling with whom he bargained for my arrest. On the night of the 5th this Judas came with Inspector Milling and a large force of police. The informer pointed out the house but had neither the manliness nor audacity to come in and betray me with a kiss.
>
> The police were so cautious that some of them stripped off their shoes in order to make no noise on their approach, fearing a person or dog may give an alarm. Some guarded the outside and the approaches to the house while others forced their way in and with torchlight searched every compartment they saw in the house, still failed to find the den. So they returned outside to get more minute information from the informer who remained in the dark. Having found this they re-entered and went directly to the spot where the den was, removed the old clothes box which covered it, looked into the hole, saw Reynard, ordered him out, presented revolvers to his head, and put manacles on his hands. This happened three months after the burning.
>
> There was one of the policemen, named Sergeant Scully, who was very anxious for promotion, showed more eagerness than any other to grab me. He came without shoes or stockings, was the first to lay hands on me in the den, and presented his revolver to my head. 'Ah! Scully,' said I[1], if I got twenty yards from you, it would take you and all your men to capture me. But you have caught a hare asleep. So now boast of your victory with your informer in the dark and part of the bribe in his pocket.'

[1] Lynchehaun MS.

When my dear sister heard of my arrest by the treachery of her unfaithful husband she sickened and died in confinement a few weeks afterwards. The cupidity of the informer was not satisfied as he got only part of the promised reward for his treachery. But to make up for the loss, by forgetting my sister, and marrying a young girl with a large fortune, then getting her brother to forge a note for him, which brought them into so much trouble that one of them got three months imprisonment and the other sped off to America. After all this illgotten money the informer feigned to bankrupt, closed on his creditors, sold his house to a cousin, fled from his second wife and went off to England. His wife had to return to her father after her health and wealth being shattered. After a few years waiting in vain for his return home she followed him to England. Very few know what has become of them since. So what is ill-got is ill-gone. But if ever J.L. gets his hands upon him he'll get a mauling.

As one man's downfall may cause another man's promotion, so it fared with Lynchehaun and Sergeant Scully. From his being a sergeant in charge of a small barrack at Achill Sound, the time of James Lynchehaun's arrest, he was soon promoted to Head Constable and removed to a large town, and a few years later promoted to D.I. or District Inspector, and later to second grade D.I. He may not end at that!

CHAPTER XI
Trial at Castlebar: The Prosecution

The trial opened at the Crown Court in Castlebar shortly after 11 a.m. on Monday 15 July 1895, before the Right Honourable Mr Justice Gibson.

The Judge sat, the books of crimes were opened, the Jury panelled, the culprit placed on the dock, eminent lawyers arranged on right and left of prisoner, some for and some against him. These gentlemen of legal lore declaimed, shouted and spouted so as to drive terror into the hardest heart; even the very walls of the courthouse reverberated their thundering threats, some denouncing the tyranny of the Landlady, others the brutality of the culprit at the bar. These QCs shook their wigs and rent their gowns, and clenched their fists, trying to make the best case either for or against the prisoner who remained stolid at the bar, awaiting the decision of the Jury and the sentence of the rigid Judge Gibson. Such a display of forensic was rarely witnessed in the courthouse at Castlebar.

Over nine months had passed since the crime was committed. Three of these the prisoner had spent on the run and in hiding and six in jail. Yet he looked none the worse for wear, rather as if he relished being at the centre of a public spectacle: 'As he stepped into the dock all eyes were turned upon him but he bore the trying ordeal unflinchingly. He was very well attired and his calm soft-featured countenance created an impression decidedly in his favour' (*The Western People*, July 20).

The importance the authorities laid on a conviction was shown by the fact that the prosecution was led by The MacDermott, Attorney General for Ireland, who travelled from Dublin, accompanied and assisted by his barrister son, Charles, as well as others.

The MacDermott was the senior representative of an ancient minor ruling family in Co. Sligo, one of the few aristocratic Gaelic families to avoid total dispossession and exile in the seventeenth century, holding on desperately in the ensuing time to a measure of gentility and importance. The heads of these few families, such as The MacGillacuddy of the Reeks, the O'Conor Don, and The MacDermott of Coolavin, asserted their respectability by affixing the English definite article to their surnames, sometimes by having their wives called Madame instead of Mrs, minimal gestures without force in law, which sought to extract from society the respect given to a baronet, if not even to a peer of the realm.

Also acting for the Crown were J. Taylor, QC and H. J. Richards, BL. The instructing solicitor was Mr Malachi J. Kelly.

The accused was defended by Dr Falconer of the Leinster Circuit and by J. J. Louden, BL, instructed by Mr Myles J. Jordan.

The selection of a jury was so important that the issue of a case might depend on it rather than upon the evidence. Ideally a jury should consist of a random selection of twelve of the accused's peers, sober, respectable men, not easily swayed by passion or prejudice. But in Ireland juries empanelled at random could rarely be trusted to reach an honest verdict when there was any political, social, or religious matter at issue. Accordingly, the process of empanelment varied somewhat from English practice. In cases of felony, such as this, the prisoner's solicitor had the right, without showing cause, to challenge up to twenty jurors. The Crown, on the other hand, had no such right, but could ask any juror to 'stand aside', an advantage limited only by the number of jurors in supply.

Things, at first, did not look too favourable for the Crown. The MacDermott pointed out that the answering of jurors was very unsatisfactory and he would ask his Lordship to have the absent jurors called on a heavy fine. His Lordship agreed. The long panel was read through for the second time that morning and it was demonstrated again that there was a very meagre attendance, up to sixty-one gentlemen of position in the county having chosen to absent themselves. The MacDermott, however, agreed to go on with the trial. The trickiness of the position, and the procedures involved, can be appreciated by a comment from *The Old Munster Circuit* by Maurice Healy (1939, p. 212):

> A good solicitor always armed himself with a copy of the jury-panel well in advance; sometimes he was able to prove that the panel had not been constituted according to law in that the jurors thereon had been arbitrarily or unfairly selected. In such a case he would instruct his counsel to move to quash the panel, and, if successful, would thereby paralyse the business of the assizes until another could be formed. On the assumption that the panel had been well struck, his next duty would be to inform himself of the personal character and outlook of as many members as possible, and to mark his list with emblems of a descending scale, discriminating the most dangerous from the merely dangerous, the doubtful, the possibly favourable, the good friend, and the ferocious partisan. The presence of a single one of the last variety would ensure that the worst that could happen to his client would be a disagreement of the jury. But when the names came to be called in Court it necessitated all the skill of the expert gambler to put one's challenges to the best advantage. With only one left it might be the wiser course to let a doubtful man go unchallenged and reserve the last for the possibility of a dangerous man being called. The Crown had no right of challenge; they could order a juror to 'stand by', but if the list ran out without a jury being completed, the Crown had then to go back on their 'stand-bys' and the presence of one of these on the jury was not calculated to improve the chances of conviction.

Lynchehaun's solicitor, Myles J. Jordan, according to *The Western People*, 'exhausted' his challenges, but significantly, in view of Maurice Healy's comments above, the number of jurors named as challenged numbered nineteen. He kept a challenge in reserve up to the last. The Crown 'excused' two jurors for good reasons, and ordered thirty to stand aside. Despite absentees, challenged, 'stand-bys', and excused, a jury was successfully empanelled. From the names one would guess that the Crown had secured seven or eight Protestant or Unionist jurors; five or six were Catholics and therefore, to a greater or lesser degree, doubtful in the eyes of the establishment. The foreman, Matthew Fahy of Clogherna, had an almost unmistakably Catholic name. One might fairly say that the Crown, acting within the law as it stood, had made a creditable effort to 'pack' the jury but without complete success. So far as possible the prosecution would stress the brutality of the crime, the sex of the victim, and avoid having it appear to have any political or agrarian complexion.

The indictment contained five counts:

Firstly — That on the 6th October, 1894, he, James Lynchehaun, feloniously and unlawfully wounded one Agnes MacDonnell with intent to kill and murder.

Secondly — That he caused her bodily harm with the same intention.

Thirdly — That he feloniously and unlawfully did wound her with intent to disfigure and maim.

Fourthly — That he feloniously and unlawfully did wound her with intent to do grievous bodily harm.

Fifthly — That he did wound with intent to commit actual bodily harm.

The MacDermott opened the case. His speech is given in full, as taken from the court records and printed in *The Western People*, 20 July 1895, conflated, to some degree, with the version given in the Supplement to the *Mayo News*, printed on the same date. There is no reason to suppose that the reported versions are incorrect or unfair in any way. Here the text of the speech will occasionally be interrupted by comments.

> May it please your lordship and gentlemen of the Jury, it is now my duty on behalf of the Crown to state to you the facts of the case which the Crown is prepared to prove in evidence. I will begin by saying that you will have evidence as various and as conclusive as ever was addressed to the intelligence and conscience of a jury, and that should place the guilt of the prisoner at the bar beyond any doubt, beyond any yea or nay. He is not being tried on the capital offence, which might have been the case. Providence, perhaps in mercy to the woman who was attacked, a mercy which has fallen indirectly on the prisoner himself, has saved him from completing the crime which undoubtedly the evidence shows he intended to commit that night. Now, before I draw your attention to the evidence immediately applying to the case I ought to tell you something about the relative positions of Mrs MacDonnell, the lady who was attacked, and the prisoner James Lynchehaun. She is the wife of an Irish gentleman, a barrister in London, and some time in the year, I think, '87

(*Comment:* correctly '88).

> she acquired by purchase out of money of her own this small property in the Island of Achill. She lived in London, but sometimes came to Achill and resided in a house called the Valley House, near to which was a village called the Valley. Some time before the 6th October of last year her housekeeper died, and she consequently came over from London to take charge of the house, and was the only person living in the house on the night of this 6th October. When she first got this property her agent was a Mr Salt; next she had a gentleman named Sweeney; and thirdly she had as agent for a period of three months, or so, or rather as steward, the prisoner, James Lynchehaun. In addition to being in her employment for a short

time he had also a power of attorney, which was not signed, describing the terms under which he was to be in charge of this lady's property, and he was set out in that document as 'James Lynchehaun, grocer'.

It appears he held two small houses from her, in one of which he carried out the grocery business, and with some success; and besides that he had a small farm of land which he purchased from a man named Burke for £11 with her consent and which was known as 'the Scraw'. When he became her agent, or under-bailiff, he was receiving from her an annual salary of £15 a year. Now, for some reason or another he did not give her satisfaction, and at the end of the three months she dismissed him from her service. Further, owing to the dislike she entertained to him, either from his misconduct or whatever may have been the cause of it, she served him with a notice to quit of the premises where he carried on the grocery business, and she also sought to determine, and I think did determine, his tenancy of the holding called 'the Scraw'.

The notice to quit was wrongly served, because it was the unstamped copy that was given to the prisoner instead of the stamped one. A similar mistake occurred with a second notice, and then a third notice had to be served, this time in due form, to determine the tenancy on the 29th September '94 — a date which is very important to this case.

(*Comment:* No proof is adduced (nor considering Mrs MacDonnell's dislike of using stamps, is it likely that it could be) that a 'stamped copy' ever existed, that is, previous to the third notice. There is a strange omission here. The prosecutor is naturally anxious to show his chief witness in as good a light as possible. Hence, it would seem, he is reluctant to mention the date of Lynchehaun's dismissal (see p. 39, above) because to do so might suggest that Mrs MacDonnell was so incompetent, so dishonest, or so pennypinching that, through constant lack of stamps, she could take three years to accomplish a commonplace and simple legal procedure. He is also probably anxious to make the dismissal of Lynchehaun seem as near as possible in time to the crime in order to make the motivation all the more immediate and adequate).

You can easily judge from the foregoing that if there was anyone in the world who had a grievance to avenge or a loss to avert by attacking her as she was unquestionably attacked this night, it was the prisoner, Lynchehaun. He was a dismissed servant. She had taken from him his little holding of land and had served him with a notice to quit to determine his tenancy in the house where he carried on the grocery business on the 29th September, '94. We have some evidence under his own hand of the spirit in which he regarded her, and of the lengths to which he was prepared to go to have satisfaction. She gave receipts for rent without attaching thereto the usual stamp and thereby subjected herself to a penalty. She will prove herself that they were merely conditional receipts as she had not a stamp about her at the time; but anyway

(*Comment:* The hasty 'but anyway' shows an anxiety to be done with this line of reasoning which could hardly convince even the speaker. Mrs MacDonnell, indeed, made a statement in court in answer to a question put by The MacDermott: 'I had not a stamp in the house when they brought the money, and I gave receipts on condition that they would be brought back to be stamped.' Far from 'proving' anything this statement could, without great unfairness, be dubbed a brazen untruth by an unfriendly counsel. It was surely a landlady's business to have stamps in the house on the day she held her rent office. Her record of failure to stamp notices to quit hardly supports her veracity in this case; furthermore, to ask tenants to make a second journey from as far away as the limits of her estate at Dugort on account of such an elementary failure on her part, would be asking too much, even in those days of oppressive landlordism. The truth is, rather, that being literally a penny-pinching woman she used the penny stamp as sparingly as possible, and, dealing, as she thought, with a crowd of timorous and ignorant peasants, had no doubt that she would get away with it.)

on the 2nd March, '92, Lynchehaun wrote to the Collector of Excise in Galway, enclosing a copy of a receipt which he got from Mrs MacDonnell without the usual stamp, saying that this was always her practice, and that in the interests of justice the writer felt compelled to bring the matter under the notice of the Inland Revenue.[1]

On 7 March following he again addressed the collector of Inland Revenue as follows:

Sir — Enclosed is a receipt given by Mrs Agnes MacDonnell to Edward McPadden. I also enclose you one dated '88 given myself by her son. The receipt is in her own handwriting.

To this communication some reply was sent by the collector, because the prisoner again wrote him:

Sir — In reply to yours on the 9th inst. I beg to inform you that Mrs Agnes MacDonnell's postal address in the Valley House, Dugort P.O., Achill; or 19 Belsize Square, London, N.W. This Mrs MacDonnell is a small proprietor here. She lives here presently, and will probably be here for a good part of the year. She is an extensive farmer. Any information or assistance that I can render will always be forthcoming. This woman is so economical that to affix a 1d stamp to transactions such as are now before you would in her opinion be sheer extravagance and waste.
      Yours, etc., James Lynchehaun

Now, these letters indicate the feelings which as far back as the year '92 dwelt in this man's breast. Well, notwithstanding those letters, in the year '93 she was collecting rents there and he came in, apparently in a penitential

---

[1] The *Mayo News* gives the text of the letter: "Sir, a poor man places the receipt, a copy of which I enclose, in my hands, in order to have your attention directed towards the custom of the woman who gave such receipts. In receipts given for £10 she does not stamp them. I have a receipt given for £10 not stamped. In the interests of justice I think it very proper to have this case brought under the notice of the authorities."

spirit, and asked her to allow him to assist in collecting the rent, but she said "Certainly not". I have said enough, I think, to show you, gentlemen of the jury, the feeling that existed between the prisoner at the bar and Mrs Mac-Donnell, and this will now lead up to the fearful attack made upon her on the night of 6th October while residing alone in the Valley House.

(*Comment:* The MacDermott has, not unfairly, shown Lynchehaun as having at the same time the character of an informer and of a landlord's hack. This could not but lose him the sympathy of jurors with leanings towards either the national cause, or, more narrowly, the Land League).

On the day of the 6th October there were a number of persons working in her employment at the Valley. There was a woman named Bridget McNeally, also known by the name "Grealish". She acted as her servant, coming in each morning and going away in the evening when her work was done. There was also a man named Matthew Gallagher, and his son, John, who was a herd of hers; a mason named Calvey, a man named Deasy [Vesey, *Mayo News*], and a young man named Pat McNeally, a son of Bridget McNeally.

Some time about 7 o'clock they finished work for the day and left. In one of the outoffices in the yard there were some sheep, in another house a mare and foal, and in a loose box in another of the houses a young mare.

(*Comment:* The MacDermott, if correctly reported, has his facts somewhat mixed up. There were only two, not three, outhouses involved, one for the sheep, and one for the horses. Michael McGinty's precise deposition shows the true facts with regard to the horses: 'Before leaving I fed the *horse* in the stable. That was *the stable* on the right hand side of the yard as you go in the gate. There was only *one horse* in that stable. There was a mare and a foal in a loose box *in the same stable*'.)

The yard itself was surrounded by a wall and protected by a gate which was pushed back on wheels, but the gate was rarely opened, as a door in the centre, called the "wagon door" gave sufficient ingress and egress for all purposes. On this 6th October Mrs MacDonnell, who was a very active and industrious woman, had been up at 5 o'clock, and being tired after the day's work, she retired to rest shortly after the workpeople left, seeing that everything was secure for the night.

(*Comment:* The MacDermott then explained to the jury the situation of the Valley House and outoffices from a wooden model (made by a Mr Lindsey) placed on the witness table[2] and continued the narrative.)

Now about a quarter after eight o'clock Mrs MacDonnell was aroused from bed by a loud knocking at the door. She went down the stairs in her nightdress and looking out through the kitchen window saw the outoffices on fire. The Jury will remember that the gate had been securely fastened for the night so that whoever was knocking on the door must have gained surreptitious entry into the yard by climbing over the wall. She ran downstairs, as I have told you, in her nightdress and to her horror, not alone saw the flames shoot up in the air, but what she feared more, the prisoner, James Lynchehaun, outside the door.

(*Comment:* The MacDermott told the Jury, not once, but twice that Mrs MacDonnell ran down the stairs in her nightdress, and no doubt he thought it a useful image of a frightened and distracted woman to present to the Jury. But, despite his wooden model, he had not yet fully grasped the layout of the house and the habits of its solitary inmate. Mrs MacDonnell, probably for reasons of labour saving and economy of heat, occupied, as she explained later in giving evidence, a small room on the ground floor; she did not have to run downstairs. The Counsel for the defence will eventually make the same error. Horror, and a fear greater than that of fire, were her reactions to the sight of Lynchehaun,

---

[2] Counsel here, pointing to the model, went over the several buildings in the yard, showing the entrance and the places in which the horses were stabled, and in a corner of the yard there was a large barrel of petroleum, (*Mayo News*). Elsewhere the 'barrel of petroleum' is referred to as a 'barrel of tar'.

The MacDermott said. He was hardly quite right here. Fear, as will be seen below, was only to come later. Why should she fear? When asked in court if she had summoned Lynchehaun for trespass she answered, 'Not for trespass. There has been nothing serious between him and me.' She had no feelings of guilt, and did not regard her efforts to evict him from his home as 'serious', despite the fact that he was the only tenant whom she had ever sought to evict. Neither in her evidence in court, nor in any of her four depositions, is her initial reaction to Lynchehaun shown to be one of fear. She got the keys for him at his demand, and when he released the horses she ran across the yard crying out to him 'There are sheep in there'. She then ran back to the house, for she was still in her nightdress and was not to get her cloak until later. It may also be noted as important that there is no evidence that she wore shoes or slippers, and that her running around the stony yard in bare feet could possibly have accounted for some of the injuries to her toes.)

As to that there cannot be the smallest particle of doubt, for she not only saw him but spoke to him. He said: 'I have come to call you, the stables are on fire, give me the keys until I let out the horses.' She was struck by this and she took the keys down off the nail on the wall where they were hung and gave them to Lynchehaun and she saw him go into the stables where the horses were. When he released the horses and put them out through the 'wagon door' he caught hold of Mrs MacDonnell round the waist and tried to push her into the flames. She struggled with all the strength she had, and this portion of her story will be borne out by the fact that one of her legs was scorched from the ankle to the knee. Some persons got alarmed and a young girl named Mary Gallagher Tom with others saw the flames and went into the yard and there saw the man Lynchehaun with his arms round the waist of this woman, and she saw him trying to force her towards the flames with considerable force.

She thought at first that he might be trying to save her but the more she looked the more she saw the intention of Lynchehaun, and she used the remarkable words towards him which indicated the opinion she then formed of him: "Keep away, you murderer". And she saw the poor lady thrown in the door, her head towards the door, and her feet towards the house. She went over and took the lady up off the ground where she lay, the poor lady saying to her in imploring tones "Take me away from that scoundrel". There you have, gentlemen of the jury, the prisoner caught red-handed this evening, addressed first as a "murderer" and later on a "scoundrel" by this lady who threatened and menaced him with the consequence of the crime he had intended. At this time, and it would seem to be a feature of the case, he had in his possession the keys of the gate and the stables which she had given him.

She went in the kitchen door and barred it inside, and Mary Gallagher endeavoured to induce her to open it. And Mary Gallagher returned to the wagon gate at which there were half a dozen persons assembled and immediately afterwards Mrs MacDonnell, wrapped in a cloak, returned to the yard, carrying a little fox terrier in her hand, passed through the wagon door, told the people to try and put out the flames, and then went round to the front of the house and made in the direction of a stack of hay near a whin fence. And our case is that when she rose to return the prisoner came up and hit her a violent blow on the head which dashed the light out of her eyes and deprived her of consciousness and stretched her on the grass. She remained dazed by that blow for days, and I will have to refer to the circumstances again inasmuch as it will serve to account for some discrepancies and inaccuracies in part of her evidence.

The prisoner was not satisfied, however, with the blow he struck her that reduced her to unconsciousness, but afterwards maltreated her in the most shocking manner. She thought she had gone back from this point to get the little dog, she thought she was going to get assistance, she thought she had returned, that she had gone in and shut the door. No, she took the dog and cloak with her and the cloak was found near to where she received the injuries that I shall describe. When she passed out through those people she disappeared, but she was not the only person who disappeared. Two persons disappeared at that moment; the poor lady disappeared filled with terror, Lynchehaun disappeared and it will be for you to say what he disappeared for when I tell you that within fifteen minutes from the time she left the yard that same James Lynchehaun followed round to the front of the house and near the haystack he reduced her to unconsciousness. As to everything else he did, he was not satisfied with this. Perhaps in all the history of human escapes there was never a more marvellous escape — almost a resurrection to life — than this poor woman had that night.

The doctor will describe to you in detail her injuries. The temporal bone of her head was fractured, she had two large cuts on the head besides, her nose was eaten off by human teeth to the very cartilage, a portion of her lip was also eaten off, one of her eyes was injured for ever, and the other reduced to a pulp, being literally kicked out of her head, some of her ribs were broken, her body was covered with contusions all over, while there were injuries on her stomach and other parts of a most abominably cruel character, and marks on her throat of an attempt made to strangle her. And this is the man for whom, we are told, there is some sympathy in Achill. Then with regard to her body wounds he had kicked the lower part of her person, her urethra and private parts were broken, some of her ribs were broken, her body was all filled with contusions from kicks. This was the condition to which this woman was reduced by her assailant. Another remarkable thing came out upon the examination of her body. The lady stated that, when she fell in the house, he seized her by the throat and attempted to strangle her, and the doctor found the distinct marks of the four fingers on one side of her neck and of the thumb on the other where he endeavoured to strangle her. The women were running up and down carrying the water from the lake within a few hundred yards of the house, Bridget McNeally and John and Matthew Gallagher, Michael and James McGinty, who will all be examined.

The McGintys did not come to the house until 10

o'clock and they took a short cut which took them to the front of the house near the haystack. On the way to the place Bridget McNeally was told something about a moan being heard from near the haystack and, rushing there, she found her mistress lying near the hedge of whin bushes growing along the fence and she was quite unconscious. One of the girls states she saw her little terrier dog out on the road. She heard a slight moan and she was afraid to go near it, but the other woman, ultimately coming up, found the body apparently dead. She immediately collected other women. When the Gallaghers and the McGintys arrived the body of Mrs MacDonnell was found, and that was important to remember, so that the injuries were inflicted on Mrs MacDonnell between the time the horses were let out and the immediate disappearance of Lynchehaun. When the Gallaghers and McGintys arrived, on their way to give assistance, they saw this lady in the hands of the women who were about taking her to a place of security, the house of Michael Gallagher, the tailor. When they took her into the house some of the women said she was dead, but Bridget McNeally said, 'No, if I could warm her I might bring her to life', and she placed her opposite the fire and two or three men were sent off for the doctor and the police. While the men were away what was James Lynchehaun doing? Mrs MacDonnell will swear he inflicted that injury upon her. It will be proved that the prisoner went into the house of a woman named Mary Gallagher Tom and said, 'You are the only person who can free me.'

And she replied, 'Others saw you as well as me.'

He then said, 'No one will tell of me if you don't' and she made answer 'I am the one that can guilty you', to use her own peculiar phrase. You have him then immediately afterwards going about to try and silence evidence which he knew could be brought against him if she spoke. Is that an indication of innocence or guilt? Now I come to the next appearance of the man. While the neighbours were trying to extinguish the flames, and pull down the burning roofs, he came into the yard. His face was scraped and bloody, he had a semi-circular cut on his hand, and the form of the cut was important. There was blood on his trousers, he wore no boots or cap, and he carried in his hands, for some unknown purpose, two stones and presented the appearance of a man who had imbibed a quantity of drink to keep up his spirits after, as we say, committing this great crime, and that he continued taking drink that night.

(*Comment:* The evidence as to how Lynchehaun spent the hours before his appearance at the fire does not suggest that he had taken a large amount of drink that evening. He had dealt competently with Mrs MacDonnell's sheep and horses hardly a quarter of an hour before. Where did he get a 'quantity of drink' after the alleged crime?)

He was asked what he was doing with the stones, but could give no explanation. Where was his cap? He pulled it out of his breast and put it on his head and then proceeded to give, or pretended to give, some assistance with the others to put out the flames. He described himself on this occasion as having been going to bed, or just in bed, when he was aroused by the alarm of fire, and that he ran up in the condition I have described to you, his presence in the yard being after Mrs MacDonnell had been beaten and left lying by the ditch.

And when he came into the yard he said 'What's up?' as if he had never been there that night before. Then he proposed to assist them but instead of doing so he was trying to prevent them. He pretended to assist but said 'To Hell with the old sheds', as if he wanted the conflagration to take place. He said to the woman who was trying to save her 'Leave her there and don't get yourself burned by remaining here.'

He was there for some time, and remember he afterwards came there when the McGintys had been in the yard with the Gallaghers and he said 'What's up?' The McGintys and Gallaghers had been aware on their way up that Mrs MacDonnell was injured and her body found so he never reappeared in the yard until all the injuries were inflicted which ruined and so disfigured her that all happiness is forever effaced from that woman's life from the condition in which he has left her.

Then there is the statement of Judy Cooney addressed to the people quenching the fire, 'Mrs MacDonnell is dead — you will all be arrested.' When Lynchehaun disappeared for the second time it was to try and get Mary Gallagher not to give evidence against him. The doctor and police arrived at half-past twelve. The Big House was not then on fire. The sheds to the back were disconnected from it and the wind was blowing in an opposite direction and the jury will be made perfectly certain that the main house was independently set fire to and set fire by Lynchehaun, after he inflicted the injuries on this woman.

When the doctor arrived Lynchehaun had the audacity to enter Gallagher's house where Mrs MacDonnell lay. Lynchehaun was then more under the influence of drink than at the earlier stages. When the doctor examined her and asked for a little whiskey to give her to drink Lynchehaun went out and brought in a little whiskey in a cup and the doctor gave some of it to the woman and it helped in restoring her. The doctor asked how this thing happened and Lynchehaun said it was in letting out the horses. 'They threw her sky-high, she insisted on letting them out in spite of my advice.' He told Sergeant Dusting the same and when Sergeant Dusting asked 'Who are they?' Lynchehaun pressed him on the foot privately and said in a whisper 'Arrest Matthew Gallagher, arrest Johnny Gallagher and arrest Tom Calvey, mason. It was they who did it, they threw the building on her.' Are these signs of guilt or innocence? No one was there with blood upon him but James Lynchehaun. Nobody invented falsehoods but James Lynchehaun. Nobody accused innocent men but James Lynchehaun. Why was he alone distinguished by the course he took that night? Mrs MacDonnell would swear Lynchehaun struck her in the field and the doctor would describe her injuries and a very remarkable thing was that the doctor found up in one of the wounds some of the whin bushes from the hedge; the fellow who went there had the whin bushes on his shoes and kicked them up into her body.

The Big House was set fire to about half-past one o'clock, the fire originating in the room of this lady. I will go back to tell you that the yard wall which was covered with glass was broken for about three feet and drops of blood were found on the outside of the wall, on the inside of the wall, and on James Lynchehaun's hand was found a semi-circular wound, just such a wound as would be caused by the glass. He let out the horses and on the side of the door and on the post of the horse-box blood marks were also found and it was thereby concluded that he crossed the wall into the yard. The person who set fire to the main house entered by the pantry window and blood stains were found on the shelf inside. Was it the prisoner at the bar who did it? You have the proofs against him. First you have him tracked in blood and secondly you have this, that in the debris of the room of this lady where the fire commenced were found the keys which on that night had been given to Lynchehaun to open the stables. Who carried the keys there? Lynchehaun. Who dropped the keys there? Lynchehaun. Who went in the pantry window? It was the same blood-stained ruffian, bent on general destruction and conflagration. It might be said in his defence he was drunk, but *in vino veritas* — there is truth in wine and a man when he is under the influence of drink is likely to let out things that he would not let out in other moments, and every statement he made that night was designed to acquit himself and stain the character of others. The horses did not do it for two of the horses were stabbed themselves, the Gallaghers or McGintys did not do it, and then he invented the notion that she herself did it that night in order to get money from the Insurance Company. The prisoner at the bar said he got the cut on his hand going in the pantry window to extinguish the flames, admitting thereby that it was he who went in the pantry window. Lynchehaun was arrested at 7 o'clock next morning, taken to the police barracks, and he there made a statement:

'Isn't this an extraordinary offence? I was called out of my own house by Judy Cooney; she came up with the two Gallaghers. I was just going to bed and had my shoes off when I saw the blaze. I ran down and saw her (Mrs MacDonnell) in the middle of the flames. I rushed in and caught her and shoved her out, and she fell in the yard, and when she got up I asked the keys of the stable from her, and she gave them to me. I ran and led the mare and foal out of the stable. I saw no more of her till I saw her in Gallagher's house. The poor woman is destroyed. I don't think she will live. I don't know how it occurred. She must have fallen or struck her head against something. The galvanised roof might have fallen on her head. I was the bloody fool not to have remained in my own house, but sure if I was in London she would say that I did it; but I don't know what they arrested me for or the woman didn't know what she was saying. She said to Mr Carr she was in her own house. I am nicely fixed if the old devil dies. That mason of hers, Calvey, is a queer lad, and the Gallaghers too. Gallagher gave up his position last Saturday morning and left Mrs MacDonnell, as they were not agreeing with one another.'

Now that statement is wholly and entirely untrue. The prisoner knew well what he was about. He had a various career. He was at one time a schoolmaster, and afterwards joined the police force, not the Irish police. If he were an innocent man why should he invent the contradictory stories and seek to transfer the guilt of his crime to other people, and insinuate that Mrs MacDonnell had fired the place herself in order to get the amount of her insurance? The jury would have it in evidence that over and over again he expressed the wish that she might die, and that he used language about her of a character too indecent to bear repetition. On his way to the barracks next day he asked to be brought to his father's house to get a change of clothes.

(*Comment:* This is incorrect. He asked to be brought to his own house. His father's house was not even on the island.)

The policeman in charge said he could not do that, but that he might leave word to have another suit of clothes supplied to him from his father's house but that they would take charge of the clothes he was then wearing. They went to his father's house, and the prisoner had a conversation in Irish with the father's boy

(*Comment:* Tony Lynchehaun was James Lynchehaun's 'boy' not his father's.)

and asked him to bring him a suit of clothes, and shortly afterwards the boy rode off on a horse and carried a bundle of clothes round to Dugort barracks where the prisoner was allowed to undress himself and make a change of clothes, putting by the old ones in a corner of the room in the barracks. There was a policeman placed in charge of him and he asked the constable in the most artless way to go and inquire how Mrs MacDonnell was getting on. The constable refused to leave his presence however. Then after a little while he suggested to the constable to go down and light his pipe and he again refused. Then another policeman less cautious, came into the room, and he unfortunately went out of it for a few moments, and when he returned the boy, and the horse, and the parcel of clothes were gone. They must have been put out through the window by the prisoner but all efforts at pursuit proved useless. On the 20th October the prisoner was brought into Castlebar for examination and on the way home he passed by his father's house

(*Comment:* The MacDermott is very confused. Lynchehaun was not being brought into Castlebar 'for examination'. He was being held there, but had to be brought frequently to Achill to be present at depositions, and then to return again to his temporary 'home' in Castlebar Jail. The incident described consequently happened on a journey to Castlebar and not to Achill.)

and suddenly jumped off the car and vanished. Two hundred policemen were in search of him day and night but they were unable to discover his whereabouts. It was suggested that he had left the country, and while on the run he wrote a letter to District Inspector Rainsford purporting to come from Lancashire in order to throw his pursuers off the scent. The letter was as follows:

Kirkarn, Lancashire
Sir — I beg to inform you ...

(*Comment:* The letter from James Lynchehaun's autograph is given above, p. 93. Before being read out in court the letter was changed or conventionalised and there were some omissions. Racy or Hiberno-English speech was paraphrased. 'Croly was death on me' becomes 'Croly was hostile to me'. In 'he will put her to death surely' the last word is changed to 'principally'. 'Nook and turn' becomes 'nook and dell'. 'Crossed into Doohooma, thence to Blacksod, into Iniskea' is reduced to 'crossed to Blacksod'; 'You were coming by Hickey's car' is misrepresented by 'You were getting off of Hickey's car'. There are some omissions. After 'to have an opportunity to buy the Valley House for himself' the transcript omits 'On this subject I will write to her husband'.)

The MacDermott dwelt on the clever manner by which the prisoner attempted to mislead the police — the envelope showing that the letter was actually sent over to Lancashire by some means and posted there — while he was all the time hiding in Achill in a hole dug in the floor of the house of a man named Gallagher, covered over with earth and a box to escape detection, and there he was found at three o'clock in the morning naked, his clothes hanging on a peg in the room. Was he (The MacDermott) on all the facts, not justified in saying that a clearer or more powerful case was never presented to a jury. Was there room for sympathy or doubt? They were there trying a man who attacked a defenceless woman and treated her worse than a brute would have done. Of course if there was any real doubt the prisoner, if he were ten times as guilty as the Crown believed him to be, was entitled to the benefit of it; but this could not be a capricious doubt or one evolved out of counsel's ingenuity, but based on solid reason. The MacDermott then closed his statement, having spoken for upwards of an hour and a half.

Mrs MacDonnell was the first witness for the prosecution. Even now when close upon a century has passed, it would be as ungracious as it probably would be untrue to accuse her of deliberate perjury. But convinced as she was of Lynchehaun's guilt on every possible count certain 'facts' seemed to follow upon her strong conviction, and she gave evidence accordingly.

The MacDermott recognised that there were many contradictions and inconsistencies in her depositions, and these he attributed, naturally and conveniently, to her shocking experience. During the trial she was hysterical, emotional, imperious, and gave the impression that, with a certain perversity, she took pleasure in the tragic drama in which she was a principal participant. According to contemporary statements, and the most obvious interpretation of her mode of life, she was to a degree eccentric. It is unnecessary to stress that it would be unsafe to accept her uncorroborated evidence in details, such, for instance, as the important matter of James Lynchehaun's boots.

She was the first witness to be called to the table. 'The prisoner eyed her keenly as she came up, but a muscle in his face did not change' (*The Western People*).

She told the court how she had come to buy the Achill property, how she came to employ the prisoner, the names of those who served her, and finally she came to the point where on the evening of 6 October she heard a knock on the kitchen door. 'It was then a quarter past eight; I rose and went to the kitchen window, and saw the stables on fire; I put on a large cloak, and saw through the glass the prisoner...'

The MacDermott, pointing to Lynchehaun, asked 'Is that the man you saw?'

She turned, stood with arms outstretched, fixed her eye — the reporter owing to her tragic blemish had to vary the conventional phrase — on the prisoner in the dock, and in a firm voice, said emphatically 'That is the man'.

Here the witness, whether consciously or not, has been guilty of a trifling untruth, but one with a purpose. According to a statement of hers in her third deposition she did not at this point put on a cloak; indeed her state of comparative undress during the incident in the yard is one of the factors which made Mary Gallagher Tom watch the scene with such horrified fascination, and to show relief when she subsequently acquired a cloak on returning to her house.

It is greatly to be doubted that Mrs MacDonnell was merely confused. Rather, having given the matter some thought since her third deposition, she realised that she could not admit publicly that under any circumstances she would appear before James Lynchehaun, or any other man but her husband, clad only in a nightdress.

Her evidence was less than satisfactory when she came to describe the attack that Lynchehaun made upon her near the whin bushes. 'I ran to the haystack, and looked around to see if there was anyone, and there was no one to be seen, not even my servants; when near the haystack I made up my mind to return to the house and try and dress myself and summon my servants; I saw a man coming towards me, who proved to be Lynchehaun; he had something in his hand; he gave me a tremendous blow and I felt as if I had been shot into a thousand pieces.'

'On the head?' asked The MacDermott.

'On the back of the head. I lost consciousness then.'

'Have you any doubt as to who assaulted you on this occasion?'

'I am positive it was Lynchehaun. It was a clear bright night.'

His lordship, naturally wishing to visualise the scene clearly, asked 'How near was he to you?'

'He just passed me, and was about a foot below, or rather on a level with me. I recognised him as he passed, and just as he passed he gave me a tremendous blow on the head. I was only conscious at intervals for some days afterwards.'

Her account was not satisfactory to Dr. Falconer. He was apparently worried, as was his Lordship, by one fact. Mrs MacDonnell represented herself all the time as facing Lynchehaun, and recognising him as he passed by. How, under these circumstances, had he given her a blow on the back of the head?

'Was the person who struck you coming directly towards you?,' asked Dr Falconer.

'He was walking in and out of the whin bushes.'
'Coming towards you?'
'Yes.'
'Coming toward you? Did you say he was not coming toward you?'
'I decline to answer your impertinent question.'

His lordship intervened on behalf of the witness, saying that she had given direct evidence.

'I said he was walking in and out of the whin bushes,' said Mrs MacDonnell, 'as if he did not wish to be seen. He was dodging in and out. I cannot tell you more plainly than that.'

'When he hit you he was behind you?'

'Not more than a foot. Where I was struck is close by a path, which would only be used by my own work people, and they were prohibited using it. I made four depositions; I cannot recollect the date; in the first deposition I may not have said anything about Lynchehaun having struck me.'

Dr Falconer read out the deposition and there was no mention of Lynchehaun's having struck Mrs MacDonnell. The examination continued.

'Did you summon Lynchehaun for trespass?'

'Not for trespass. There has been nothing serious between him and me.'

'Did you ever tell Miss Fitzgerald, your nurse, that whoever it was struck you it was not Lynchehaun?'

'No; I never said anything of the kind, to her or to any other person. I could not say such a thing.'

'Can you say that while in this condition the constable had conversation with you?'

'How dare they! Not one of them dare ask me a question. To come into my bedroom!'

Mrs MacDonnell's indignation and asperity suggests that she had forgotten many things. At least two policemen, Constable Joseph Morrison and Sergeant Joseph Dusting had taken statements from her as she lay in bed at Michael Gallagher's house on the night of 6 and the morning of 7 October.

Mrs MacDonnell gave evidence which, if we accept it, may throw some light on the immediate circumstances of the crime. But first to return to her meeting with Lynchehaun at about 8.15. After the release of the sheep and the horses Mrs MacDonnell stood in the yard clad only in her nightdress when Lynchehaun seized her. It is suggested by The MacDermott, and indeed by the general folk tradition, that this seizure was unprovoked. This, however, does not appear to have been so. In the second of her four depositions Mrs MacDonnell describes how Lynchehaun had just released the horses from the stables. She said: 'I then went over to the burning flames, for I was so startled to find him in the yard and so convinced that he caused it, that *I must have said something to him. I don't know what it was.* He then said "Is this your gratitude to the man who came to save your horses?" and he then put his arm round my waist. I was in the midst of the flames at the time and he tried to force me into them. I struggled and came to the wagon door. I called to the women as I rushed out of the yard to help to bring water to put out the fire, and I then went towards the haystack.'

There is no need for deep speculation as to what it was that Mrs MacDonnell said to Lynchehaun. Despite her plea of bad memory in this respect, her own words ('...so convinced that he caused it...') and his answer, as quoted by her, implies that she accused him of incendiarism. And this interpretation is supported by Brother Paul.

On Lynchehaun returning the keys to Mrs MacDonnell, she accused him of incendiary (*sic*); he denied the charge and threatened to strike her. She drew her bulldog revolver and threatened to shoot him. He snatched it from her, and taking her bodily, carried her towards the flames. She screamed, and a courageous girl, named Mary Gallagher, ran to rescue and cried to James Lynchehaun, 'What are you going to do, you rascal? Do you wish to burn the lady?' At these exclamations he let her go. But she, being so inflamed with passion, very imprudently followed him about the yard repeating the accusation of incendiary.

It may well be true that Mrs MacDonnell kept a 'bulldog revolver' by her bedside, as Brother Paul tells us elsewhere. But, clad only in her nightdress, she can hardly have 'drawn' it in this dramatic manner. However, the important point of the whole incident is that the words of Lynchehaun, as quoted by Mrs MacDonnell (and admitted by her under Dr Falconer's cross-examination) are words of outraged innocence. If this be true it would seem to follow that, so far, no offence had been committed, neither 'surreptitious entry' nor arson. It was the repeated accusations of incendiarism that goaded Lynchehaun into his first apparent attack on, or threat to, Mrs MacDonnell, his dragging her towards the flames. This would mean that there was no premeditation, that there would not have been any crime had not Mrs MacDonnell, shocked and exhausted, chosen to leave her workers and tenantry and seek the isolation of a hayrick, thirty yards from her hall door. The great crime, the attack on Mrs MacDonnell, was, it would appear, the result of a sudden fit of insane and ungovernable rage by a man who, according to general report, had had such fits of insane violence before.

General tradition, Lynchehaun's great friend and biographer, Brother Paul, The MacDermott, and presumably the Jury, all regarded Lynchehaun as guilty of the burning of the stables and of the house, as well as of the vicious attack on Mrs MacDonnell, and hold that these crimes were premeditated. The MacDermott's eloquence, and the natural human desire for a simple, rather than a complicated solution, would urge the Jury towards the conclusion that not chance, not a possible second or third criminal, but one person and one alone, James Lynchehaun, had effected every evil that occurred that night.

There is one act of which Lynchehaun was thought guilty that might turn the minds of many against him, and that, curiously, whether in middle-class English or Irish psychology, might weigh more heavily than arson, and even compete strongly as a revolting outrage with the mutilation of the lady's body. This was the stabbing in the flank of two of the threatened horses.

When Lynchehaun went into the stable to release the horses he was hidden from Mrs MacDonnell's sight for a short time, possibly for a number of seconds, hardly more than a minute. Speed was of the essence of the operation. When the horses were recovered next day they were found to have been stabbed in the flank; that the stabbing was done in the stable is suggested by the fact that traces of blood were found there. Lynchehaun, it was thought, in those tense moments when he was alone with the horses and unseen, had committed this wanton and senseless deed. No bloody instrument was found, either in the stable or on Lynchehaun's person. Proof of his guilt in this matter is entirely lacking. The act might have been committed earlier in the day by somebody with a grudge against the owner, and of these there were many; indeed, at this period mutilation of a landlord's animals was a not uncommon outrage. When Lynchehaun released the horses he was doing so either to ingratiate himself with the landlady or for purely humanitarian reasons. He was in total command of the situation, and the insane rage, inspired by the accusations of incendiarism, had not yet laid hold of him. There is nothing known of him otherwise to suggest that he would commit an act of cruelty against an animal. The mutilation of the horses must remain as one of the minor mysteries in the case.

Mrs MacDonnell's evidence was followed by that of Mary Gallagher Tom. Then others came to the table, the McGinty brothers, Dr Croly, Tom Calvey, John Gallagher, Mary Gallagher Tom, Senior, and the police witnesses.

The Jury, in finding Lynchehaun guilty, must have taken the view that certain defence witnesses had agreed together to take a certain line, or that Lynchehaun's wife Catherine, and the Lynchehaun family, had put pressure on them to do so. According to Mary Gallagher Tom's evidence, and that of her mother, Lynchehaun himself had attempted to ensure the younger woman's silence. Catherine, according to Michael McGinty, had made efforts to influence himself and his brother. He made a deposition on 19 January 1895, and under cross-examination by M. J. Kelly the Crown solicitor said 'The defendant's wife did not hold out any threat to me.' But his succeeding words are a flat contradiction of this: 'I recollect in the month of October last her coming to my father's house. She asked my mother where me and my brothers were. My mother said I was in bed, and my brother was out. She said that she heard that me and my brother had too much to say against her husband; that if we hanged him we wouldn't hang her, that she would be in the Valley after us'.

The case for the prosecution closed at 7 o'clock on Tuesday evening.

CHAPTER XII
Trial at Castlebar: The Defence

On Wednesday morning Dr Falconer of the Leinster circuit opened the case for the defence.

I appear with my friend Mr Louden as counsel for the prisoner at the bar whose trial and whose fate you are the ultimate arbiters of. I quite agree with what The MacDermott said to you as to the horror of the crime that was committed that night. I do not stand here, nor does my friend, to justify the treatment which that poor woman received. I concur with every word The MacDermott has said in describing his horror of the act. But while I agree with the description of the feelings of The MacDermott I ask you to beware of the object for which he stated them with such power and skill. When you hear of an act which was repugnant to your sense of decency and humanity you are apt, if you are a man, to say 'The scoundrel, if I could catch him'.

I ask you, not because it is the natural feeling that would come to any manly mind and mouth, to be careful and consider, because of your objection to crime, whether you would not fall easily into the delusion that that man was guilty merely because he was charged. Of course if he was guilty mercy would be thrown away upon him. The MacDermott described the crime with pathos, the effect of which might be to make you anxious to convict the prisoner. I do not put it that way to you, but that might be the effect of the skill and ability with which he stated the case to you if you are not particularly on your guard against it.

There was another matter mentioned by The Mac-Dermott which I gladly ask you to follow. When you find police witnesses in favour of the prisoner their evidence ought to be conclusive. The MacDermott, that great criminal lawyer, skilled in prosecuting, and trained in all the arts and forensic ability to wind the web of evidence to prove guilt around the prisoner, recommended you, if you have reasonable doubt about the man's guilt, to give him the benefit of it. He said that it should be a reasonable doubt upon your mind and not a doubt arising from the ingenuity of counsel. I think that if you only compare the men on each side you will have very little reason to call upon the ingenuity of counsel. In the first place you have representing the Crown a man who is the most skilful and eminent Crown prosecutor that ever served a government in this country, at all events in my time, most successful in procuring convictions, most successful in doing his duty. On the other side you have a comparatively junior member of the circuit here and a stranger you know nothing about. Therefore, instead of the ingenuity of counsel for the prisoner raising any doubt — the last resource of a baffled Crown prosecutor who cannot make a case good in evidence — I would ask you to say to yourselves when you go into the room to consider your verdict how much of the feeling on your mind against Lynchehaun was due to The MacDermott's cleverness, ability, and skill, and how much of it was due merely to police evidence. How much of it was due to persons who might be anxious to exculpate themselves, and how much was due solely to persons like Mr Rainsford whose evidence would be above suspicion? How much of it was due to men in positions where they were bound to justify themselves, and how much of that was due to what I call, to a certain extent, tainted witnesses?

This was a dreadful crime. The indignation of the civilised world was aroused at it; but you are not to allow your indignation to make you convict the prisoner in the dock without the clearest proof. You will see the nature of the evidence and if there arises in your minds that reasonable doubt which The MacDermott himself anticipated you will be entitled to give the prisoner the benefit of it. The English law closes his mouth. He could tell his story. The law did better for the man than that: it says that he is presumed to be innocent until you could not find him innocent without breaking your oaths. In consequence of that provision of the law the only way the prisoner can state his case is out of the mouth of the constable. The prisoner's case is not the concoction of Mr Louden or myself, or his very clever solicitor, Mr Jordan. It was a statement made to Sergeant Scully which was the beginning and foundation of the prisoner's case. He said 'I was called out of my house by Judy Cooney'. She was proved to have called the attention of Bridget Grealish or McNeally to the conflagration, and why did not the Crown produce her? 'I was just going to bed at the time and I had my boots off'. That was the material point, that he had his boots off. I would remind you that not a single witness said that he had his boots on and if you are satisfied of that the ruffians by whom Mrs MacDonnell was done to death did not include the prisoner at the bar. This is the beginning of this man's case. The first part was that the Crown did not produce Judy Cooney and the second was that he went there without boots. These facts by themselves would be sufficient, because the charge against this man is a charge of having practically done the woman to within an inch of her death. But whoever it was that hurt her the person was represented as wearing boots and this man who was going to bed had no boots on. I am going to call testimony in his favour you little expect, from the lips of Mrs MacDonnell, as sworn on the 8th October. There was a marvellous coincidence which if they lived in the ages of faith would show you that truth will prevail. First this man told Scully exactly what Mrs MacDonnell told the magistrate Mr Carr. He said — 'When I went out I saw Mrs MacDonnell in the middle of the flames.'

(Counsel then read Mrs MacDonnell's deposition in which

she described her discovery of the fire and James Lynchehaun at the back door, that she walked across the yard in her nightdress and that the accused put his arm round her and tried to throw her into the burning stuff.)

Lynchehaun told Sergeant Scully when he went down he found her in the middle of the flames, that he shoved her out, that she fell and that when she got up he asked for the keys of the stable. Mrs MacDonnell says 'He then asked me for the keys'. Did not the coincidence in regard to the acts, the coincidence in the succession of events, prove that Mrs MacDonnell's first story was right and the story this man told was right. That was the man's case. After this what does he go on to say? 'She gave them to me and I let out the mare and foal.' Mrs MacDonnell on the table said he did so and that the mare rushed out very quickly. What did he do then, this man against whom so much was alleged? Mrs MacDonnell naturally was in such a state of fright she could not tell and gave three or four versions of it — he tried to drag her into the flames, that there was no one there, that there were no men there, but they knew there were from other sources. The prisoner's case was that instead of trying to drag her into the flames he was trying to drag her away. She was undoubtedly in the middle of the burning when she went out to see where the horses were and what he was doing. Mary Gallagher told them he was struggling with her for twenty minutes. Did they believe that? Did they believe that powerful man would not have succeeded in his purpose sooner if he so desired it? And instead of pushing her into the burning stable he pushed her into the stable not on fire. Her own statement was that she fell into it. After that she was quite incapable of giving one scintilla of evidence or making a statement they could rely on. She said when she got out of his hands she ran away to the haystack. Do you believe that? You are not to suppose for a moment I am charging Mrs MacDonnell with attempting to state falsely anything she recollected, but what I suggest is she did not recollect it. Directly she got away from the touch of his hands she said he went down to the haystack. Is that true?

Mrs MacDonnell now says she might have gone into the house. She believed she did because, forsooth, Tip her fox terrier was upstairs in the bedroom and she must have gone into it because he had come out, as if he could not have come out through the window or twenty other ways. If there was a syllable of truth in Mary Gallagher's evidence — and I do not suggest she was telling the truth at all, I suggest she was not telling the truth — but if there was any reliance to be placed on what she swore — did she not swear that after getting from the fire Mrs MacDonnell went into the house, shut the door and locked it and Mary Gallagher felt her going upstairs and thought she was gone upstairs. Now Mrs MacDonnell never made any statement of having believed even that she had gone into the house until she stated it to Mr Kelly, the Crown Solicitor, a week or ten days ago. Counsel asked her how she came to believe it then for the first time, apparently that she got to know that other people said she had gone into the house when she heard the evidence read to her from the newspapers in January last. I do not suggest Mrs MacDonnell would tell a falsehood — that is not my case. My case is that she was so dazed she did not know what she was saying when she stated she went right down to the haystack without entering the house. How can you believe she was accurate or had the means of being accurate in regard to other matters? Now if there is one thing certain it is that she did go into the house that evening. She did not recollect it herself and, if she did not, how could she recollect what passed afterwards in the dark? She went into the house and Mary Gallagher called to her to come out to get her friends. I cannot conceive the cause why a woman like this Mary Gallagher would say that this lady — you could tell she was that from her manner and voice on the table — who had come out into the yard, etc., who had gone into the house in her dishabille, would be better to be out amongst the crowd of women and men. I put it to you, would it not have been better had Mrs MacDonnell remained in the house when she got in and locked the door? When she came out Mary Gallagher spoke to her and said 'Don't you know me, my lady?' My lady did not appear to know her at all. I am leading up to this to show how little you should rely on Mrs MacDonnell's identification of the person who struck her. She told them distinctly on that table she saw nobody, spoke to nobody, while she was rushing from the flames in the yard to the haystack in front. Mary Gallagher said she spoke to her but there is one thing as certain as you are sitting in the box: before Mrs MacDonnell went to the haystack she met a number of persons outside the wagon gate and gave them directions and permission to go in and try to save the stables. Now what do you think of Mrs MacDonnell's recollection and accuracy after that? One of the men, Sweeney I believe it was, asked her for permission, and those women there, and yet she said she looked up and down, searched high and low, and that there was not a man there at all. If they believed the evidence of Mary Gallagher and the other witnesses there were several people in it, that they asked permission to go in and that she told them to go. Notwithstanding that, she said she did not see a single man there. It was clear proof that the woman was out of her mind and when she could not recollect the people there she could not recollect who she met and gave her that destructive blow. That is the case I suggest to you. The case for the Crown is so weak you could not commit upon it. I put it to you there was not one of the police, not one of these unfriendly — I do not want to call them enemies — not one of the police or people who ventured to save that poor woman, ever alluded to Lynchehaun as having attacked her down in the grass. He was always at the fire at the stables. There was no doubt but he had his hand on her. That constitutes common assault. We do not deny that, but that was not what the Crown relied on. In the struggle in the flames Mrs MacDonnell may have got bruised. Far be it from me to suggest that she did not but there was one curious thing: she had a chemise on her and if the prisoner kept her in the fire the chemise, down about her feet and ankles, must have been scorched. It was not produced, but it will be produced, and I am instructed there is not a sign of fire about it.

(His Lordship intervened saying that it was going to be produced. 'Is it worth troubling about?', he asked.)

I do not suggest the police are keeping it back. Mary Gallagher said the man had her twenty minutes in the flames or where the flames were and I am instructed there was not a burn upon it, and what a fool the man would be without boots to keep himself in the flames twenty minutes. I could understand if he was trying to put her in and not go in himself.

(His lordship intervened to say that he had no note of anything like what he was telling the jury. 'Mary Gallagher was asked would it be twenty minutes and she said it might be'.)

My case is that she was not in the flames at all because the poor lady would have got greater burns than she did. The case for the Crown is a very weak case and is open to the very doubt that The MacDermott mentioned when he was stating it to them. I made a mistake about the woman being twenty minutes in the flames, but it was not for what occurred in the yard but for what happened out on the grass the prisoner was being tried. My case is that he tried to take her away out of the flames instead of trying to put her into them. But let you take the probabilities. Imagine for a moment that this man had been wicked enough to go and set fire to the stables; why would he have gone and called attention to it? People of common sense know a person who commits a crime tries to conceal it and run away to escape observation. I venture to say whoever did set fire to the stable was probably the last person to come up to it. What would bring him there if he had done it? He could only have done it with the object of injuring her property and what was the evidence? That he went there and asked for the keys to let out the horses for fear they would be injured by the fire. The Crown could not have it both ways. If they say this man set fire to the place I would ask how did they explain to you that he presented himself to Mrs MacDonnell and as she admitted herself was saving her horses. It is not because an eminent Crown Counsel makes a statement and puts up witnesses you are to convict unless the evidence satisfies you. If Lynchehaun was the guilty ruffian the Crown represents him to be why did he go and rap at Mrs MacDonnell's back door and call her attention to the fire? Was that the act of a man who would set fire to the stables? If he wanted to burn the stables why did he save the horses? It will be proved Judy Cooney saw the flames and went and knocked up her neighbours, amongst them this man. He went up and he found the place open. You know Mary Gallagher was there and women and men too. Why is this man singled out? This is the question. What did he do that night to make himself liable to this charge, supposing he is innocent. It is a curious work of the mind. Mrs MacDonnell came out, saw her place in flames, saw Lynchehaun there and connected Lynchehaun with the flames, immediately supposed he had set the place on fire and immediately supposed everything was done by Lynchehaun.

(Counsel then described the nature of some of the evidence to be given.)

When Mrs MacDonnell went from the wagon door to the haystack it was quite dark. She was so absolutely dazed that she did not know what she was doing. I suggest that the reason why she said she saw Lynchehaun there was that she was after having an interview with him, a struggle if you like with regard to the fire, and she thought that everything was Lynchehaun in her fright. I put it to you that a lady under such conditions as she herself declared, in the darkness of the night, was unable to distinguish and to tell you with confidence who it was that struck her. Is it not a curious thing that the people who came to the fire by the paths near the haystack did not see Lynchehaun there? Somebody struck the woman but there was not a single witness but the lady herself to say that Lynchehaun was in the lawn when Mrs MacDonnell was there. It is not an obligation on the prisoner to prove who committed this crime. It is the duty of the Crown to prove that no person but the prisoner could have committed it. I suggest that you have not been told the whole story by the witnesses for the Crown. When the women were passing up and down between the river and the burning premises they must have passed within a few yards of where Mrs MacDonnell lay, but there was not one of them to say that they had seen her. I submit that Mary Gallagher must have seen and heard a great deal more than she told you, and if you believe that she has been concealing anything that might be favourable to the prisoner you will not act upon her evidence. When Mary Gallagher Tom was asked by Mr Louden as to some conversation she had with Johnny Gallagher she said she did not remember, while Johnny Gallagher admitted that there was such a conversation, that he asked her was she in the yard that night. In his deposition he said he was anxious to get 'witness' out of her to prove against Lynchehaun 'as he said me and Calvey should be arrested for this'. You will find that the prisoner went to Tailor Gallagher's house like the rest. It will be proved that he was there before the doctor or police came, and undoubtedly he brought whiskey there. In none of her [Mrs MacDonnell's] depositions made after the occurrence did she refer to the assault in the lawn. Her depositions had reference altogether to the scene in the yard only. Lynchehaun's case is that he knew nothing of what occurred to Mrs MacDonnell except what was known to the others there. As to the alleged statements of Lynchehaun, he asked them to pay no attention to the rambling utterances of a drunken man. As to the fire at the Big House it will be proved to you that from the time Mrs MacDonnell was brought to Tailor Gallagher's house Lynchehaun remained there under police supervision and could not, therefore, have set the house on fire. The statements made by Mrs MacDonnell in Gallagher's that night can not be used against the prisoner unless you are satisfied that the prisoner was listening to them and had an opportunity of contradicting them. I would point out that Constable Morrison, in his deposition of February 4th, said that Lynchehaun was sleeping at the time. As to the escape on the 20th October, there is no man would not endeavour to escape if he got the chance, and the incident does not point to the guilt of the prisoner. If the police were guilty of negligence or breach of duty is Lynchehaun to be blamed for that?

(Dr Falconer then read the letter from Lynchehaun to Mr Rainsford, bearing the Kirkham postmark and submitted that it was a joke.)[1]

Mrs MacDonnell, who does not appear to be an Irishwoman, does not seem to have been happy in her relations with her tenants, and there were persons who had infinitely greater motives for the crime than Lynchehaun had. I would point out that Mrs MacDonnell had appointed and dismissed three agents before Lynchehaun was appointed sub-agent and there was not the slightest suggestion that she had done him any wrong that would have been likely to call forth revenge. She never distrained his cattle, she never summoned him for trespassing, she had no real cause of quarrel with the prisoner.

In conclusion, we all pity Mrs MacDonnell, and it would be very desirable that the outrage should be punished, but it would be a sorry thing, indeed, if people were convicted without sufficient evidence. The law does not act as an avenger. There is a Power above that has the power of revenge; you have only the power to judge by the evidence and the law is that you cannot give a verdict against the man in the dock unless the evidence compels you to do so. I do not ask for mercy because, if the man were guilty, he did not deserve mercy at the hands of justice, but I ask that, if you have any reasonable doubt as to the evidence, you should give the prisoner the benefit of it. Foul as was the outrage committed a worse outrage would be committed upon society and a greater wrong done to the law and a greater insult given to humanity if you, for the sake of clearing the country of a stain, made yourselves a party to convicting a man without sufficient evidence to compel you to do so.

[1] For the letter see p. 93.

The first witness for the defence was Judy Cooney, a first cousin of the prisoner. On the night of 6 October when she saw the fire at the Big House she first ran to summon Bridget McNeally. Bridget told her to go and get Matthew Gallagher. James Lynchehaun's house was on the way, so she knocked on his door and pushed it in. She heard Lynchehaun talking to his wife, but did not see him. In her hurry she only spoke to Catherine Lynchehaun. It is to be assumed, although she could not say so since she did not witness it, that as she rushed on to Matt Gallagher's, Lynchehaun left the house, racing to the fire. Meanwhile Judy went on, and then, on Matt's instructions, ran to call his son, Johnny. She was a long time knocking at Johnny's before getting an answer, and when she was let in Johnny and Tom Calvey were putting on their clothes 'on the floor'. She then made for the Big House, and overtook Matt Gallagher on his way there. When they came as far as the whin bushes they were in time to see Mrs MacDonnell being lifted off the ground. Judy said that she never came any nearer to the fire, and denied that she had called out to those in the yard, 'Come out or you will all be arrested', that is, she denied that she had been one of 'the cursing women'.

Constable Costelloe gave in evidence from his notebook a statement alleged to have been made to him by Judy Cooney on 15 October 1894: 'I did not call James Lynchehaun, shopkeeper, the night of the fire; I didn't see him at the fire, but he might have been there.'

In some way, which the reports do not make quite clear, District Inspector Rainsford's testimony, no less than that of Constable Costelloe, was in direct conflict with Judy Cooney's.

Dr Falconer called the attention of the court to the fact that the incompetency of District Inspector Rainsford as a police officer had been proved by the result of an enquiry which had him transferred to Thomastown, Co. Kilkenny in consequence of the escape of the prisoner while under arrest. But the Judge and The MacDermott rallied to the defence of the disgraced officer, who was not present to defend himself, and Dr Falconer was compelled to apologise. His Lordship finally said that either Judy Cooney or the

District Inspector had committed perjury, and it was for the jury to decide which.

Mary Lynchehaun Pat gave evidence that she lived in the Valley, and was a 'far out' relation of the prisoner.

> On the night of the 6th October a lot of children came and gave the alarm that the Big House was on fire. I went to the Valley House and saw Mrs MacDonnell outside the wagon gate in a chemise and cloak. There were a lot of men and women there. I heard a voice which appeared to be that of Denis Sweeney say something and Mrs MacDonnell said something like 'Save the place'. The people then went into the yard and set about saving the place. They had sticks in their hands. I saw Charley Malley, several others, and James Lynchehaun, the prisoner, amongst them. They were putting out the fire. I heard a shout at the outside gate about half an hour after I went to the yard. I ran to the outside. The prisoner was in the centre of the yard at the time. I saw him occasionally since I went there. I saw the women going down the green and I followed them. Bridget McNeally had Mrs MacDonnell in her arms. I put a shawl about Mrs MacDonnell. I went to Tailor Gallagher's. The prisoner came in not long after the others. The doctor or police were not in at that time. From the time I entered the yard until I heard the shout Lynchehaun was in the yard.

Cross-examined by The MacDermott witness said that Lynchehaun could not have been taking his supper at the time Mrs MacDonnell was found. She did not see any blood on him, but she was not close to him.

> He might have blood on him without me seeing it. He had no boots on. I saw the side of his jaws and there was no blood on them. I saw no scrape on his face. I saw his hand bleeding in Michael Gallagher's.

She admitted that her husband owed the prisoner a few

pounds; her husband and the prisoner were six-of-kin.[2] She denied that she ever had any conversation about the crime with the prisoner's wife, or with any of the Lynchehauns.

Mary Fallon, examined by Dr Falconer, said that she was a spinner, and that she sometimes worked for Mrs Lynchehaun. She was working there that night and James Lynchehaun and 'the little girl' were there. Her reference to 'the little girl' is curious, for the child in question was a boy. But at that time throughout the west of Ireland, in peasant communities, boys, sometimes even up to their twelfth year, were dressed in the same clothes as girls. This was not, as has often been said, to disguise the sex of the little boy, in case the fairies might take him. The dressing of young boys in such clothes had originally an obvious hygienic purpose, and had been a common European custom which survived (perhaps still survives) in the west. Mary Fallon's misapprehension is curious but explicable. She continued:

> James Lynchehaun was after his supper sitting beside the bed. He had his trousers and shirt on. I took no notice of him when I came in. He had no boots on. He had his stockings. A knock came and Judy Cooney cried out the Big House was on fire. Mrs Lynchehaun went out to the door to look at the fire. James Lynchehaun made a remark. Mrs Lynchehaun went out into the street. Lynchehaun ran out past me and Mrs Lynchehaun and I don't know what he did after that.

Under cross-examination by The MacDermott she elaborated her statement.

> I go about to all the neighbours spinning. I did not see James Lynchehaun coming in because he was in before me. I worked with candle light. I slept in the kitchen and it was little sleep we had that night. When I came in James Lynchehaun was at a table beside the bed at the

---

[2] Irish *col seisir*, 'a relationship of six' = second-cousinship. First-cousinship would be expressed by *col ceathrair*, 'a relationship of four'; the intermediary relationship between first- and second-cousinships would be expressed by *col cúigir*, 'a relationship of five', or, in English, five o' kin.

end of his supper. There was a candle lit on the table. That was about half an hour before Judy Cooney came. Lynchehaun had no shoes or coat on. He never spoke a word to me that night. I did not hear him telling his wife that he let out the horses or that he saved Mrs MacDonnell. Anthony Lynchehaun was not in the kitchen when I was in it. A boy named Gallagher was in the room where I was spinning. He came into the kitchen after James Lynchehaun left. I did not go to the fire. I did not hear that Mrs MacDonnell was injured until I got home. Mrs Lynchehaun and I were standing looking at the fire for about half an hour.

A few more witnesses gave evidence for the defence: Michael Gallagher, the tailor, Thomas McDonogh, one of Lynchehaun's roadworkers, Michael Sweeney, son of Denis Sweeney, and Dr William Jordan who acted as *locum tenens* for the medical officer of Castlebar Jail, and who examined the prisoner on his first admission there.

The jury, having been charged by the judge, retired and came to its decision, in half an hour according to Brother Paul, in forty-five minutes according to the evidence given in later years at Indianapolis.

The short recess suggests that no great consideration was given to the case, the easiest line being taken by accepting the view of the whole affair as given by The MacDermott in his opening speech. The reconstruction of the crime attempted here, if put forward at the time, might have secured some mitigation of the sentence.

Lynchehaun returned home at about 7.30 on the evening of 6 October, having had a modest few drinks with friends and fellow workers. He was in a good humour, and showed no signs of elation or depression. When he came in Catherine served his evening meal as he sat to table, jacketless and without shoes, relaxing in the warmth of the kitchen and easing his feet after a hard day's work. About eight o'clock, whether by Judy Cooney or some other, the alarm was raised. Lynchehaun rushed out as he was, grabbing a cap but still jacketless and without his boots. He rushed up to the house by the shortest route, scaled the wall in an instant, and, having aroused Mrs MacDonnell and obtained the keys, released the sheep and horses. All this was the work of minutes, and the thought must have crossed his mind that, having done the landlady such a service she would at last soften towards him and suspend her notice of eviction. But on his returning the keys she accused him of incendiarism.

The collapse of his hopes, the injustice of the accusation, the repetition of the charge of incendiarism, together with the bitter knowledge that in a matter of days she would encompass his total ruin aroused him to a state of passionate and vengeful hatred: he seized her and dragged her struggling towards the flames. He was temporarily baulked by Mary Gallagher Tom's intervention. But after a few minutes, his passionate anger unslaked, Mrs MacDonnell's unforeseeable withdrawal into isolation enabled him to work out his passionate vengeance.

A minor mystery in the whole case is the intriguing matter of James Lynchehaun's boots. Nobody saw Lynchehaun wear boots that night. It was anything but certain that kicking with a heavy boot had been responsible for some of Mrs MacDonnell's injuries. She claimed in court that the damage to her toes, mentioned in Dr Croly's report, was caused by Lynchehaun's having crushed them with the heel of his boot during the incident in the yard. But there is no other evidence, and, especially for these moments, of which she had initially no memory whatsoever, her uncorroborated testimony is far from sufficient. The lack of boots would point to extreme haste in leaving his house, to an absence of premeditation, for what criminal would set out in his stockinged feet to scale a wall covered with black glass? Furthermore his lack of a coat or jacket on that cool October night is negative support to the view that he wore no boots.

The police would, of course, have clinched the case had they discovered Lynchehaun's blood-stained boots in the vicinity of the house. But apparently no boots, blood-stained or otherwise, could be found. Had they been, they would have figured prominently in the case, in The Mac-Dermott's opening speech, and the defence witness Mary Fallon would have thought twice before swearing that Lynchehaun had left the house in his stockinged feet. Very curiously the Index to the police reports in Dublin Castle has a relevant item: '8128 Regina versus Lynchehaun, expenses producing boots in evidence' (reference no. 13364). But as has happened with much of the Lynchehaun material, originally preserved in Dublin Castle, the indexed document has disappeared. It is possible that such documents were removed by officials for use in the case of Edward VII versus James Lynchehaun (or Thomas Walshe) in Indianapolis in 1903.

The Jury, after their brief consideration of the case filed in, and the foreman, Matthew Fahy, gave their decision that the prisoner was guilty on all counts.

Judge Gibson, pronouncing sentence, said: 'James Lynchehaun, you have been convicted after a spirited and able defence by counsel — a gallant defence made in a hopeless case — and no one who heard the evidence could have a shadow of doubt of your guilt. It was by a miracle of the Almighty you are not now in the dock convicted of murder, and that I am not now imposing a sentence which would send you a month hence to a felon's grave. The Jury could find no other verdict without being false to their oaths. An able man, you might have obtained brilliant success for yourself.'

Lynchehaun spoke for the first time: 'I am in the prime of life, my Lord, I'm only in the prime of life. Have mercy on me.'

His Lordship continued: 'I pity you from the bottom of my heart, but I cannot pass any sentence but one. Your crime is murder, except for the accident that by a merciful interposition of Providence this woman was endowed with splendid courage and vitality, though, poor wreck, she will live for a few and miserable years. The sentence of the court is penal servitude for life. God be merciful to you and soften your heart.'

Brother Paul describes the scene in the courthouse:

The father and brother of the prisoner left the court on hearing the verdict of the Jury, not willing to hear the Judge pronounce the dread sentence. But his faithful wife remained by his side to the last. When she heard the Judge pronounce the sentence which was to separate wife and husband for life, she screamed as if about to lose her life, and the culprit declared to a friend that her screams grieved him more than the sentence of the Judge.... The court was densely crowded during the trial, but more so from the time the Judge charged the Jury until the Judge pronounced the sentence of penal servitude.

After hearing the dread sentence Lynchehaun's friends returned home loaded with grief, while he returned to prison loaded with chains, there to weep over his misdeeds.

CHAPTER XIII
Imprisonment and Escape

There are not at the moment available any official sources from which can be learnt the details of Lynchehaun's years in Mountjoy and Maryborough Prisons. Brother Paul's *Narrative* is the only source — that is, until we come to 7 September 1902, the date of one of the most daring prison escapes in Irish history. But first, there is Brother Paul's account of Lynchehaun's seven-year spell in prison.

While in Castlebar Jail he was often reported and punished by the chief warden who was one of the Crown witnesses. But to the ordinary wardens Jim was thankful.

After a detention of fourteen days in the County Prison, Castlebar, he was removed to the convict prison, Mountjoy, Dublin. A more appropriate name would be 'Mount Sorrow' for a dungeon of misery.

From Castlebar to Dublin he was escorted by a Sergeant Slone and two constables to one of which prisoner was handcuffed for greater security. On his arrival in Mountjoy Prison, Dublin, Jim was inspected by doctors and Governor and searched even to nakedness for fear of having anything concealed.

He spent seven years in this convict prison under close observation owing to an official document accompanying his papers intimating that he said he would escape again. This may have been reported by some of his enemies in order to add rigour to his confinement.

After nine months' probation he was located in an underground workshop at the tailoring trade at which he became an expert in a short time. He being naturally quick in parts and apt to learn, he soon became so skilled at the machine that all critical jobs were sent to him. This man was a compound of good and evil.

Although he got very stout and flabby at this sedentary occupation, still his health was declining from such close confinement underground. He made several applications to the Governor and Board for a change of occupation, especially to the farm where he could breathe the fresh air. But all his applications were unavailing,[1] as they did not wish to give such a clever strategist a loophole to escape again, and give them three months more trouble in searching for him. They thought it wiser to keep the jailbird in the cage than let him have another chance of escaping.

Lynchehaun brooded very much over what he considered undue confinement and his versatile mind often turned to means of escape. But the discipline in Mountjoy Prison is both severe and rigorous. Notwithstanding, bold Jim was determined to make the attempt were it not that his fancies were fed by hopes of a releasement, or at least a mitigation, on the King's coronation day.

The wished-for day came and went without bringing the least mitigation to the prisoners, except a little consolation in the form of a coronation dinner given on the 26th June, 1902. Jim said he refused to partake of that dinner and told the Governor he wanted none of his pottage. 'What I want on the day of this joyous event is a mitigation of my sentence'.

He also petitioned the Lord Lieutenant over the irregularity of substituting an expensive dinner in lieu of a mitigation of sentence for prisoners on this day of grace. But it did not reach him for the Governor suppressed it.

About this time Lynchehaun's brother was in Dublin and got a memorial drawn up and signed by most of the sirs and prominent Orangemen in the city, requesting the Lord Lieutenant to release Lynchehaun on Coronation Day.

However, the request was not granted although it may have something to do with what followed, as the prisoner was removed four weeks later from Dublin to Maryborough convict prison. Whether it was fearing attempted rescue by a Dublin mob, or for his greater security, is not known.

Although Lynchehaun's request was not granted on Coronation Day it appears to have borne some fruit afterwards. For in four weeks later, i.e. on the 22nd July 1902, he was removed from

---

[1] *unavailable* (MS).

Dublin to Maryborough convict prison, there to tease oakum instead of stitching cloth.

While on his journey between the two prisons, although accompanied by a strong escort, his mind was occupied in plans of escape. The landscape between Dublin and Maryborough is charming in July. All nature seems to bloom. The odour of the flowers wafting over the meadows regaled his olfactory[2] nerves and the warbling of the birds delighted his ears; the lambs sporting in the fields reminded him of the happiness of freedom, while a goat which he saw tied to a stake reminded him of the state of bondage in which himself was in.

While in this mood of mind he repeated the following soliloquy of Alexander Selkirk while in the isle of Juan Fernandez.

> O Solitude! where are the charms
> which sages have seen in thy face?
> Better dwell in the midst of alarms
> than reign in this horrible place
> (meaning his prison).

The impression which the beautiful landscape, and freedom of all animals which he saw (except the goat), left on his mind was not easily effaced. Thoughts of freedom haunted his mind both by day and night. His mind was occupied with plans to escape.

He was only a few weeks in Maryborough when he requested a special interview with the Governor of the prison. The object of his interview was to get permission to work on the farm, feigning his health was impaired by too close confinement. His request was refused, and he was told positively that he should be prepared to enter the tailors' shop underground as soon as it would be filled up.

This news was discouraging to Reynard and frustrated his hopes of escape for the present, like Androcles from his cruel masters, who preferred the company of the brute animals to sensual ones.

On 8 September 1902, the Irish morning papers carried the sensational news that James Lynchehaun had broken out from Maryborough Jail. *The Freeman's Journal* gave a brief biography of the escapee, and an account of the escape sent in by its local correspondent on the previous evening:

[2] ollfactive (MS).

Last night about ten o'clock the notorious prisoner, Lynchehaun, made his escape from Maryborough convict prison. He was domiciled in one of the cells of the new wing, from which he managed to break loose in some extraordinary fashion. Thence, it would appear, he made his way up the great staircase (the upper portion of the wing being unoccupied), broke out on the garden roof, and descended into the yard below by a down-pipe. With the aid of two planks and a rope he succeeded in getting over the outer wall— some twenty-seven feet high — at a point situated at a considerable distance from the new wing. He is still at large.

In the course of a lengthy article on Lynchehaun entitled 'Man of Achill', in *Iris an Gharda* (February 1951), R. J. Bennet reconstructed the escape from contemporary evidence:

Later, as the evidence was pieced together, additional details were provided, and an attempt was made to reconstruct the manner of the prison break of the most famous of Irish convicts. The prison was described as a four-storey structure with four galleries reached by the great stairs. The top gallery opened on to a roof garden surrounded by a parapet wall.

Some time before the Prisons' Board had called attention to the insecure condition of the exit to the roof. As luck would have it Lynchehaun himself was detailed on Saturday to erect a new iron gate there. This was completed with the important exception of the lock. All the time the prisoner was studying his surroundings and his chances of breaking out. He had studied the device by which, when the cell door was bolted, a white mark was shown. He had further noted that the lock was inspected at a late hour or not at all. He had a book from the prison library and out of it on Saturday night he took a small piece of white paper with which he made white the black portion of the indicator. With a piece of wood he plugged the socket of the lock bolt so that it did not shut.

Thus the cell door was open when, judging by the

indicator, the warder thought it was closed. With a second wedge-shaped piece of wood the cunning fellow secured the door so that the warder, when passing and testing it, could not push it in by the ordinary thrust of his hand. He then made up his bed so that it presented the appearance of a man asleep under the clothes.

When the great moment came for Lynchehaun to pad out in his stockinged feet we may be sure his heart beat fast. For it was for such a moment he had been hoping for over six years. With the exception of those ten weeks or so in the winter of 1894-5, when he had broken free and gone 'on the run', and the activities of hundreds of police kept him stealing from cover to cover in Achill, he had been under arrest since the 7th October, 1894.

In less than a minute the escaping convict must have been out of the gate to the roof. It was well that he had, like most Achill Islanders, served 'before the mast' in his youth and manhood.[3] As it was, the air-shaft which projected from the wall presented as little difficulty to him as the rigging of a vessel to a sailor. He grasped and slid down by it though the spikes tore his stockings, which he threw off in the yard.

Owing to the building of the new prison section the prison yard was literally piled with scaffolding, planks and ropes. With the aid of a plank the convict, active as a cat, clambered up the wall at a corner where the ground inside was highest and the ground outside was lowest. Now, with the aid of a knotted rope, secured across a cleft in the wall, he descended safely to the other side.

He was free — free at last! But he was in convict garb and bootless and so easily recognisable. A wrong turn might easily lead to an alarm and his speedy recapture. Once back in prison years would be added to the long years already waiting to be served, and he would be under such close surveillance that he could never attempt escape again. Nevertheless he must go onwards. And onwards he glided stealthily into the darkness, deter-

---

[3]This detail may or may not be true — it appears to be known from no other source.

mined to sell his life dearly if there was any attempt made to interrupt his flight.

His apparently locked cell door and the dummy figure in the bed deceived the warders and, as it was not till next morning that he was missed, the fleeing convict had a clear start of several hours.

James Lynchehaun, probably when in America, gave Brother Paul a verbal account of the escape which, while describing the same event, differs in many details from Bennet's reconstruction. Here, for instance, we are given the additional graphic detail that the book used as an aid to escape was a Phillips' *Atlas*. Brother Paul had absolute confidence in his own version. In contradicting an unimportant detail of the escape given in *Lloyd's Weekly* (9 October 1902) he says: 'The means of escape given at p. 87 is more correct, as they are Jim's own words as related to the writer.'

Brother Paul's version, based on Lynchehaun's subsequent telling of the event, shows the prisoner being nearly caught in the act of escape by the warder, Bob Nicholls, who then raised the alarm. Since official sources were reluctant to give details, Brother Paul's account is, not impossibly, the truer one. It might, on the other hand, be Lynchehaun's heightening of the story for later retelling. Like Christy Mahon, the Playboy of the Western World, Lynchehaun was an incurable romancer. Exclusive to Brother Paul's *Narrative* are the efforts of Michael Lynchehaun while in Dublin to secure his brother's release. The *Narrative* also, as seen above, tells of Lynchehaun's rejecting the celebratory dinner given in prison on the occasion of the Coronation of Edward VII, a matter which will be later presented, but with a vastly different interpretation, in the courtroom in Indianapolis.

Lynchehaun was employed in plastering on the top of the fourth ward from which a staircase leads to garden from roof of prison, the door of which was locked with an ordinary stock-lock screwed on by two-inch screw-nails. While plastering on top Jim took keen notice of all these fixtures and of the surrounding shrubs and woods and knew where to run for cover if he could escape.

At the plastering job Jim had for companions two notorious 'stags' (a slang name for informers) who conveyed an account of his actions, observations, and trip to the outside of the roof, to the notice of the prison officials. The result was that an additional door or gate was ordered to be put on outside the former door.

When Reynard saw the gate ascending by the winch as an additional barricade to prevent his exit, his heart sighed deeply and his whole frame trembled, knowing that he was betrayed by the 'stags'. While his heart was sighing with sadness he tried to keep a fair face, went on with his work, and seemed indifferent to all that was going on around him. Yet he did not wholly despair, knowing he had an inventive brain to contrive other plans. So while his hands were engaged at plastering his mind was engaged at planning new modes of escape.

Next day he was working alone in an empty cell at plastering where he matured some of his plans. He saw the gate hoisted for fixtures at 3 o'clock on Friday. But, happily for Jim, the fixtures were not ready for putting on till the following Monday.

Jim, seeing that the time for maturing his plans and putting them into execution was limited to two days, set to work. And on Saturday night he continued to make a sample apparatus which prevented the lock-bolt from entering the socket in the cell doorjamb. It was made so firmly and so accurately that it did not interfere with the closing of the door. Having one of Phillips' *New Atlases,* he cut off a clean margin and pasted a bit of it, the size of the indicator, on the lock. This was to show that the door was locked, while it was only pasted on the inside as a deceiver by cunning Jim. And to prevent the door yielding to the warder's test it was well tightened on the inside.

Jim made a turn-screw of a broken saw for taking off the two-inch screw-nails which fastened the lock on the garden door. Next he fixed a dumb-man, made of clothes, in his cell bed, laid his shoes on the floor and his coat on a plank as usual, so that if the warder came in he may think, by the deceitful appearances, that the prisoner was still in bed.

When all these arrangements were made, and all appeared quiet, about 8 p.m. Reynard commenced his daring and dangerous escape from the convict prison. But in reality it was then his real troubles began, as the following narrative will plainly show. He, as it were, leaped from the pan to the fire.

On the night of the 6th September 1902 the daring convict took away the aforesaid apparatus from the cell door, watched a time when the warder was not near, then stepped quietly to the top part of the prison which was unoccupied and where he had been plastering for some days previous. He there unscrewed the six two-inch screw-nails which fastened the lock to the garret door, then gained the outside of the prison roof.

By this time he had only shirt, drawers and cap on, as he did not wish to have any of the convict clothes on, fearing discovery. He had procured a long rope from where he was plastering the day before. This he so fastened as to enable him sling down by its means. After fastening the rope he made the descent. But the rope not being well fastened, as often happens with things done in a hurry, it snapped, and the fox fell to the ground, a distance of twenty or twenty-five feet. Luckily he fell on a heap of coal which spread under him and thus broke the fall a little. Still he was unconscious for an hour, his leg was sprained and a large lump on his head. And to add to his misfortune he was nearly captured, as the extern guard walked over to where Jim was concealed behind a thick shrub beside the surgery door. The guard, seeing the sleeves of his shirt, asked 'Is that the doctor?' Jim made no answer, but giggled and scampered away as the doctor, while the warder took no further notice, being convinced it was the doctor playing the ghost with him, as he was accustomed to go to the surgery by night to get medicine for the patients.

Lynchehaun, being fearful of an alarm being raised by the guard, he attempted to climb the ivy which clung to the principal wall at the outer gateway, but the brittle and deceptive thing broke beneath his hands. Although it was a climbing thing itself still it refused assistance to a brother climber, as if the green and red (blood-stained) would not agree.

It being now about 10 p.m. the Governor and Chief Warder entered the outer gate while the fox was concealed behind a small shrub not five feet from them. The Governor asked the Warden did he take the numbers yet. 'Not yet, sir', was the answer, 'as I expected you in every moment.'

When they passed by Jim crept along the dark corners of the prison yard and reached a quiet part of it where he found a long, heavy plank which he contrived to put up by the wall. But, owing to his previous fall and wounds, he was unable to raise it high enough on the boundary wall to enable him reach the top of it. However, he succeeded in putting it so high that by crawling on hands and feet to top of the plank he could touch the coping-stones of the boundary wall with his fingers, but was yet unable to crawl to the top of it.

The snapping rope which caused his former fall, he still carried it, and hoped it would do better business for him now than before.

He flung a noose of it to a coping-stone and succeeded in transfixing it there. By this contrivance he scrambled to the top. When there he viewed around to see which direction was best to run, then said 'Hurra for liberty! The fox is on the chase again'.

At that moment one of the chief warders, a bad pill named Bob Nicholls, saw Reynard on top of the wall. He drew down the plank and blew his alarm-whistle fiercely, then said to Jim 'Come down, you ruffian'.

Jim answered 'Ah! Goodbye Bob', and so saying slung down on the outside by means of the rope and scampered off to the shrubs.

As it took some time for warder Bob Nicholls to get his men together and around the gate to the back wall where Jim escaped, the run-a-way had a good start of them. Still, as Reynard ran in a zig-zag way amongst the shrubs, he did not make a long way forward. And as a large number of the warders were after him, who knew the surroundings better than he did, they soon closed in upon him, so much as to snap the cap off his head and ordered him stand or they would shoot him. Others cried out 'Have you him, have you him? Shoot him, shoot him!'

But needless to say that Jim did not obey, and he that was running for life out-ran those who were running for pay. Even if he knew they would shoot him he would not stand, thinking it was as good to die by the ball as to lead a dying life inside the walls of an underground dungeon.

So the more they shouted at him to stand the better he ran, making little account of his sprained leg or lumpy head or yet of his lacerated flesh which was torn with the thorns in the shrubs and briars through which he passed with only a shirt and drawers to protect him — these were his coat of mail against the darts of man and nature. Clothed he entered the prison, naked (almost) he is going away. A dread spectacle in a civilised country — what will shelter him from the inclemency of the weather?

CHAPTER XIV

On the Run: Maryborough to Glasgow
Brother Paul's Narrative

The authorities were at sea. In spite of all pretences, from district up to Castle level they had not a single worthwhile clue as to Lynchehaun's whereabouts; the period from the moment he broke jail on the 6 September to his sudden reappearance in Chicago, eighty-two days later, would be virtually a blank were it not for Brother Paul's *Narrative*.

Brother Paul can only have known of the events of this period from Lynchehaun himself, and the adventures, no doubt, would have been spiced up in the telling. There are, in the *Narrative*, two mutually exclusive accounts of how Lynchehaun got to America. Either he sailed in luxury as a fare-paying passenger or he worked his way in the engine-room of a steamer. The first appears to be true, and the other, to which Brother Paul prefers to give credence, is doubtless Lynchehaun's fiction. The American evidence, given in court, favours the less romantic version: he landed in New York, having sailed from France, as a fare-paying passenger called Thomas Walshe, an *alias* of which Brother Paul is aware.

Brother Paul has, of course, to be careful not to mention names, for to help Lynchehaun in his flight from the law was itself a criminal act. Hence 'friends' are necessarily anonymous, or, like the one in Glasgow, designated only by initials. There is little doubt, as already suggested, that his devotion to Lynchehaun led Brother Paul to go outside the law, to be Friar Tuck to his Robin Hood. He was, it may be taken, 'the sincere friend' to whom Lynchehaun wrote from Antwerp seeking family help, and through whom money had been channelled back. To any suggestion that the letter from Antwerp might be a fiction of Brother Paul's, it can only be answered that it is too well done, that Brother Paul would be incapable of writing it. The letter illustrates the depth of Lynchehaun's religious feelings as do the New Testament and the manuscript Latin Gospel of St John from his troglodyte days. Lynchehaun, like many another, experienced at different times contradictory emotions and feelings, all doubtless true and valid at the moment of experience.

Lynchehaun, then, we may take it, wrote to Brother Paul, revealing his whereabouts. Brother Paul on receiving the letter paid a reasonable and professional visit to the National School at Achill Sound. He gave the head-teacher his news, and the teacher, who lodged at Neal Lynchehaun's house in Pulranny, passed on the news to the Lynchehaun family. All very neat, and nobody would suspect the elderly brother who had as interests in life the combating of heresy, the education of the young, and a little harmless shooting and fishing for relaxation. Brother Paul continues his description of the escape:

The prison gang, having lost sight of their quarry in the dark, had to retrace their steps, and report their loss to the Governor, while Jim made towards the railway in the direction of Mountrath and walked much that night. Yet by some fatality, he found himself next morning in a field of oats outside the prison grounds. During four nights he could not reach beyond a radius of four miles from the prison, though travelling much each night. In fact he was so bewildered that he thought himself mesmerised. He hid and slept like a frightened hare by day and travelled much by night. Being starved with hunger, parched with thirst, and almost perished with cold, having only a shirt and drawers on, and these partly torn with shrubs, he ventured to approach a small farmer's house for relief. The old farmer got scared at seeing a human being in such a condition in a Christian country in these times of plenty. He asked who he was, where he came from, and what caused him to be in that wretched condition. Jim made answer 'I am a misfortunate deserted soldier who will drink all I can get. Please give me some food and old clothes to cover me'. The old farmer supplied him in part. But as the clothes were old, and small for big Jim, they did not last him long.

Having appeased his thirst and hunger at the old farmer's house, and putting on an old trousers, he wrapped a bag around his shoulders, then set off, bare-footed and bare-headed, more like a scarecrow than a human being, in search of a safe hiding-place till night come on — then he would prowl about till morning. Strange to relate that after another night's weary travelling he found himself next morning at dawn close by the old farmer's hut again. On seeing him the old man exclaimed 'O what is wrong?'

'I know not,' said Jim. 'I thought to be twenty miles from here from all I walked during the night. I must be bewitched.'

However, the poor unfortunate got another feed, and then scampered off with his sack on his shoulders to seek a hiding-place till night would spread its pall over him when he could make another nocturnal journey. The sack which the old farmer gave him served for many useful purposes....

The unfortunate suffered great privations for a month after his desertion. His food for nine days consisted almost completely of turnips, and oats which he rubbed between his hands and shelled with his teeth. He may chance on a few blackberries which he picked as a luxury. He hid in the cornfields by day and wandered about at night.

When brought almost to the brink of despair he ventured to call on a few farmers for a little food or drink, but found some of them very unhospitable, especially the Protestants, who refused him even for a drink of clean water. One went so far as to say he ought to be reported to the police and arrested for an able-bodied man like him to be wandering about in a semi-naked state. 'What are you and why travel thus?' Answer: 'I am a poor unfortunate deserter from the army who pawned my clothes to get the price of drink. Still my thirst is such that I cannot extinguish it, hoping such weakness will never seize hold of you. But the habit to me is like a second nature. Please bear with me this time and I shall never trouble you again.'

After these rebukes Jim was more cautious in approaching farmers' houses. He now contrived a new plan. He got some turnips into his old sack, carried it on his shoulders, and when, in great need of food and drink, he ventured cautiously to some farmers' house. If he found they were Catholics he would ask would they buy some prayer-books. But he would neither press them nor show them ware. Then he would ask for food. If he learned that the family were Protestants these very Catholic prayer-books turned out to be Protestant bibles, the true Rheimish version. But all the time selling a pig in a bag. If they did not greatly want them he would not take the string off the bag as it was well tied.

When night approached the so-called bibles and prayer-books were thrown away and the old sack utilized either as a blanket to sleep on or as a coat to wrap around his shoulders. So the old sack served for many useful purposes. When approaching a farmer's house and a cross dog with naked teeth attempted to bite him Jim took the sack from his shoulders and made it intervene between his bare legs and the dog's naked teeth. When crossing barbed wire fences or thorny hedges it was his only armour of defence. When creeping or hiding amongst shrubs or briars he protruded this sack before him as a war-engine to break down the barriers and clear the way for the fugitive.

While hiding amongst the thorny shrubs part of his occupation was extracting thorns from his flesh by means of other thorns. At other times he would try to sleep, then suddenly start up like a frightened hare so that he got not one satisfactory sleep during a month. The only comfort he had was that the weather was fairly mild and that the cornfields afforded him a little food and shelter. If his flight happened in any other month besides September his lot would be even harder, as neither corn, turnips nor berries would be matured; neither would the corn crop be tall enough to afford him a secure hiding-place.

Of all Jim's narrow escapes the narrowest was from a herd of frightened cattle which ran like mad animals after him on seeing his scarecrow appearance crossing the farm in which they were grazing. As they made a regular stampede, ran and bellowed after him, Jim had to run for life towards a whitethorn hedge into which he jumped with his sack before him. Even with this shield his body was well tattooed.

For nine days after his escape from prison he feared to approach any human habitation for clothes, food or drink, living chiefly on oats. This caused severe thirst. To add to his misery he suffered from insomnia which caused a severe headache and dizziness; so much so that whenever he met a river or well he feared to stoop to drink lest he should fall in. Here again he utilized his sack for a drinking-cup by casting a corner of it into the water; and when well saturated he would pull it out, put the wet corner to his mouth and suck it like a sponge. Oh, perversity of humanity! What sufferings caused by one evil deed!

Jim on the Point of Despair

Owing to the horse-food which he used for nine days his bowels did not operate all that time. Add to this thirst, headache, cold, sleepless nights and anxiety, all which brought him to the point of despair. And so he resolved to end his miserable life by laying his head on a railway track that the next train may chop it off. But the end of his days was not yet arrived and God was pleased to give him more time for repentance. Hoping he may make good use of it!

While he was in this state of despair the mercy of God came to his relief by causing a haemorrhage which relieved his severe headache and dizziness. This happened before the arrival of any train. Thus relieved he got up, asked God's pardon for the rash deed he was about to do. Though bad it is to kill another it is much worse to take away our own life and die in despair.

After this relief he took courage, went in search of a turnip to eat, and water to wet his bag which he sucked, then meditated on which way to go. As he feared to go on a direct line he was making zig-zag routes about Maryborough for nine or ten days while the police were tracking him very closely. To add to his misfortunes his feet were swollen from thorns and walking on the railway tracks by night as he feared to tread on the public roads lest some detective may nab him.

Even the railway was not wholly free from danger for this fugitive, as the police were accustomed to ask the guards did they see him on the line. As Lynchehaun suspected that such inquiries would be made, he wisely slipped from tracks to the slope on the approach of a train and there lie on the shady side till it passed.

Jim made so bold one night as to approach near a station where he concealed himself behind some egg-boxes. His object in doing so was expecting to hear something said about himself by guards and policemen. While so concealed he heard the guard tell the police that he saw with the aid of the head-light a man sitting on a ditch. 'O', said a bobby, 'it's nothing unusual to see a man sitting on a ditch — that's no information.'

Hearing this Jim learned that even the railroad and its slopes were not free from danger so he knew not where to go for safety.

At one time he would travel during a night towards Cork, then regret having done so, change his plan and travel the next night towards Waterford, regret again, direct his course in some other direction. Finally he settled on Dublin where he expected to meet a friend, and his hopes were not ill-founded.

After two or three weary nights' travelling he at length reached the suburbs of the city about twelve at night when all honest men are supposed to have retired for rest and only fugitives and the like are on the run.

On reaching his friend's house he knocked gently. A young lady-friend got up, opened the door, but almost fainted at seeing the frightful appearance of a human being such an hour.

To ease her troubled mind Jim told her immediately the cause of his being there in such a state of misery at such a late hour. This eased her mind. She got him food to eat, water to wash himself, then stowed him away into a private little room where he remained till the next night. Luckily all the boarders and the whole family were in bed when Jim arrived so that none saw him that night nor next day but the faithful girl who wept with compassion at seeing him in such miserable condition.

Although they knew of his being in prison apparently they knew not of his escape therefrom until he made his ghostlike and unexpected appearance to them that night.

The next night when all appeared quiet in the city Jim, after supper, was provided with a suit of second-hand clothes, a cap, a pair of old shoes, a little basket, some bread and a coffee can and a few pounds to pay his train-fare to Belfast and his boat-fare across the Herring Brook.

Thus fitted out he started on another perilous journey. A friend rode slowly on a bike before to convey him by the most private way to the station for the Belfast train.

Going on the late night train he reached Belfast at dawn of day. But not knowing the way to Glasgow steamer docks, and seeing none to give him information, he got uneasy and confused.

However, he was not long in this state till he met with a lad who had been boozing all night. Jim accosted him and asked would he be pleased to show him the way to the docks. The lad consented and walked with Jim to put him on the right way. Suddenly they were met by a policeman who was on night duty. Bobby wanted to know their business at that early hour. 'I am going to work at the docks, sir.'

After this Jim walked along with his basket in one hand and his coffee-pot in the other, not wishing to speak much, fearing his Connaught brogue may discover him, while the drunken lad who had the Belfast slang, kept jawing with the bobby, and may have got arrested for all Jim knew.

During the altercation between laddy and bobby cunning Jim sneaked away towards the docks where he learned with regret that the Glasgow steamer would not sail for Ardrassan till evening.

Now what was Jim to do? Where was he to hide himself from

the watchful eyes of police and detectives? The inventive mind which furnished him so often with plans suggested a little stratagem to spend the day away from much observation. He picked up an old newspaper, went into a closet where he sat for a few hours, as if to ease nature, with his cap drawn partly over his eyes to conceal his face from any person who may have occasion to call in. While in this posture he held the old newspaper in his hands reading it, as it were. Fearing being remarked if too long there, he left it and went to another where he acted in a like manner, and thus spent the day until the hour for sailing to Glasgow arrived.

When the long expected hour arrived Jim was the first to get his ticket and the first passenger on board. He then stowed himself away into a sequestered part of the ship where he remained till it removed from land. Then Jim said 'Good-bye, Erin! It's with mingled grief and joy I leave you, grief at leaving my home and relatives after me, and joy at the prospect of freedom from prison and English law.'

Although Jim was now sailing on the seas and coming near the Scottish shore his fears were coming back to him, well knowing that Scotland was part of British Dominions and that he may be arrested there any day.

On his arrival at Ardrassan he hastened to Glasgow where he sought for some employment but not with a crowd.

He soon got employed as a dray-man, taking manure and refuse from one place to another. At this employment he remained about two weeks at 24/- per week. Of this he paid 12/- per week for board and had to pay in advance as, being a stranger, they would not trust him. With the remainder he bought a second-hand suit of clothes and some under-clothing which he sadly needed as the old duds were not fit for a sweep.

While at this job he kept his face as black as if he were hauling coal in order that he may not be recognised, and lodged in a backward lane.

Although he worked by day he fretted by night and suffered from insomnia so that he lived a dying life between hope and fear. He procured the daily papers, especially *The Freeman's Journal*, which he scanned closely to see were there any reports about him. In them he read of several arrests in different parts of the country on suspicion of being the far-famed Achill troglodyte and escaped jail-bird. These reports increased his fears.

Even in Glasgow he had many narrow escapes. At one time when driving his dray-horses along the public street he narrowly escaped coming in contact with an electric tram-car, which was loaded with passengers, while crossing the railway-track. There is usually a policeman at each of these crossings. So the bobby who had custody of that crossing, seeing the danger of dray and tram coming into contact, ran towards Jim, took hold of him, shook him and said 'You stupid fellow, do you know how to drive a car but this way? Who are you? Where are you from? What's your name?'

Jim answered with a trembling voice 'My name is Jim Dooley, sir. I came from Drogheda a few days ago. I am not long at this work, but if your honour please to let me go, sir, this time, I will be more watchful again, when I see that big car coming, to keep out of its way, as it may run over my dray and hurt myself and the horses.'

At seeing his simplicity, and hearing his humble appeal, the policeman let him go with a caution. On Jim getting off he said 'Thank you, Mr Officer. I won't be in the way of that fast-running car again.'

Continuation of Jim's Actions in Glasgow

While Jim was conducting his dray in the streets of Glasgow he felt as timorous as a frightened hare. He suspected every man who looked sharply at him was a detective sent to arrest him. One day, especially, he observed a tall clever-looking young man, who had all the appearance of a detective, staring at him sharply. That evening he told his employer that he was suffering from diarrhoea and wished to be excused from work the next day. In fact, uneasiness of mind sickened him. The boss excused him and Jim remained retired in his bed-room next day.

The day he refrained from work he spend reading newspapers. In one of these he observed the name of an old acquaintance, a trusty friend, who lectured in a certain hall in the city the previous Sunday. His heart bounded with joy, thinking he was a friend on whom he could rely with confidence for help and counsel in his great need. At least he knew his friend would not betray the confidence placed in him. The great difficulty now was where to find this friend as he had not his address, neither was it mentioned in the paper.

When the pall of evening fell over the city Jim started out like a night raven in search of its prey, and followed crowds of men who were returning from their work. He listened attentively to their accents and conversation to try and discover if they were Irish. If he found they were not he would leave them and mingle with another gang.

Finally he remarked that one man spoke with a true Irish brogue. Jim tipped him on the shoulder and asked if he were Irish. On being told he was Jim asked was he at a certain hall on last Sunday when such a person spoke there. 'Yes,' said he.

'Do you know where that gentleman boards?'

'No, but I can give you the name and address of one who knows.'

'Thank you very kindly,' said Jim.

On his getting the address he soon got out the house of Mr F. J. who happened to be a neighbour when in Ireland but did not know Jim then owing to his altered appearance and dirty countenance, which he purposely kept that way for fear of recognition. However, he asked him where the friend he was in search of lived. On Mr F. J. telling him, he requested him to go and bring him to him. While F. J. was doing so Jim began to wash his face and hands that he may not appear like a chimney-sweep before his dear friend. In the meantime the friend arrived while Jim was washing his hands, but had not as yet touched his sooty-looking face so the friend did not recognise him, not seeing him for over eight years previous.

Jim wrote his name with a bit of lead pencil on a little scrap of paper, handed it to his friend, at the same time squeezed his hands and lips to give him to understand that he was to keep it secret. On the friend reading it he wondered and looked at the black man, thinking he must have come out of a coal mine.

Finally the friend looked at the scrap of paper again and read aloud 'James Lynchehaun', and looked at the black man again. At this Jim squeezed his lips and shook his head, as to say 'Don't let these people know who I am'. At this the friend asked him into a private room where he got more information from him. Then Jim washed his face and followed his friend at a distance of seven or eight yards to the private hotel where the friend boarded; there they took supper in a private room together.

Then and there they had a long, private conversation about Jim's escape from the convict prison, and how he came to Scotland, and now how to get out of it and arrive on the continent either of Europe or America. The want of money seemed to be the greatest obstacle.

At this interview some plans were arranged for his relief in the near future. In the meantime Jim resolved to go to work with his dray to earn what would pay for his board at least. He also wrote, under a fictitious name, to an old acquaintance in Dublin to send him a few pounds that would enable him tide over this ordeal. His request was granted; for he got £2 or £4 which put him in high hopes. But this small sum was not sufficient to take him to America, that land of freedom to which he wished to go.

CHAPTER XV

On the Run: Glasgow to America
Brother Paul's Narrative

Now what was he to do? To remain in Glasgow was dangerous, to go to America he could not, for want of means; to go to France he considered useless as he did not understand their language and had neither friends nor acquaintances there.

After meditating on these different places he resolved to go to Belgium as the nearest port on the Continent and then write to some friends for money that would pay his fare to America. So he went with his £4 to a clothier's store, bought a suit of ready-made clothes and a Scotch cap, carried a cane in his hand and appeared like a gent in his £2 suit. Being thus fitted out, he took the train to Hull. Then went to the booking office and paid for a first-class return ticket to Antwerp.

Although he was a pauper in pocket, he acted as a millionare in the purchasing of the ticket. This was to deceive detectives; and make them think that a jailbird would not act the gentleman in taking a first-class return ticket. And if he wanted to escape he would not pay for the return. Most likely that this stratagem saved Jim from being arrested, as he saw two clever young men whom he suspected of being detectives in the ticket office who had a consultation at a distance from him, and one of them went to the ticket agent to ask him something. Jim thought the conversation was about himself, as there had been detectives in all seaport towns, and they get the photos of all convicts with a description of their age, height, etc., etc. However Jim was much relieved from his uneasiness by seeing the ticket clerk shake his head as much as to say 'No, No! He is a gentleman to return!'

An anonymous Achill informant gave some corroboration of Lynchehaun's habits when travelling: 'Another interesting thing about him was that when escaping anywhere he always purchased a return ticket to ward off any suspicion of his not returning'.

Getting on board the vessel like a first class swell, a few hours sail brought him to the shore at Belgium. Being now in a strange country, without friends or employment, with only a few shillings in his pocket, he felt nearly as troubled as before. To add to this he learned that there were English emissaries in every European port and that they may arrest him and demand his extradition from the Government. So the misfortunate fugitive did not find perfect security either on land or sea. Thus an evil conscience pursues a man more closely than all the detectives in the world. However, he had some grounds for his fears; for if arrested he had no redress as he was not a recognised citizen.

Let us leave him to his fate in Antwerp for a short time and return in thought to Ireland and find out what was occurring there about him.

For two months after his escape from prison his father's house near Achill Sound was narrowly watched by patrols of police night and day, also that of the surrounding country. Even the National Schools were visited by detectives to listen to the children chatting, thinking they may find out something about him which they may have heard from their parents at home.

The school next Lynchehaun's father's house was especially watched. There was a lad of a teacher who had charge of that school for one year as substitute while the regular teacher was in Training College some years previous to Jim's escape. This lad, who was not a native of the place, got fairly well acquainted with the locality. He left there on the return of the regular teacher from training. But learning of Lynchehaun's escape and of the reward for his arrest, or information leading thereto, he returned to the locality as an old friend, but actually as a detective, and was in the school trying to get information from the scholars the time that a sincere friend knocked at the school-house door. As luck would have it the regular teacher came outside and kept his hand on the latch while talking to this sincere friend who brought him important news about Jim's location and asked to send him aid to take him out of the British Isles. This regular teacher was a man who could be trusted with such information and he boarded in old Lynchehaun's house.

While the sincere friend was conveying his important message in a few short words, relays of police and detectives were patrolling the road, passing and re-passing within a few yards of the school, and another lad in the school.

The writer was informed that the lad of an ex-teacher who acted as a detective concealed himself by night in a dry arch of a bridge near old Lynchehaun's house, in order to listen to the conversation of passers-by, thinking they may say something about Jim that would give him a clue to his whereabouts.

When Lynchehaun's friends learned of where the lad was concealed they walled up one end of the arch and set a fire at the other end; the smoke almost suffocated him, so he screamed and begged leave to escape and was never seen in that locality since. So this story was told to the writer.

As soon as old Lynchehaun learned where his son was and the miserable condition he was in, paternal affection touched his heart and he resolved to send relief to his Prodigal Son by some means or other. It was difficult as the Lynchehaun family were so well watched and detectives at all railway stations and dock ports in Ireland.

With all the British precaution the cash reached Jim in Belgium when he was in very, very, great need of it indeed. Oh! what joy this timely relief caused him while penniless in a strange country.

Jim's letter to a friend from Belgium, after getting the £40 cash, was couched somewhat in the following words:

My dear friend,

The long desired relief has come to me which I will soon utilize to cross the broad Atlantic and try to reach the land of freedom where there is work and food for all. If once there I have a number of friends to assist me. I know not which is best for me, to go as a first class swell in a saloon or privately in a merchant ship. However, I hope the English authorities will not go to the trouble of extraditing me either here or in America. They may let the matter die out and I will help them in doing so.

Both they and I have lost much valuable time, I running from them and they running after me. Yet you never saw a fox that got so clear from so many hounds as I did from my pursuers. I have baffled all their ingenuity.

If I get safe to America I am resolved to lead a new life according to your advice to me. As drink has caused my ruin I'm resolved to refrain from it in future.

Intelligent men ought to make a good livelihood in a free country like America when some ignorant boors have done so.

The following instance struck me very forcibly. It is this. As

I had a few pounds to exchange for foreign coin I applied to a saloon keeper for same. This man had his drawer filled with gold, silver, and notes. Still he was unable to multiply £4.8.0. by 12. At seeing this I said to myself 'If an ignorant man like you have accumulated so much cash what ought a genius like me do with my inventive brains? I who have baffled the great British forces of police and detectives, magistrates and gaolers, etc., etc.' So while there is life there is hope. You'll hear more about me yet.

A word about Antwerp before I leave it. Suffice to say that we Irish appear to be a century behind the age, not only in scientific advancement but in religious devotion. Here on Sunday masses are being said from 6 a.m. to 12 noon, and as many as five masses being said in the same church at the same time, and a crowded congregation at all. One priest is constantly giving holy communion.

The splendour and majesty of the church, the devotion, decorum, respectability and social standing of that immense congregation, would suffice to strike awe into the head of an atheist and cause him to venerate that holy place and say 'This is truly the temple of God'. O how often did I reproach myself for being such an unworthy member of such a holy Church! I now resolve to amend.

This cathedral is beyond my power of description. There are two oil paintings of Rubens' representing the death of our Lord on the Cross and his descent therefrom, and unless the spectator touched them with his fingers he would think they were really flesh and bones, so well has this great artist imitated nature.

Such specimens of manhood and womanhood as I have seen in this model city cannot be excelled in any part of the world. Here there are none deformed, hunchback or dwarfed children, such as those I saw in Glasgow. A beautiful exterior corresponds with a pure interior. When I contrast what I have seen in Catholic Antwerp with what I have seen in Protestant Glasgow and other Scottish and English towns the difference is as great as that between light and darkness.

In the English and Scotch seaport towns, where drunkenness, theft, immorality and irreligion are so rampant, their evil effects are visible in their offspring. You may find the mothers drinking in the public house while the infants are crawling like frogs in the puddles or sidewalks. At another time you may see a child of five years trying to carry an infant, then let it fall on the flags and disjoint its arm, leg, or back, and so deform it for life, while the unnatural mother is boozing in the alehouse.

These bow-legged, hunchback and dwarfish children are the offspring of drunken and irreligious parents whose God is their belly and whose end is destruction. They imitate Bacchus rather than Christ for the brand of Cain appears to be on them. You may say all this comes well from Jim. Why does he not reform his own life? Well, he is resolved to do so. His visit to Antwerp may help to his reformation.'

So much for Belgium.... While these commotions were going on in Ireland and suspicious persons were being arrested in the British Isles, Lynchehaun was sailing over the breakers of the Atlantic. He stated to a friend that he embarked at Antwerp on a first class steamer as a first class passenger, knowing well that first class passengers would not have to undergo such a scrutiny at Castle Gardens as third class passengers would.

The following narrative may be more truthful.

While Jim was in pecuniary need in Belgium, and not knowing when he would get help from Ireland, he resolved to work his passage on board of some merchant vessel. He happened to meet a burly Scotchman who had spent his money foolishly and was now as penniless as Lynchehaun. It appears that the Scotchman was once wealthy and not accustomed to hard work. But in his straitened circumstances he had no better means of getting to New York than to work his passage on board of some ship going there. So himself and Jim agreed to go to the docks and offer their services to some captain that would take them across on these conditions. Luckily they found a merchantship ready to sail, Captain being a Scotchman and, wanting such men to stow coal into the furnace, he agreed to take them on board next morning. On Jim's return to his boarding-house he found to his great joy an Irish letter with a goodly cheque awaiting for him. This he cashed and preserved for future use on the western side of the Atlantic, not knowing how much he may need it there.

Next morning, Jim and Scotch went to the dock and on board of the merchantship, then about to sail for New York. Jim had now two causes for joy, having his money in his pocket and a free passage for throwing in a little coal as he thought. All being nearly ready to set sail Captain asked which of them would go down to the engine room for the first shift of four hours. They argued over the point — finally lots were drawn and it fell to the Scotchman to go down for the first term.

After the big soft Scotchman being four hours in front of a red-hot furnace, drawing out red coal and replacing it with black coal, his flesh was partly burned red and black, his face and neck covered with perspiration and coal dust, the shirt fastened to his back. In this condition he returned exhausted to deck after his term of four hours being ended. He there fanned himself, and then stretched on deck as if about to die and exclaimed 'You often talk of the punishment in hell. I say there is no hell can be much hotter than that furnace-room where I have spent four hours which appeared to me as long as four weeks at farm labour. If I have to go down again I shall cut off a leg or arm in order to disable myself from suffering such burning for twelve days which this slow ship shall take to cross the ocean'.

While Scotch was bemoaning his misfortune Jim was ordered down. He, being used to hard knocks, entered the fiery ordeal without flinching, endured it as a punishment for his bad deeds. Jim believed in the reality of hell fire, but for Scotch it only painted a picture. Lynchehaun's four hours being ended, he ascended from furnace-room to deck. Scotch was again called upon to replace Jim but he refused to obey orders. Captain said he would chuck him over board if he would not comply with his agreement. After a long altercation the canny Scotchman went down, but was not long there when he disabled himself by drawing red cinders with a long iron rake from the furnace on his feet. The doctor went to examine him and declared him unable to work and ordered him to the ship hospital. So Scotch went, as it were, from hell to purgatory.

This was a sorrowful story for Irish Jim as he had to do the work of two now. He descended to the pit with an ill grace, but he should comply, otherwise be put in irons and half starved, or perhaps chucked over board to become food for the sharks. It was a trying ordeal but he complied with orders and tried to make the best of a bad matter. Such is the life of man that while he tries to escape from one species of trouble he may meet with something worse. The life of man on earth is a warfare. With very short spells of relief Jim had to spend his voyage stowing coal into the furnace. The result was that his flesh was nearly melted with perspiration and burned with heat, blisters on his skin, nails burned off his hands, and his face as black as a nigger's with sweat and coal dust. In this miserable condition he is stated to have arrived at New York Harbour.

A lady-friend who knew and expected him went on board to seek for him. After looking around at the sailors and passengers in expectation of finding her dear friend Jim in order to take him to her home, she almost lost hopes of finding him, and was about to leave the boat when unexpectedly a black-looking man came on deck from the coal room. The lady recognised him but he did not recognise the lady. However, she got so frightened at seeing him in such a miserable condition that she fainted. A crowd gathered round her but none knew her. Jim approached to see what was wrong, when, to his great surprise, he there saw his dear ladyfriend in a fainting condition on account of his misfortune. On her recovery she tenderly embraced and saluted him: 'O Jim dear what has reduced you to this pitiable condition? Have you got any clothes except these dirty duds?'

Jim answered 'Don't fret. I am all right. My clean clothes are in my hammock. If you wait I shall get them on.'

He went downstairs and borrowed a second-hand suit of one of the sailors, returned on deck to his lady-friend who brought him to a clothier's store where she bought a new suit for him, then requested he would retire to a certain house for a week or two in order to recover from his burns and miserable appearance.

After a short sojourn in New York he went to Pittsburg and from thence to Cleveland. Learning there was a search after him he fled to Chicago. He went amongst his relatives for a short time, but he acknowledged they gave him very little assistance, especially after learning that there was a female detective who wanted board and lodging in the very friend's house in which Jim was concealed. This lady detective said she was in search of a friend of hers. Lynchehaun's friends, thinking they may get into trouble, ordered him leave. They also left that house and rented another in a distant part of the city.

So Jim had to leave there and seek employment for a living; he went to work on a railway until the winter frost froze him out. Being now out of employment in the midst of a severe winter, and almost as friendless and penniless as ever, he knew not what to do. A thought occurred to him to buy fish for the few shillings he had left. These fishes he hawked from house to house; as the season was unsuitable for fish trade he was unable to make what would pay his board, so he was soon again in hard luck.

In the latter part of November 1902 Mr. Michael Davitt lectured in Chicago, and, as he was an ex-convict, Lynchehaun thought he would sympathise with him and let him know could the English government extradite him. If Davitt was an ex-convict it was for an honourable cause, that of trying to free his country from foreign yoke, while Lynchehaun's was a dishonourable one, that of arson and attempted murder. So when Jim went to interview Davitt the latter despised him and refused to converse at any length with him; he even went and reported him to the Mayor of Chicago who ordered police and detectives after him.

Next morning Jim saw an account of the above in the papers.[1] Jim immediately wrote letters to the press contradicting most of the statements in the morning papers. After posting these and not waiting for an answer he fled from Chicago and went to Indiana where he sought for employment in a meat cellar deep under ground. There he contracted cold and rheumatics from which he still suffers.

Early in 1903 Jim wrote pressing letters to his wife in Ireland to collect what money she could and go over to America to him. Finally he said if she would not go quickly he would never do for her, and that she and his brother Michael were like two old hags, unworthy of having such a brave man as himself amongst them. Owing to these pressing letters the poor wife resolved to share his misfortunes sooner than offend, prepared to go as soon as spring opened favourably. With all her privacy she was pursued by detectives...

It appears that as soon as she reached Cleveland that he met her there and took her farther west, as the very day before his arrest he and she wrote a joint letter to their friends in Ireland stating how nicely they were except that he had contracted rheumatism from working in damp cellars in cold storage. He also enclosed a letter with addressed envelope which he got from a detective in Westport, but written in Tom Lynchehaun's name (Tom is Jim's brother), requesting to send James Lynchehaun's address and all information to him for safety sake. Jim Lynchehaun was clever enough to discover this insidious snare to entrap him and so forewarned his brother Tom at home to be cautious.

[1] See page 183.

CHAPTER XVI

The Authorities Give Chase

In the prison Lynchehaun's escape led to pandemonium. Warders were sent out in every direction, the police were notified, £100 reward was offered and speedily increased to £200. Four warders were relieved from all duties pending an enquiry by the Prisons' Board.

On Monday 9 September, the evening train through Castlebar to Achill was packed with police. A description was issued. Lynchehaun, it was said, was of stoutish build, of middle size, having grey or blue eyes, a regular nose set in fair, rounded features. A tramp in Tipperary, said to answer to the description, was arrested and released three times by different parties of police.

An ex-RIC man, who, if he were alive to-day, would be over a hundred years of age, was twenty-three at the time, and a new recruit to the force. In 1951 he described to R. J. Bennet how, when he was stationed at Kilcommon, Co. Tipperary, there had been a reported sighting of the desperado:

> On a chilly night he was taken out on patrol duty with his ageing sergeant. The sergeant would much rather have been indoors at the fireside, but orders were orders, and he could only take a few glasses of real Irish whiskey to fortify himself inwardly, and his great-coat and cap to fortify himself outwardly, against the chill night winds.
>
> Their 'beat' lay through a local cemetery and the young policeman said nervously 'Surely to God we won't find him here, sergeant?'

A blast of wind whistled eerily as the sergeant, terrified, replied hoarsely 'To tell you the truth, boy, if he's here I hope he's safe with the dead.'

He was not found there, dead or alive, nor was he discovered in any of the scores of other places, ranging from Waterford to Sligo, where he was reported to have been seen. But about two weeks or less after Lynchehaun's escape, information reached the authorities, which they believed reliable, to the effect that he had all the time been in hiding in the Raheen district, about eight miles from Maryborough, where he was reported to have secured refuge, food and a change of clothing from a family.

Brother Paul culled some items from the contemporary press:

Lloyd's Weekly (9-10-02). Lynchehaun is a well educated man with marvellous aptitude for disguise, and has had a remarkable career. He is about 5ft 9½ inches in height, of very powerful build. His eyes and hair are light brown and his complexion is fresh. He has a noticeable scar on the first finger of left hand. This scar he received while breaking and going through Mrs MacDonnell's window the night he committed the arson. It remains as a lasting mark of his evil deeds.

From an unnamed source or sources Brother Paul copied two further items:

MANY MISTAKEN ARRESTS

Police search for him began immediately after his escape from prison. Four warders were severely punished and afterwards suspended. A reward of £100 was offered for information as to his abettors in escape.

From all parts of Ireland came tidings that he had been seen or heard of. A clergyman near Dublin was detained on suspicion, a harmless missionary dragged from a train at a road-side station, a lunatic held by the police till the Clonmel Asylum Authorities stepped in to answer for him.

A poor man in Kilkenny had to run the gauntlet of being arrested on suspicion on two different occasions.

As the police portraits of Lynchehaun got better known throughout the kingdom people in England, Wales and Scotland (including a well-known English clergyman) had also to free themselves from the suspicion of being the fugitive.

A WARDER'S ODD MISTAKE

Early in January 1903 the Manchester police arrested on suspicion an ex-soldier named Meakin whom a Maryborough warder emphatically identified as the missing convict. The suspected man showed his army discharge from serving over two years in South Africa together with the medal bearing his name. And though he was the very image of Lynchehaun as portrayed in the 'Police Gazette' he was, of course, discharged with magisterial regrets and without a stain on his character.

There was consternation amongst the police authorities over the whole of Ireland. Apart from the central and embarrassing fact of the total disappearance of such a well-known prisoner, a number of related and incidental questions now agitated the authorities. Had James Lynchehaun left the country and, if so, by what means did he leave it and where did he go? Was his escape to be connected with the visit to the prison a few days before of Michael Lynchehaun, 'the Dublin brother'? Did the brothers at their meeting speak in Irish or in English? Were any prison officials party to this disgraceful episode?

A central figure in the hunt for the fugitive came to be 2nd District Inspector T. O'Brien of Tubbercurry, Co. Sligo, as, by the middle of October, it was suspected that Lynchehaun might be somewhere in his area.

He issued instructions to all Head Constables and Sergeants under his jurisdiction.

RISING PATROLS

Escaped Convict, James Lynchehaun, County of Sligo Tubbercurry, 19-10-1902

You will please have two rising patrols at each of your stations until further orders between the hours of 12 midnight and 6 a.m. in each week commencing on the receipt of this order.

These patrols should leave Barracks at different hours and to be armed with revolvers.

The patrols should lie in ambush and at likely places where this criminal would possibly pass.

If coughing, smoking, talking, or noise, be occasioned the patrols would be perfectly useless.

These morning patrols to be returned in the usual weekly list.

Nine days later O'Brien sent an enquiry to the District Inspector in Maryborough.

Tubbercurry 28-10-1902

It being currently rumoured about here that one of Lynchehaun's brothers had been seen drinking in and about Maryborough a couple of days or so prior to his, the convict's, escape, I shall feel much obliged if you let me know is there any truth in the rumour.

T. O'Brien
2nd DI

The District Inspector at Maryborough was on leave but a reply came post-haste from the Head Constable in charge.

Maryborough, 29-10-1902

Lynchehaun's brother was in Maryborough a week before the convict escaped. He came on a visit, and he interviewed Lynchehaun in the ordinary way in prison, but he only remained 5 hours in the town, and no connection could be traced between the visit and the escape.

It is rumoured they spoke in Irish but that is denied by the warder who was present at the interview.

Investigation of all the circumstances connected with the convict's escape has shown that he got out of prison and away from Maryborough unaided at the time by any person within or without the prison.

Lynchehaun's brother was traced from Maryborough

to Dublin, Roscommon, Claremorris and Achill where he arrived on 5th September before the escape,

J. Fitzgerald, Head Constable.
(DI on leave).

T. O'Brien responded:
Escaped convict, James Lynchehaun
Tubbercurry 30-10-1902

I am much obliged for your report.

Can you say if there is any truth in the rumour that Lynchehaun, on his escape, stopped for four days with a farmer near Maryborough? Also if the convict has a brother in Dublin?

T. O'Brien
2nd DI

An answer was sent immediately:

Maryborough 1-11-1902

There are theories but no reliable or definite information has been got as to where, or how, he went, or with whom he stayed or elsewhere. The Dublin brother is the person referred to overleaf.

J. Fitzgerald, Head Constable
(DI on leave).

After a few days T. O'Brien submitted the file on the missing convict to the County Inspector.

Escaped Convict, James Lynchehaun, Co. of Sligo
Tubbercurry 5-11-1902

Submitted with a request that enquiries be made from the Inspector General as to whether any clue has been obtained regarding this criminal's movements since his escape on 6th September.

It will be seen that I have special rising and other patrols on the look out for Lynchehaun, but since the receipt of Head Constable Fitzgerald's report I have grave fears that collusion has been practiced in this case. I know the Lynchehauns and I can safely say that they are a wily lot and the moves of the Dublin man have filled me with a presumption that the convict is still at or near Maryborough, or that he has left the country as merchandise.

T. O'Brien, 2nd DI

Five days later the Inspector General returned the file to O'Brien.

O'Brien's suggestion 'that he has left the country as merchandise' was marked by N. M. Davies, the County Inspector, with a large A, and he then wrote in the file:

Sligo, 10-11-1902

If A is to be utilized as information it might be well to say in what form of merchandise the convict has left or may attempt to leave the country.

N. W. Davies.

At this point the discussion of the hypothetical becomes ludicrous.

Tubbercurry 11-11-1902

I should rather think if he is gone, that he left in a sort of a crate.

T. O'Brien, 2nd DI

The file was received in Dublin Castle and drew the comment:

Our latest information is that Lynchehaun is still in the country. However, it cannot be wholly relied on as accurate, but we must still act as if it was.

The Inspector General is glad to learn that you still maintain the search for the fugitive and that your efforts are not relaxed.

Though Michael Lynchehaun did visit his brother James in Maryborough Jail a short time before the escape there are no grounds for believing there was any collusion between the jail officials and the convict or that any fixed time for the escape could have been arranged.

J. Considine, DI 13-11-1902

When Lynchehaun, who since his arrival in the United States had been known as Thomas Walshe, approached Michael Davitt, he necessarily abandoned his anonymity. The wires hummed and by 29 November Dublin Castle, and the Irish people in general, knew that Lynchehaun was at large in the Middle West of America.

On 17 December a report marked *secret* was received at Dublin Castle containing the amazing suggestion, arising out of the case, that 'an unostentatious eye' be kept on the residence of Michael Davitt at Ballybrack, Co. Dublin.

SECRET
Co. of Sligo
Tubbercurry 15 December 1902

A few days ago when on duty with Sergeant Cronin of Cloonacool he informed me that Constable Marley, or his wife, had got an extract from an American paper as to Lynchehaun being in Chicago.

I proceeded this morning to execute Revenue warrants in Cloonacool and got the newspaper extract on opposite margin from Constable Marley but he cannot say from what paper it is taken. Judging from the print it seems to me to be like the *Irish World*.

I have dwelt over the matter and I look upon the business as being strange in coupling Mr Davitt's name with the alleged transaction.

There is, no doubt, something at the bottom of this publication and perhaps it would be well if an unostentatious eye was kept about Mr Davitt's residence at Ballybrack.

T. O'Brien, 2nd DI

T. O'Brien had examined the newspaper cutting in a very cursory manner. It was not, as he thought, from the *Irish World* but from the *Evening Journal* of Chicago:

> ### FAMOUS IRISH
> ### CRIMINAL HERE
> ### JAMES LYNCHEHAUN, INCENDIARY and PRISON BREAKER
> ### Is Now In Chicago
> ### CALLS ON MR. DAVITT
>
> Special Dispatch to the *Evening Journal*
>
> *Chicago, Nov. 18.* James Lynchehaun, Ireland's most noted criminal, incendiary, attempted murderer, prison breaker and fugitive from justice, for whom hundreds of police have searched Ireland since he escaped from Maryborough Prison, September 6, is in Chicago and the local authorities may soon have him in custody.
>
> Lynchehaun made what was probably his most daring move when he approached Michael Davitt, the noted Irish leader, in the Grand Pacific Hotel.
>
> Mr Davitt saw the noted Irish fugitive approaching. Astonished and surprised, he stepped aside and scrutinised the man as he advanced.
>
> 'I want to speak to you privately,' said Lynchehaun.
>
> 'I do not want to see you,' replied Mr Davitt. 'I know who you are, and I do not want you even to speak to me.'
>
> The noted criminal retired and Mr Davitt regretted having permitted him to escape and reported the facts to the police.
>
> Lynchehaun was sentenced to Maryborough Prison in 1894 [*sic*] for life for burning the house of Mrs Agnes MacDonnell and trying to kill her. He escaped from his guards two weeks later but was captured the following winter and sent to Maryborough.
>
> He escaped from there last September.

J. Considine submitted T. O'Brien's letter and enclosure to the Under-Secretary with the comment: 'We have already heard something about Lynchehaun being at Chicago.'

It would seem that it was Davitt who, whether deliberately or not, first set the American law in motion against Lynchehaun. The news item reported from the *Evening Journal* is given in substantially the same terms in the *Chicago American* of 29 November which runs:

> Lynchehaun, for it was he, retired, and Mr Davitt regretted having permitted him to escape. Later, while in Mayor Hamson's office, Mr Davitt told of his encounter with Lynchehaun, and Inspector Hunt at once sent several of his best detectives to seek out and arrest the criminal.

R. J. Bennet, writing of this incident, says that it is unlikely that Davitt set detectives on the convict's track, and that the reporter who wrote the news paragraphs later admitted that he was relying much on rumour. But Lynchehaun, unhappily for him, had heard the same rumours, and, now in hiding from American as well as British authorities, wrote a letter to the *Chicago American*.

> Sir,
> I beg to state for your information, and that of your many respectable readers, that the statements that appeared as emanating from Mr Davitt are not only exaggerated by him but grossly misleading and incorrect.
> I was convicted on the indictment 'assault with intent to kill'. The lady injured was my landlord, and my being under service of immediate eviction was the basis on which the Crown based its charges. It is true that I left prison, but I can aver that I did not break as much as one pane of glass in the effort. Having served eight years in prison I considered that I have suffered enough for an assault which, if committed by an English landlord on an Irish peasant, would not entail three months' confinement.
> My landlady for three years previous to the assault spent that term in litigation to have me evicted from my home and land reclaimed by myself.
> Her outoffices got on fire, which spread to her house,

and unfriendly and unfair administrators of justice charged me with the crime. She is alive and well and strong as any woman on her estate, and it is not more than two years since she was bound over to keep the peace for twelve months for firing a revolver shot at one of her tenants named Denis Sweeney.

She brought all her misfortunes on herself by crossing the wrong man. An Englishman or an Englishwoman would make a great mistake interfering with me. It is true that I applied to Mr Davitt for an interview, which he declined; but why he should become a public informer of me, who never did him any injury, is more than I can understand. The world is wide for me, and if the British Government is anxious to have me back in prison I hope that it won't be through the means of Mr Davitt or any other Irishman who knows anything of the means by which prisoners are convicted in Ireland.

James Lynchehaun

Lynchehaun now went underground again and was to surface next in Indianapolis. If he was to be extradited, he had chosen Indianapolis as a place where he would get a fairer trial than, say, Chicago. It had, for him, the advantage of having a large population of Irish, many of them from the western counties and, indeed, from Achill itself.

Meanwhile back in Ireland the ballad singers plied their art. This was very near the end of the period of anonymous ballad-makers who were a feature of the Irish and Anglo-Irish scene from the late seventeenth century to the first decade of the twentieth. Not unnaturally they seized upon Lynchehaun as a worthy subject. The art of ballad-making was largely oral, and no printed Lynchehaun ballads have survived. Of the two given (both perhaps fragments of one original ballad) the first was collected from John McHugh for the *Irish Folklore Commission*.

> Some years ago here in Mayo
>   We had a great outrage;
> A lady's place in Achill
>   Was almost set ablaze.

The lady too was cruelly used
   And taken was the man,
To Castlebar Jail they did repair[1]
   And bring brave Lynchehan.

If you heard the murmuring
   On every barrack wall,
'Surely we will capture him
   If he's not gone abroad.

And even then, we'll have him still
   By extradition law,
And surely we will chain him down
   For fear he'd climb the wall'.

The second fragment was remembered from childhood by Mrs Fleming (Kathleen Gallagher) who was born in Erris, Co. Mayo, some eighty-seven years ago:

I'm Lynchehan, I'm Lynchehan,
   I am that very man,
I'm Lynchehan, I'm Lynchehan,
   Let them catch me if they can.[2]

The British forces can't do that
   Now since the chase began;
Sure the people know where e'er I go
   That I am Lynchehan.

A cattle drover from Mayo
   Was taken for me twice
Whilst I was looking at the foe,
   Sure this was very nice.

And then as well down by Clonmel
   They took an engine man;
They stopped the train, 'twas all in vain
   For here was Lynchehan.

---

[1] 'prepare' in McHugh's text.
[2] John McHugh also had this verse.

Some years ago here in Mayo
   They had a hunt before
After years of trail they captured me
   On Achill's rugged shore.

Three hundred warriors on my track,
   Sure many a mile they ran,
O'er barren ground before they found
   The famous Lynchehan.[3]

---

[3] The rhyming of the last syllable of the name as -han rather than -haun suggests that Lynchehaun himself may have been the author of the ballad.

CHAPTER XVII

Trial in Indianapolis

Although the Irish authorities knew that James Lynchehaun was somewhere on the American continent by the spring of 1903, they had no idea of his exact whereabouts. But the Lynchehaun family knew and Catherine was aware of her ultimate destination when, in late spring, in answer to pressing letters from James, she and her son crossed over to Liverpool. On 18 April, as Mrs Walshe and son, they boarded the s.s. *Campania* bound for New York, unaware of the fact that they had as fellow passengers Sergeants Young and Arthur[1] of the RIC.

They landed safely and Catherine came to realise that she was being followed at every step. Undaunted, but still pursued, she boarded a train for Cleveland, Ohio. There the pair somehow shook off their pursuers and had a joyous reunion with husband and father. Thomas and Mrs Walshe and son set off for Indianapolis where Tom worked for the prominent and wealthy Irishman, Maurice Donnelly, manager of the Terre Haute Brewing Company.

The three lived quietly and in moderate prosperity for almost four months. But somehow Sergeant Young, whose unrelenting pursuit of the escaped convict had led him to Chicago, and who was working in close co-operation with the American detective agency, Pinkerton, got wind of the fact that an Irishman, answering to James Lynchehaun's description, had been sighted in Indianapolis.

[1] The name of Sergeant Arthur is found only in the *Narrative*.

He hastened there and immediately, knowing Catherine Lynchehaun's habits, began to frequent the churches. His piety was rewarded when he came upon her as she knelt in prayer at St John's Cathedral. He followed her to her home on the near-westside of the city.

Early next morning, on 25 August, she was awakened by a hard knocking at the front door. When she opened it she was confronted by a United States Deputy Marshall, Sergeant Young of the RIC, and two private detectives of the Pinkerton Detective Agency, one of them a top operative, E. J. Weiss. The men gained admittance and the Deputy Marshall arrested Lynchehaun under a warrant sworn out against Thomas Walshe.

The sensational news of the arrest of Thomas Walshe, and of his identity with James Lynchehaun, spread throughout the city in a matter of hours.

Leaders of the Irish community, including Maurice Donnelly, came quickly to the jail. A Defence Committee was set up without delay and a firm decision was arrived at to defend Walshe or Lynchehaun 'at all costs'.

The committee included the elegant but penniless J. P. Mahoney, a member of Clann na nGaoidheal, an Irish revolutionary organisation in the United States, which had as its object the ending of English rule in Ireland. Within days money started to pour in from church door collections and from Irish societies, at first from Indianapolis, then in an ever-widening circle from every state in the Union. Lloyd B. Walton in the Indianapolis *Star Magazine*, in an article entitled 'When Indianapolis Got its Irish up', (18 February 1973) says:

> The Irish rebel was the most popular prisoner in the jail. Sheriff Metzger said, 'More people come to see him than all the rest of the prisoners in the jail'.
>
> Once 74 sympathizers talked to him through the gates, and the telephone jangled constantly with people sending their best wishes. The sheriff said that the chief fear of the Irish was that Lynchehaun would be 'spirited away' — he constantly got phone calls in the middle of the night asking if the prisoner was still there and if he was all right.

The amount subscribed was so great that on the conclusion of the legal proceedings in Indianapolis the committee had sufficient balance in hand to publish in book form what purported to be a complete account of the proceedings:

AN IRISH AMERICAN VICTORY
OVER GREAT BRITAIN

Complete Proceedings in the Great Extradition Case of Edward VII v. James Lynchehaun, as Tried in the United States Court in Indianapolis.

The claim to 'completeness' is misleading. The book contains 130 pages. It has pictures of the twelve Irish members of the Committee for the Defence of Lynchehaun, of the counsel for the defence, the Hon. Ferdinand Winter, Henry N. Spaan, the Hon. Addison C. Harris, and United States Commissioner, the Hon. Charles W. Moores who was to adjudicate, but unfortunately, none of the defendant. It contains the speeches for the defence made by Spaan and Harris, the important decision given at great length by Judge Baker on the place of trial, and finally the judgement of Commissioner Moores. But since the book is strictly a partisan document little space is devoted to the prosecuting counsel, Jesse La Follette of Indianapolis, and Charles Fox of New York.

The feeling of the time is shown by the words of the secretary of the committee, William L. O'Connor: 'There is no depth of meanness to which the British government will not sink when it is persecuting an Irishman for some trivial offence. It is not a year since Irish Members of Parliament in prison were compelled to wash the clothes of outcast women. It would be a crime for this government to return him to England.'

The Indianapolis Committee, doubtless composed of moderate nationalists as well as extremists, made it quite clear that they were fighting for a principle, and not for James Lynchehaun. In an 'explanatory statement' they say: 'The Committee desires it to be understood that this battle was fought on principle to establish a sacred right, the right of asylum for political offenders. *At no time did the personality of the defendant enter into the case'.*

The italicising of the last sentence is as significant as the omission of a portrait of James Lynchehaun from the book. It means that a substantial number of committee members had the gravest doubts as to his character and personality.

At the arrest of Lynchehaun the 'English detectives' — that is, the Irishman Sergeant Young and Pinkerton's agents — produced a 'certificate of conviction' of Lynchehaun in the British court and the British government at once made the claim that 'the prisoner, being an escaped convict, should be returned immediately to the demanding government'.

The Irish, in the Committee's words, felt 'that, if the English government's demand was allowed to go unchallenged in this case, precedent would be established, which would, in years to come, deprive many a soldier of liberty from securing shelter under the protecting folds of the American flag, that glorious emblem which waved in battle over the Irish Brigade in the Civil War under the leadership of the "escaped convict", General Thomas Francis Meagher, who was "sentenced to death by the same English government".'

The case against Lynchehaun was based upon an extradition treaty concluded between the United States of America and the United Kingdom in 1842 and some amendments to that treaty made in 1889.

Normally an extradition case would be that of a government seeking to extradite a criminal who had escaped from its jurisdiction soon after committing his crime, and the purpose of the extradition would be to bring him, for the first time, before the bar of justice in his own country. But Lynchehaun presented a type of case that had not occurred before in that he had already been convicted. There could, the British held, be no review of a United Kingdom conviction by an American court.

Besides this there were constitutional differences between the two entities involved in the treaties. The United Kingdom was governed by a common law. But in the Federal scene of 1903 there were — to quote a subsequent court judgement on this case — 'no common-law crimes of the United States, and ... the crime of murder, as such, is not known to the national government, except in places over which it may exercise exclusive jurisidiction'.

To appreciate the subleties of the Lynchehaun case — which became a leading case in Federal law — these differences between a unified state such as the United Kingdom, and a genuinely federal state such as the United States, must be firmly borne in mind. In order to extradite a supposed criminal from the territory of one of the contracting parties it would be necessary, according to the treaty of 1842, to show that the criminal act alleged to have been committed in one area would also be a criminal act if committed in the other. Thus it would be necessary to show, in whatever court in the United States, that Lynchehaun's supposed criminal acts in Achill would also be criminal if committed in Indiana, or New York, or New Jersey, or in whatever state his arrest took place. This, of course, meant that Lynchehaun's original crime would have to be examined anew in the United States and this is what was to happen. There could be no extradition if the original crime was political.

In the light of these general considerations one may look at the events in proper sequence.

At the first sitting of the court before Commissioner Moores on 7 September 1903, the case was only partially tried in order to give counsel for the British time to send to Ireland for a corrected record of the prisoner's conviction.

At the next meeting the counsel for the British Crown dismissed the proceedings before Commissioner Moores, but immediately afterwards caused the re-arrest of Lynchehaun on a warrant from the United States Commissioner, John A. Shields, in the Southern District of New York, a warrant which had been issued as far back as 6 June. The British authorities would probably be glad to have the case tried in New York and to escape from the strong Irish resistance that had been organised in Indianapolis.

Counsel for the defence replied to this move by seeking, on the petition of Thomas Walshe, a writ of *habeas corpus* from Judge Francis E. Baker of the United States Circuit

Court in Indianapolis. Judge Baker granted the writ and made the important point in law that an extradition case must be tried in the place where the arrest is made:

> I shall hold, until controlled by explicit legislation or until the Supreme Court shall by definite construction declare that the makers of the treaty intended that an accused person, presumably innocent, could be taken from Alaska to New York for the purpose of a preliminary hearing, or that an American citizen, presumably innocent, could be taken from Australia to London, for the purpose of a hearing, that no such intention was within the views of the makers of the treaty, and that they intended that when the basis of the extraditability of the crime was made the law of the place where he was found, that the hearing would be had there, similarly to the hearing where he would be committed for trial if the offence had been committed in the place where he was found (*Complete Proceedings*, p. 21).

The prisoner was released, and re-arrested again immediately upon a third complaint made before Judge Baker who thereupon issued a warrant directing that the case for extradition be heard before Commissioner Moores. The matter of the place of the trial had been disposed of and to secure the release of the prisoner it was incumbent upon the defence to prove that Lynchehaun's crime had been political.

Much was made of the fact that the Attorney General for Ireland had conducted the case. Lynchehaun told the court of the procedure involved in empanelling a jury. The defence had twenty challenges, and when nineteen of these were exhausted only three jurymen had been selected. The Attorney General now had a clear field. As each member of the panel came forward he was asked 'How much rent do you pay?', and he had the right to challenge any man who paid less than £40, that is, two hundred dollars. By this weeding process the Attorney General had, in a large measure, selected large property holders. His next question was 'Are you a member of the Land League?' and if the answer was 'yes' the would-be juryman was told to stand aside. The third question asked, according to Lynchehaun's dubious testimony, was 'Are you a member of the Brotherhood?' With regard to the matter of empanelment Addison Harris recalled to the mind of the court an event that had occurred in that very room in his own memory.

A jury was being empanelled to try a case of a political party nature. Certain people in a certain county in the state of Indiana were indicted for violating the national election laws of the country. The government employed to lead their case General Benjamin Harrison who, it was said, had come to be not only the leader of the bar in Indiana, but in the world.

After the prisoner had exhausted all his challenges, the jury was turned over to General Harrison. When he said that the prosecution was content with the jury Governor Hendricks arose and addressed General Gresham who sat on the bench saying, 'Everyone knows what is to be the result of this trial.'

Said General Gresham, his eyes flashing with fire, 'Governor Hendricks, what do you mean, sir?'

'I mean that I am informed that this panel consists now of ten men who are Republicans and two men who are Democrats, and the prisoner is a Democrat; and I say it is not a fair jury.'

Gresham said to the officer of the court: 'Is it true that in filling your panel you have only called Republicans?'

'It is, your Honor'.

'And why did you do that?'

'Because this is a political case, and I put in a jury that would render a proper verdict in support of the government.'

Judge Gresham said 'We have been friends for life, but you are discharged for the purpose of this case'.

Then he turned to a bailiff. 'You were in my regiment, I believe?'

'Yes, General.'

'Did you ever disobey a command of mine?'

'Never'.

'Will you obey me now?'

'Yes, General, I will.'

'Mr Clerk, issue a new venire to this bailiff'.

Then, addressing the bailiff, he said 'I put you in charge of the jury during this trial. You go out and bring men of the best character that you can find in the city of Indianapolis, take no excuse, and bring men of both parties to make up a new jury, because it shall never be said, so long as I preside in this court, that a man charged in politics, has not had a fair jury'.

As the case against Lynchehaun continued, the defence built up a picture of the two main participants, and of the incident at the Valley House on 6 October 1894, that bore but a distant relationship to that which had emerged from the evidence given at Castlebar. Lynchehaun was closely interrogated as to his motive in assaulting Mrs MacDonnell.

Q. Now I will ask you if in your conduct that night you were actuated at all by any motive of personal feeling directed against Mrs MacDonnell on your part?

A. Not the slightest personal motive.

Q. And what was done there, you may state what that was the result of.

A. That was the result of the combination of the tenants and of the Irish Revolutionary Brotherhood men.

Q. Now, what was the object in view in treating her in that way that was discussed at the meeting of the Irish Revolutionary Brotherhood?

A. To send her back to England, sir, to send her out of the country back to England.

Q. And what you did there that night, you may state whether or not that was done in furtherance of carrying out the plan that you had advocated from the public platform, that is, to regain the lands of Ireland for the Irish, to drive out the landlords, and to establish a republican form of government in Ireland.

A. That was the sole and only reason.

Q. Did you show any personal motives at all against the

>   woman as an individual, apart from this general motive?
>
> A. Not the slightest.
> Q. So far as you know, did any of the parties have any personal grudge against the woman?
> A. Not personally.
> Q. Did you talk with them on the subject?
> A. I knew the feeling of every man, woman, and child on the estate: I knew their feelings so far as the tenants were concerned.

Some of the new evidence, that is, evidence which had not emerged in Castlebar, may possibly be true; as, for instance, that Lynchehaun since the year 1881 had been a member of the Land League and of the Irish Republican Brotherhood (in Court always referred to as 'Revoluntionary' rather than 'Republican' to avoid any unfortunate misunderstanding in the American mind). Davitt's immediate recognition of him in Chicago suggests that they had met before, perhaps at a Land League meeting in Achill or elsewhere in west Mayo. The likelihood of his having joined the IRB on his return from England in 1881 is less easy to judge. The issue is complicated by the probability that perjury was indulged in by Lynchehaun and some of his supporters to an extent that would seem incredible to the stern puritanical and Protestant lawmen who argued and judged the case.[2]

The trial lasted for nine days. As time went on Lynchehaun flagged visibly. Brother Paul quotes from an Indianapolis newspaper as it described the scene.

> Yesterday Mrs Lynchehaun, sad and nervous, sat through the hearing with her little boy at her side. The husband sat near them when he was not on the stand.
> And in face of the burden of separating this man from his wife, which element ordinarily would enter strongly into the decision of the case, Moores must decide the case entirely on the law. Not one

---

[2] The *Mayo News* published an account of the 'Complete Proceedings' on Saturday, 10 October 1907. They refer to the evidence regarding the events at the Valley House, etc., on 6 October 1894 as 'flagrant perjury'.

whit of sympathy for the man and his wife and child can enter into the decision. It is not very often that a judge has such a case to try or such a decision to make. In jury trials at least, there are few cases into which sympathy for the man and his family would not enter to a large extent into the verdict.

The strain is telling on Lynchehaun, he is nervous, his features are drawn, his eyes are never quiet, and he no longer has the self-controlled demeanour he displayed when he was first taken into court, several weeks ago. During the past few days, as he sat for hours in the Federal courtroom, his wife and little son close by him, and the courtroom packed with sympathetic friends and keenly interested spectators to this legal drama, he has shown plainly that the strain is wearing him down. He answers all questions, either from his attorneys or those of the opposite side, quickly and nervously. And he answers all questions distinctly. He has a marked Irish brogue.

The court was presented with a picture of James Lynchehaun as being the most important revolutionary in Achill at the time of the crime. Accounts of the IRB in Achill, its aims and methods, were given by a number of people 'who belonged to the Brotherhood', their names being Conway, Vesey, McNamara, Corrigan, Lynch, and the prisoner; two other witnesses, O'Mahony and Donnelly, gave evidence as to the operations of the IRB in other parts of Ireland.

Of the evidence of these witnesses, that of Thomas J. Lynch, 'a reputable citizen of Indianapolis, and a former resident of Achill Island' is quoted at length. The possibility was hardly adverted to that in this case Lynch was probably an anglicisation of Lynchehaun and he would thus have been at least a distant relative of the accused. The questioner was Henry Spaan.

Q. Now, what was the contention of the tenants, as to what rights they asserted over the land? What did they claim?

A. This land came down to them from time without record, from their great, great ancestors, and they naturally felt that it belonged to them; by right of title it belonged to them, and their ideas were to banish by any means whatsoever, to banish them from the place so that the lands would belong to the people.

Q. Were those matters spoken of in public meetings?

A. Why, certainly, that was the drift of those meetings, and the object of them.

Q. Now then, the tenants, their theory was that the land having been occupied by them and their ancestors from time immemorial, of right belonged to them?

A. Yes, sir, they called those landlords usurpers, that usurped their rights, of what rightfully belonged to them.

(After detailing the specific cause of complaint for the charging of rent on pastureland that heretofore had been common the examination continued:)

Q. Now, you may state what expressions of feeling you heard among the people as the result of that conduct?

A. Well, the expressions of feeling were that they should do anything, burn them out, kill them out, do anything in order to banish them from the place so that they could get the place to themselves.

Q. Were those acts of the landlords spoken of at those meetings?

A. Certainly.

Q. And how were they received by the crowd?

A. Received with cries of 'Banish them', 'Burn them out', 'Get rid of them any way'.

Q. Was that conduct characteristic of all those meetings that you were at?

A. All of those meetings. Yes, sir.

Q. In conversation with people over this island, or at their meetings at other places where you got together, you may state whether or not there were expressions of similar character used?

A. It was always the same.

Q. What was the general feeling, then, of that class of people that you have described, towards the landlords?

A. Why, the general feeling towards the landlords was harsh, and they considered the landlords the English representatives in Ireland, and their feeling towards them was just the same as towards the English government, and their ultimate object was to banish both out of the country and form a government for the people and by the people.

Q. Now, I will ask you if those matters, if those doctrines of self-government, whether or not they were proclaimed in those meetings?

A. Only in Irish, because if they were spoken in English it was treason.

Q. They were talked in Gaelic?

A. They were talked in Gaelic; if talked in English they would be arrested.

(After stating that he had known the prisoner in Ireland, had attended meetings addressed by him, and had heard his speeches, the interrogation continued as follows:)

Q. Now, what were the leading ideas in his thought — in his address?

A. To, if possible, procure the land for the people.

Q. And anything else?

A. And by, as a general run of all meetings, his talk was, if possible to procure the land for the people and break the power of the English government in the place.

Q. Now, was anything said in his advocacy of any particular form of government?

A. Not in open meetings in the English language; if he talked anything like that, it was done —

Q. (Interrupting) Did you hear him talk in Gaelic?

A. I heard him talk that in Gaelic, or the Irish, as we call it.

Q. Was that at a meeting of the Irish tenantry, at a meeting of the Irish?

A. Yes, sir.

Q. What did he say in Gaelic on those occasions?

A. He said as much as that by overthrowing the landlord power it was the first step towards overthrowing the English government and in that way establish a republic like the United States.

Q. Now, you may state if you know whether or not he was considered a leading character among your people over there in Ireland on those subjects.
A. He certainly was.

According to the evidence there was a delegate meeting of the IRB in Achill on 2 October 1894, and fifteen or sixteen delegates represented the entire tenantry of the island. Lynchehaun, who was district organiser for the Brotherhood, was amongst those present. Five of the delegates were tenants of Mrs MacDonnell and there was a discussion of her exactions, prosecutions, and evictions. For the moment discussion was closed but at a further meeting on 4 October a plan of campaign was adopted. Her barn and her house were to be burned and an effort was to be made by the tenantry to frighten her. Lots were drawn to determine which member should fire the barn, which the house, and three were chosen to commit the personal assault. The prisoner was not one of these.

A few minutes after eight o'clock on the night of 6 October the fire broke out, and Lynchehaun, then at home, hastened to the scene. There he found about half the MacDonnell tenantry gathered. As he and Mrs MacDonnell stood in the midst of men and women who were engaged in spreading the fire while pretending to put it out, Lynchehaun struck her with his fist. She staggered into the arms of a party of men and women, and in the mêlée she was badly injured. Amongst those into whose hands she had fallen were the three who had been selected by lot to punish her.

It was pointed out to the court that the man Boycott, who gave a new word to the English language, carried on his oppressions in the neighbouring estate. Thomas Lynch's evidence as to the behaviour and character of Mrs MacDonnell was quoted in Henry Spaan's argument:

> This woman has been called, in this case, an old lady, and my client has been denounced because he was one of fifteen or sixteen that got together to have her whipped that night. Well, if the evidence is at all true, your Honor, that woman deserved a very good thrashing; there is no

doubt about that; and, as my client said, if she had been a man she would have been shot. Two or three instances with reference to her conduct came to light and I use those simply to illustrate the fact that they were entitled to consider her in the same class with the others. It seems that there was a little lake there where the people went to get fresh water, the freest gift of God under the sun, next to air! Who would deny a child, or a mother, a drink of water? Who would keep them away from water where it was boundless and plentiful in the shape of a lake? This woman did that. It is the testimony of Mr Lynch, not of my client, that she built a fence around the water, so that her tenants could not have good water. This act shows her character beyond any question. She was an interloper there, a newcomer there, who had bought this land at auction. She had opportunities to ameliorate the downtrodden conditions of those people who had to live on shell-fish. But instead of doing that she seemed to be actuated by a demoniacal desire to do them all the injury she could, even denying them water where it was just as free as God could give it.

Then there is the instance of the poor little boy who built a little hut out of sticks and mud to save the remainder of a flock of geese from the foxes. The woman came with two bailiffs — English bailiffs, paid by English law — and pulled down the little hut, and the geese were destroyed by the foxes that lived wild upon the mountainside and could drink God's water whenever they wanted to. It was just such acts of tyranny, just such acts of personal injustice, that made these landlords hated by the tenants.

The evidence given at Castlebar is far from suggesting that the crowd that assembled at the Valley House on the night of 5 October was in any way politically motivated. The only suggestion of political or agrarian feeling on that night was the act of the 'cursing women', who warned the people away from the house, that their presence there would be misconstrued by the police, and they would all be arrested.

But in the Indianapolis courtroom it appeared that there

had occurred in the Valley on the evening of 6 October a minor uprising of the oppressed tenantry. In every way (except, of course, scale) this minor uprising was to be compared with the American Revolution, and the 'riot' in the Valley was not dissimilar to the Boston Tea Party. With similar reservations the incident could be compared to the French Revolution. Mrs MacDonnell had been treated in a barbarous fashion. Yes, but many more grievous outrages were commited by the revolutionary populace in the years leading up to 1776. Addison Harris, under ten headings, enumerated the appalling excesses of the French Revolution, and followed with an account of Marie Antoinette, with the implication that, everything being on a reduced scale, the part of the unfortunate Queen of France was played in Achill by Mrs MacDonnell:

> So that we have to expect that whenever the passions of men are aroused by what they feel to be a political wrong inflicted upon them, and they seek redress, it finds expression in the hot crimes of passion and not in the usual crimes of a common kind. Why, think a moment of Marie Antoinette. She was the child of Marie Therese, the greatest queen of Europe; a queen who sat at the head of the House of Hapsburg which had been on the throne of Austria for six hundred years. Marie Antoinette, a girl of fifteen, comes from Vienna to Paris to be the Queen of the French. She comes, the child of luxury, a woman of culture, of great address, of powerful ability, and when the revolution breaks out she is no more to blame than anyone else of the noblesse whom the populace are incensed against. But the people, taking her as the representative of the class against which they bear resentment, taking her as the product of the system which has deprived them of their lands and made them slaves to labor, without the reward of wage — she is taken by a mob to the guillotine. The first woman in France! If you look at if from the civil side it was a cruel act, but if you look at it from the political side it was a natural act, as an expression of the fierce hate and of the deep-seated passion which the people of France held against the nobles

and those who deprived them of what they thought was their common rights in the land of France.

Making his way through the exaggerated, and sometimes perjured, evidence, Commissioner Moores gave judgement that the crime was political, that the assault on Mrs MacDonnell was incidental to, and a part of, a popular disturbance; that the popular disturbance, including the prisoner's part in it, had its origin and cause in a popular movement to overthrow landlordism. But Lynchehaun did not escape unscathed; rather was he treated with contempt in the Commissioner's judgement:

> The testimony of the prisoner as to the final act is uncontradicted and it is unsupported. Nevertheless, upon many material phases of this case, phases tending to establish his defence, his story is supported by the uncontradicted evidence of other witnesses. If it were not for this corroboration, a decision of this case might be harder to reach. The prisoner's first oath in the court that was to hear his plea for liberty was a denial of his identity. This must have been deliberate perjury. One is apt to think that a political refugee should be a hero and a patriot. And much has been said in this trial about Robert Emmet. It is a far cry from that immortal dreamer to the agitator who, after his cowardly assault upon a defenceless woman, seeks to charge against his associates the odium of a detestable crime.... Disgraceful though an assault on a woman must always be, I am convinced that, under the terms of the extradition treaty with Great Britain, this was an offence of a political character for which the prisoner cannot be surrendered. Let him be discharged.

Brother Paul shows by a single comment that he was not impressed by the defence claim that Lynchehaun was 'at the head of from 600 to 1600 men'. 'A lie', he comments, and curtly passes on. As he approaches the end of his *Narrative* he is clearly losing sympathy for his subject.

Lynchehaun still faced certain dangers. Under pressure from the British (who, no less than the Irish had a principle to fight for) an appeal was made to the Supreme Court by Henry C. Pettit, Marshal for the District of Indiana, against Judge Baker's decision given in the Federal Court in Indianapolis. A decision in the Marshal's favour would put Lynchehaun at risk again. Percy Sanderson, His Majesty's Consul General at New York, wrote to His Majesty's Principal Secretary of State for Foreign Affairs: 'I have the honour to report that the Supreme Court of the United States has granted the motion to advance the hearing of the Appeal against Judge Baker's decision in respect of the warrant granted for the arrest of Lynchehaun, and that the case has been set down for argument on the 4th of April next'.

The Supreme Court was almost as good as its word: the case was argued on 6 April 1904, and a lengthy judgement, sustaining Judge Baker's decision, was given on 2 May.

CHAPTER XVIII
The Playboy: An Buachaill Báire

When the Supreme Court, by its decision of 4 May 1904, made Lynchehaun a free man he still had a problem to face. The British would not give up. He had, after all, entered the United States under a false name and could, perhaps, be forcibly sent home under the immigration laws. But the authorities would hardly take such an action as it would inevitably create disturbance amongst the numerous, influential and ever-growing Irish community. The Irish in Cleveland took up the matter. They approached the powerful king-making Republican senator, Marcus Alonzo Hanna (Mark Hanna), who then approached the President, Theodore Roosevelt, and with his intervention all remaining difficulties were sorted out, except of course, for the British who still had not got their man.

At this time, Brother Paul tells us, Lynchehaun became an agent for an insurance company, and for extra income, taught the Irish language by night.

But these two occupations did not satisfy either his ambition or his cupidity, so he abandoned both and took to saloon business which he found far more lucrative, and easier for his rheumatic legs than travelling for an insurance company.

In January 1906, while ill, he was visited by no less a person than Charles Warren Fairbanks, Vice-President of the

United States. Brother Paul quotes for this event a press report that, doubtless with ironic intention, is in the style of a magazine article chronicling the doings of high society.

12-1-1906. An Indianapolis paper of this date states that Vice-President Charles W. Fairbanks called on James Lynchehaun, the Irish escaped convict (or, as some call him now, the Irish political exile) at his home in 1912 Howard Street, Indianapolis, and found his condition much improved. Lynchehaun had been in a serious condition for several weeks from rheumatics.

Mr Fairbanks met Lynchehaun during the negotiations for extradition in 1903–4 which resulted in his release from British custody. The sick man expressed his pleasure at having the honor of being visited by such an honorable gentleman, and said he felt 50% better since such a distinguished man condescended to visit him, a poor exile of Erin. He hopes to have so far recovered from rheumatics contracted in caves and prisons in Ireland and America as to be able to resume business in a few weeks.

His recovery was as speedy as predicted, and little more than a month later the local papers show him appearing at a cultural event which involved him closely, a lecture by the Irish republican, J. P. O'Mahoney, who had been on the Defence Committee fighting his extradition:

15-2-1906. James Lynchehaun, the Irish exile, attended a meeting of the Gaelic Society in Indianapolis, where Mr J. P. O'Mahoney gave a lecture, illustrated with stereopticon views, on the escape of James Lynchehaun from a convict prison in Ireland, and his subsequent struggle for liberty in the Federal Court at Indianapolis. Mr Lynchehaun was present at the entertainment, and was accorded an ovation. He related portions of his history in Gaelic as the views were thrown on the screen.

In the following July Lynchehaun had some serious trouble in his saloon. Brother Paul hears of it from an Indiana newspaper or journal, and tells it in his own inimitable style.

In the saloon business he made a lot of money and a lot of trouble for himself too, as the following instance out of many others will show. On the 14-7-06 a nigger named Harry Simms entered Lynchehaun's saloon; after some drinks some altercation arose between them. Lynchehaun ordered Simms leave, but the latter refused. Lynchehaun evicted him by force. The nigger went to a hardware store where he pawned his watch and bought a revolver, returned to Lynchehaun's saloon, placed himself outside the door and behind a large telegraph post, then started a fusillade through Lynchehaun's windows. As nigger was firing in, Lynchehaun was firing out. About twenty shots were exchanged between them, still neither was wounded; while nigger was sheltered by telegraph post Lynchehaun ducked behind the counter.

Police were sent for. They pursued nigger on bicycles. As Simms ran through cornfields police lost track of him for a short time. Finally they were directed by a man who was looking out from an elevated window and saw the direction Simms went. So the police and a number of town boys renewed the pursuit.

When nigger saw them approaching him he fired at one of the policemen and grazed his leather legging twice within one inch of each other. Finally he was captured, bound in irons, laid in prison to await judgement for his rash deeds. When captured he begged of the mob not to lynch him, this being the usual treatment given to niggers who grossly insult or assault white people in the southern[1] states of America.

In 1906 Lynchehaun had an unpleasant social experience. Douglas Hyde, president and founder of the young and vigorous Gaelic League, and later President of Ireland, visited Indianapolis while on a propaganda and fund-raising tour of the United States. Hyde's meeting with Lynchehaun must, for the latter, have been uncomfortably reminiscent of his meeting with Davitt some years previously. Hyde was the second great and representative Irishman to rebuff him publicly. Hyde writes of the encounter in *Mo Thurus go hAmerice* (My Journey to America) (1937):

> *Tá an Loingseachán i nIndianapolis* ... Lynchehaun is in Indianapolis. England tried her best to get hold of him

---

[1] Indiana is, of course, a northern state.

but the Irish got together and they defeated England's attempts at getting hold of him. They did that through spite and hatred of England, and it appears that they did not know that he was a blackguardly ruffian. The scoundrel himself said, 'When I die Indianapolis will be written on my heart', and, indeed, he has good reason to be thankful to the people of that city. He was on the platform when I spoke, and he came to shake my hand, half ashamed to come near me. At first I did not realise who he was, but (then) I said to him in Irish, 'I heard of you before', and I turned away from him.

In the meantime, back in Ireland the Lynchehaun legend had long taken firm root and was achieving sturdy growth. In 1904 the dramatist, John Millington Synge, visited Co. Mayo for the first time, heard the story of Lynchehaun, and associated it mentally with another case, the Aran case, where a parricide had been harboured by a western community. Towards the end of the year he had completed the first draft of his most famous play, *The Playboy of the Western World,* which, after much revision, was first produced in the Abbey Theatre, on 26 January 1907. The riots that broke out on the first production, and were repeated many times in Ireland and America, are a part of literary history. The central theme was that of a supposed murderer being given sanctuary from the police by a Mayo peasant community, and especially by its womenfolk.

In a letter to Stephen McKenna defending his play Synge says:

> It isn't quite accurate to say, I think, that the thing is a generalisation from a single case. If the idea had occurred to me I could and would just as readily have written the thing as it stands without the Lynchehaun case or the Aran case. The story — in its *essence* — is probable, given the psychic state of the locality. I used the cases afterwards to convert critics who said it was *impossible*.

Synge, however, in the course of his play, and thus preceding the criticism that ensued upon its production, has a reference to the trial of Lynchehaun in Castlebar, and to the nature of his attack on Mrs MacDonnell, implicit confirmation of the importance of the Lynchehaun case in his development of the theme. The reference has not apparently been understood.

Susan Brady, a village girl, is encouraging Sara Tansey, to follow Christy Mahon: 'Maybe he's stolen off to Belmullet with the boots of Michael James, and you'd have a right so to follow after him, Sara Tansey, and you the one yoked the ass-cart and drove ten miles to set your eyes on the man bit the yellow lady's nostril on the northern shore'.

The 'northern shore' is the Valley, Lynchehaun is the man who did the shocking deed, and 'yellow' is Synge language for 'English' or 'Protestant'. The word echoes Seán Buidhe, or 'Yellow John' which connotes Englishman; in a note-book which contains some early fragments of *The Playboy*, Synge has a translation of an Irish folksong in which the poet gets from King George 'A woman with yellow hair', the typical English colouring.

Synge's contention that the story of *The Playboy* is in its *essence* probable, given the psychic state of the locality, is not convincing. The great difference between the case of Christy Mahon, the central character, and Lynchehaun, is that Christy sought refuge in an utterly strange community, claiming to be the murderer of his father, was received, hidden, given sanctuary and respect: whereas Lynchehaun was hidden by close friends and relatives for a crime that (if marginally) was less than murder and was committed against an outsider who, at least to some degree, in a period of agrarian tension, was regarded as an oppressor of the peasantry. Synge's play, which he calls 'a comedy', must be enjoyed and appreciated without conceding to it any of the virtues of an acute sociological study, which, in the course of controversy, the dramatist seems to claim for it.

The term 'playboy', applied by Synge to Christy Mahon, is a translation of an Irish expression, *buachaill báire*, a 'hurling boy'. The term, though translated 'trickster', 'playboy', is not necessarily depreciative. The image behind the expression is that of a young man with a hurley stick driving for a goal. But the driving does not take place on a miniscule modern pitch but, when the match is between parishes, ever onward over miles of countryside or miles of beach. In its most ancient and heroic form hurley is played by the Irish hero Cú Chulainn who (though the term *buachaill báire* was not used for him, had hardly, in fact, been invented) drives a ball from his home in Mag Muirthemni in Louth to the centre of the Ulster Kingdom near Armagh. There, on a great playing field, he drives alone against a hundred and fifty youths, and compels them to admit his superiority. He is the *buachaill báire* par excellence.

In Synge's play the *buachaill báire* does not exist as such until he is built up by Pegeen Mike's imaginative appreciation acting upon Christy's own hitherto latent qualities. He becomes virile, a winner at sports, a man with a contempt for the police, and with the gifts of fiery language and poetic imagination. He is the opposite in every way of the careful, conservative, priest-fearing namby-pamby, Shawn Keogh, whom Pegeen is destined to marry.

Synge could not have known all the stories relating to Lynchehaun, for some of them happened or came into being after the creation of his play. On the other hand he could have known many anecdotes, in the same mould, concerning Lynchehaun which are no longer in existence today.

Lynchehaun was perhaps a classic example of the *buachaill báire*. He had a contempt for the law and for 'British Justice'; in fact in his arrogance he had a contempt for everybody but himself, assuming the pose of genius; that he was a winner in sporting events is not recorded, but at least, as will be seen, he was the first to drive a horse and cart over the bridge at Achill Sound after its opening in 1886. His daring is emphasised in all the stories concerning him, but it is sufficient to anticipate that which tells how, for a wager, that he might easily lose, he could set his stake as high as imprisonment with hard labour for the rest of his life.

Brother Paul gives an account of the riots that took place on the first presentation of the Synge play. His account is culled from the Irish daily papers. His other comments, his antagonism to Synge, his antipathy to the Abbey Theatre, and his highly inaccurate summary of the play are more worthy of notice.

CALUMNY ON MAYO LIFE

A play alleged to be founded on the Lynchehaun case.

Dubliners' protest against its production.

(1907). Remarkable scenes were witnessed during the last week of January in the Abbey Theatre, Dublin, when the managers of this so-called Irish and National Institution attempted to produce a drama entitled *The Playboy of the Western World*. It was written by a Mr Synge, and its plot is briefly as follows.

Michael James Cleary is a publican, living in a little drinking shop in a wild coast of Mayo. His wife[2] Pegeen helps him in serving his customers and runs the house. On the night of the story Cleary wishes to go to a neighbouring wake, where there will be 'lashins and lavins' of good poteen drink, but he cannot leave Pegeen unprotected. He appeals to her friend Mathew Gallagher[3] to stop to protect her; but Mathew declined to spend a night under circumstances that might compromise his reputation — not Pegeen's (mark the Synge touch of spleen) but his own — in the eyes of Father — the parish priest of the place. Worse followed, but omitted to be repeated here for modesty sake.

The audience strongly protested against the play as a vile calumny on Irish peasant life, particularly coming as it did from a theatre which invited the sympathy and support of the Irish nation; but the management insisted on its production with the result that a general uproar ensued ...

In an interview with a press representative the author, Mr Synge, said the idea of the play was suggested to him by the fact that a few years ago a man, Lynchehaun, who was a most brutal murderer of a woman in the island of Achill, and yet by the aid of Irish peasant women, managed to conceal himself from the police for months and then get off to America where the English authorities failed to get him extradited.

Mr Synge, the author, was drawing largely on his imagination when he described Lynchehaun as a brutal murderer of a woman, as the lady referred to still lives (1907) in her very mansion that was burned in Achill Island. As she got £1000 insurance and

---

[2] Correctly 'daughter'.
[3] Correctly 'Shawn Keogh'.

£1000 as a claim for malicious injury, with these £2000 she got it into a better state than it was before.

The writer of these pages who knows the Mayo life more intimately than Mr Synge, can state that his efforts to represent Mayo peasant women as the willing harbourers of murderers are founded on calumny gone raving mad. He has cited the case of Lynchehaun, but perhaps he does not know that when that audacious scoundrel, as he was pleased to call him, was being sentenced at Castlebar assizes in 1895, Judge Gibson paid a special compliment to the 'peasant woman, Mary Gallagher' who was the principal means of bringing the criminal to justice. He told this simple, truthful, Achill girl that she was a credit to the religion to which she belonged, and to the island from which she came, owing to how much she endangered her own life to save that of Mrs MacDonnell, who was English and Protestant, while Mary Gallagher was Irish and Catholic. This shows there were charitable, courageous and self-sacrificing women, even in the Island of Achill, west Mayo.

In June 1907, the Lynchehaun saloon in Cleveland closed its doors and the proprietor quietly disappeared from public view. In July, according to Brother Paul, he appeared in Dublin, staying at the Shelbourne Hotel and visited the International Exhibition. There would be little point in examining the hotel register, for Lynchehaun would not, of course, have used his own name.

He then went, as Mr Cooney of New York, on a visit to Co. Mayo. The high point of this trip was his visit to his parents in Achill. He left hastily, with a gift of £200 from his father, to make a tour covering northern England, Norway, Denmark and Germany.

The question as to whether or not he had visited Achill became a matter of controversy in the *Mayo News,* but the matter was eventually put beyond all doubt by communications from himself to that paper.

The first public intimation of his having visited the island was an item in the *Mayo News* of 3 August. The writing of this item is completely set apart from the general style of the paper. It was written from the viewpoint of Lynchehaun, arrogant, vaunting, contemptuous of the police and of authority, mocking Head Constable Hicks who, at the time of the extradition proceedings, had come to Indianapolis to identify him, and finally referring in a tasteless manner to Mrs MacDonnell. It is difficult not to conclude that it was contributed, though perhaps anonymously or under a pseudonym, by Lynchehaun himself, and subjected perhaps to slight editorial treatment.

A DISTINGUISHED VISITOR

Mr James Lynchehaun Revisits his Native Hills

It is stated with every semblance of truth that during the past few weeks James Lynchehaun visited his native Achill and spent a pleasant time there with his friends. It is also stated, quite unnecessarily, we think, that the distinguished visitor travelled *incognito,* and thus escaped attentions which to one of his modest temperament might have been unpleasant. The story goes that a mild-looking American gentleman of middle age arrived one fine afternoon at Mulranny railway station and, approaching a car-owner, informed him that he desired to be conveyed to friends of his named Cooney in a certain part of Achill. The car-owner, an old acquaintance, remarked slyly 'I think you want to go a little farther'. The visitor 'guessed' he did not, and declaring that his name was Cooney, said he wanted to see his friends before returning to the States. 'I think your name is James Lynchehaun,' replied the Jehu. But the traveller, nothing daunted, completed arrangements for the drive, and proceeded to Achill where, as Mr Cooney of New York, he spent a quiet but delightful day!

Not being weavers of fiction[4] we are unable to describe what the feelings of the passenger were as he drove through the scenes of his first marvellous escape midway between Mulranny and the island. We are further assured that during the past week the Mulranny car-owner received a postcard all the way from Denmark (signed by the world-famed Lynchehaun) congratulating

---

[4] The suggestion that only a creator of fiction could adequately describe his sensations is a ploy used elsewhere by Lynchehaun.

him on his sharpness and stating that he was the only individual in the whole stupid British Isles who had recognised him, without being first told who he was. We should like to see the postcard.[5] After his first escape that entertaining organ the *Hue and Cry* did us the signal honour of describing the fugitive as 'Achill Correspondent of the *Mayo News*', omitting however to state that he was an ex-policeman and an ex-National Teacher. True it was when the *Mayo News* was in its infancy James Lynchehaun sent us several well-written reports and interesting contributions concerning Achill, most of which appeared in our columns; so that we are well acquainted with his hand-writing, and shall be delighted 'for the sake of old times' to have a glance at the Danish postcard if the recipient will so kindly oblige.

Of course it sounds unlikely in the extreme that one whose precious body the great British Government spent thousands of pounds in vainly attempting to secure, and who was the subject of serious complications between the two most powerful nations in the world, would thus expose himself to the danger of once more being caught and sent to durance vile for the remainder of his natural life. But our readers do not require to be informed that Mr James Lynchehaun is no ordinary man. Quite possibly his well-known sporting proclivities getting the better of him, he longed for another run with the nimble minions of British law. Moreover, has he not already demonstrated the truth of the couplet

> Stone walls do not a prison make,
> Nor iron bars a cage.

'Mr Cooney', we are informed, is now on the high seas and will resume his more famous patronymic on landing again in the hospitable 'Land of the Free' which proved so secure a sanctuary for him a few years ago. We are only surprised that before bidding adieu to his native land he did not pay a friendly visit to Head Constable Hicks of

---

[5]The paper acquired the postcard, or rather letter-card, authenticated the writing and signature, and published a facsimile (blotting out the name of the recipient whose initials were M.M.).

Castlebar, if only to have a chat with him on extradition treaties, and other international subjects, about which they had differences of opinion when they met in the United States. But it is probable, had he done so, the Hicks reception would have been so cordial that the tourist's stay might be too prolonged for his tastes, and interfere with other engagements of a more agreeable character. Another old acquaintance Mr Lynchehaun missed was Mrs Agnes MacDonnell of the Valley house, that amiable lady being away in England. How very enjoyable her holidays would have been had she known that her former steward had selected Achill for his vacation!

'Mr Cooney' came near to disaster, being arrested at Achill Sound during his stay. A sober, and doubtless near factual account of the incident is given in an article in the *Mayo News* of 10 October:

> During his stay 'Mr Cooney' (Lynchehaun) was actually arrested in Achill Sound on a charge of breaking into the house of a man named Peter Sweeney at Pulranny. He was taking his dinner in the new hotel. The police got Peter Sweeney's servant girl to go into the dining room to identify him, which she did, as the man who went in through the window of her master's house, he and his wife being absent. 'Cooney' was accordingly brought out of the hotel by the Achill and Mulranny police sergeants to the Achill Sound police barracks where he was charged, but the little girl in the meantime had for some cause or other changed her mind and she refused to identify the prisoner as the guilty party and he was accordingly discharged.

In the early part of this century Lynchehaun's name was commonly used as a bogeyman to frighten children. This undeserved ill-fame had a mushroom growth and probably originated in the above incident.

Brother Paul has some variants of this story, which, gullible and innocent as he often was, he presents as completely different events. The most extreme of these is grossly exaggerated and even touches on the horrific.

On arriving at his native townland, he entered a friend's house where he found only a little girl aged fourteen, minding three young children. As he was going upstairs the little girl thought to prevent him. He flung herself and the child downstairs and said he would kill them if they would not stop; he began to whet a razor. As Lavelle at Achill Sound cut his wife's neck with a razor a few weeks previous to this, it drove terror into the children. On the arrival of the Master and Mrs, who were national teachers, from their school, the children told them what the boodyman[6] did, who remained only about a half an hour. The Master went to the police at Achill Sound, reported the case, got the little girl of fourteen to swear information. Next day the police who went in search of the burglar found a man answering to his description which the little girl gave, dining at Mr Patrick Sweeney's Hotel, next house to the barrack. Two constables sat at same table, put many questions to the stranger, asked him where he came from, who answered he came from the Shelbourne Hotel, Dublin (first class hotel) where he visited the International Exhibition. Police sent for the little girl to see would she recognise him, but he had exchanged cap and coats. She said it was not he. Next evening he walked into his parents and brother, embraced and kissed them, chatted with them for a few hours, then disappeared.

So far nothing has been said as to the motive for the break-in. But fortunately amongst Brother Paul's sources was a letter dealing with the matter, and doubtless written to Brother Paul himself. The break-in was apparently as innocent as any technically illegal act can be, simply a natural desire to see the old school of his boyhood.

The Continent

Dear Friend,

I have been home to see my dear father and mother. Neither fiction nor history has recorded, or ever will, such a scene. See the old people and they will tell you all, much better than I can describe or write while on my flying tour. I left a written report in

[6] A common variant of 'bogeyman' or 'boogeyman'.

Peter Sweeney's school in his absence. I drew the staple which held the lock, left the report on the desk, then drove in the staple and made off. When I get more money I shall send him price of maps, etc., and order him burn the old torn rags on the wall. All things appear to have deteriorated in value and appearance in that school since my early days.

By this innocent act the 'playboy' generated the 'bogeyman'.

On his return to the USA two letters from Buffalo to Mr Doris, editor of the *Mayo News*, provided a sensational column for the paper. The editor comments: 'They are written in pencil and one of them, only, is signed, the signature being Jas. Lynchehaun, and both are beyond all doubt, in the hand-writing of the daring outlaw. We print them just as we received them except that we omit the name of the naval officer who, Lynchehaun says, took a paltry bribe from him, and that of a respectable resident of Mulranny to whom he refers as the only man who recognised him during his recent visit.

LYNCHEHAN!

Now in Buffalo, U.S.A.

HE SENDS US TWO LETTERS

He Inspects 14 British Men-of-War

ARRESTED on Board H.M.S. THE TALBOT

HIS VISIT TO ACHILL – RECOGNISED BY HIS BROTHER'S DOG

DELIVERS A SPEECH AND RAISES A ROW IN BELFAST

EXPLOITS IN GERMANY

Dear Mr Doris,
I read your communication to 'Lloyds's' and 'The News of the World', photo was splendid.

I travelled Europe. I was at the Liverpool Pageant; shook hands to all the Admirals and Captains; was made a prisoner on board H.M.S. *The Talbot* for smoking near the magazine. The — was my friend for a shilling, and I got off on a fool's pardon.

I visited every one of the fourteen men-of-war in the Mersey. What was I thinking about. Guess.

I was in Germany, and my passport was a sod of turf. I got over all difficulties as a sailor taking a sod of German turf to America. An English tourist camaraed me; I drew a rough sketch of one of the Hamburg docks; dropped it into his pocket; gave the tip to a policeman, and this Englishman and camera were arrested and detained. All explanations were of no avail.

I had my sod of turf under my arm, and I received more courtesy and attention than if I had a passport from the Kaiser. I was dressed in true sailor fashion. When addressed I spoke Irish only.

Now comes the best part of my story. I was Coroner's foreman on my own inquest and lost at sea. The captain was a German and an Englishman was missing. I told the captain that he went over-board. I was made foreman of the jury, and returned a verdict accordingly. I had more fun over that than I had all my lifetime. I could explain more fully, but I have a way of my own for travelling.[7]

I wanted to see poor Dominick McGovern and he was dead the very day I landed.

I searched Liverpool and Manchester for a certain informer but could not find him. My guide in Manchester was one Joe McNamarra. He didn't know me.

I went specially to see my dear old father and mother. The scene cannot be described either in fiction or history.

Two policemen had an imbecile from Claremorris to Castlebar jail. The prisoner was over 6ft. 1½in. I paid his fine to the sergeant, 3s. 6d., and gave him 1s. 3d. to pay his way back home. I challenged the sergeant to wrestle

---

[7]This whole incident is very obscure. Apparently Lynchehaun was the 'Englishman' who was missing, and he presided at an enquiry into the matter. There is not, of course, a 'jury' as such in German legal procedure. The whole story may be one of Lynchehaun's fantasies.

for £1 — he declined. Three boys of the name of Calvey from Innisbeggil, Achill, were witnesses. See them.

M____ M_____, Mulranny, was the only man that knew me. I visited Neal O'Donnell, but he was in bed.

James Lynchehaun

SPECIAL

Dear Mr Doris—

I forgot to tell you that I made an excellent inflammatory speech in Belfast for the peelers. I posed as one who struck. At the corner of Queen and Main Streets I got up a row.

I want to tell you a strange but true episode. My brother Tom's dog sniffed and smelled me all over. He embraced me with all kinds of affection. I could not get him away. He put his forepaws around my neck. He followed me for miles. I fired three revolver shots to scare him. No use. I took him up by the paw, shook it and kissed him and he returned home. I spoke to him in Irish only and he went straight home. That dog is a genuine Irish hound — see him; red coat of hair.

CHAPTER XIX
The End

Some time about 1907, Brother Paul implies, Lynchehaun deserted his lawful wife, leaving her penniless, and went to live with another woman. In March 1907 he left Indianapolis — this move and the parting from his wife may have been inter-related — and opened a saloon in Cleveland, Ohio, 'amidst a host of his own friends and acquaintances'. His name, in his favoured spelling, is found in the Cleveland City Directory, 1907, and in two subsequent years: Lynchehan, James, saloon, 3414, Detroit Avenue, N.W. The business failed, we may take it, in 1909.

McHugh's narrative, very unsound as to facts and chronology, traces Lynchehaun's decline in popularity to the public rebuff by Michael Davitt, and gives a picture of him as a strike-breaker in Cleveland. It has not been possible to get any confirmation of strike-breaking activity in American sources.

All went well until Michael Davitt arrived in Cleveland[1] during his tour of America. Lynchehaun, now established as a hero among the Irish population there, sought also to make an impression on Davitt. One day he went up to him, hand outstretched to greet him, but Michael Davitt stood stiffly in front of him, and said, in a tone of voice which certainly could not be mistaken for anything but the greatest annoyance at the impertinence

---

[1] Correctly, of course, Chicago.

of the man 'I will not shake hands with a murderer'.

That finished Lynchehaun's popularity. People got to know of the incident, and gradually the facts of the assault on Mrs MacDonnell got around. All his newly made friends deserted him, and he became a sort of outcast from society. Due to his increasing unpopularity, it became very difficult for him to obtain work, and when he did get it, he was rarely able to keep a job for any reasonable length of time. Shunned by all hands, who under ordinary circumstances would be quite friendly and helpful towards him, he now found that the only people who were willing to sympathise with him or become allies were other outcasts and desperados like himself. When a strike occurred in Cleveland he organised a gang of those fellows to replace the workers who were out on strike. They were known as the 'Blackleg Gang'. But even this attempt to eke out an existence was short-lived, as the workers were extremely hostile, so after suffering, for several days, a considerable amount of abuse, mingled with threats of worse to come, the gang at last deemed it safer to leave the job.

In 1917 Brother Paul heard a rumour that he had died:

The writer, while in Achill in June of this year, was told that Lynchehaun died or was shot in a brawl in Cleveland, Ohio. As the tree was inclined so it fell.

But the rumour was false and it would appear that, already in his late fifties, having conquered his rheumatics, he could not resist adventure, crossed the border into Canada, and joined a Scots Canadian regiment under the name of McElwaine; by so doing he doubtless honoured the memory of Adam McElwaine, the 'grog-blossomed' Presbyterian inspector of schools with whom he had an unhappy encounter in his days as a school teacher. He was made sergeant, and either while on furlough or absent without leave, could not resist another visit to Achill. Brother Paul has a supplementary note on the outcome, the last in his manuscript:

N.B. His reappearance and arrest in Achill, April 15th, 1918. Lynchehaun was visiting his friends, dressed like a Canadian soldier, when Sergeant Donevan of Mulranny arrested him and placed him in Castlebar Jail on the 7th of May, 1918. He was transferred to Maryboro from which he had escaped on September 6th, 1902.

The account of his arrest in Canadian uniform has survived locally and was recorded by Bríd ní Mhaolmhuaid, but her anecdote may be a revision of one that originally told of his visit to Achill in 1907:

> One time he arrived in Achill dressed in a Canadian soldier's uniform. He left his kit at the police barracks at the Sound and went into Sweeney's where he started drinking. He spoke in Irish to people whom he recognised, but they did not recognise him (he spoke as well in Irish as in English).
> 'Don't you know who I am?' he said to them.
> 'No', said they.
> 'Don't you know who was the first man to drive a horse and cart across the Sound bridge?'
> 'Lynchehaun', they all said.
> 'The very man', said he.
> The story went around that he was on the island so the police arrested and deported him again.

In 1977 Edmund Carroll, a former member of the RIC, and then an old man, recorded on tape an account of the arrest of Lynchehaun in Achill in 1918.

> The local police had advance warning that Lynchehaun was coming to Achill. He came into Achill Sound, walking along the railway, and went to Kilcoyne's public house. He wore the uniform of a Scots' regiment of the British army, and he got lodging at Kilcoyne's. There he was arrested in his bedroom by Sergeant Donevan, an old man within two months of retirement, and Edmund Carroll, the narrator. The desperado was handcuffed to the young policeman who, with the sergeant, had the job

of bringing him to Newport. He was the finest stump of a man you ever set your eyes on. There was an old man and a *gasúr*[2] at the arrest of him, and eighteen men under arms to receive him when he arrived at Newport.

Edmund Carroll tells us that he was released after a few months, but on condition that he remain out of Achill. Other Achill sources say that he was released on the intervention of the Canadian authorities.

Carroll saw him in Achill some time afterwards but ignored him and did not report the matter to his sergeant.

In 1895, when giving judgement on Lynchehaun, Judge Gibson had said of Mrs MacDonnell: 'This woman was endowed with splendid courage and vitality, though, poor wreck, she will live for a few and miserable years.'

His Lordship under-estimated Mrs MacDonnell's vitality. She was to live on vigorously for another twenty-eight years, wearing a false nose, an eye-patch and a veil, constantly guarded by the police, farming, horse-dealing, appearing at fairs, at court to summon her tenants for trespass and nonpayment of rent, praying devoutly on Sundays at St Thomas', Dugort.

From the time of Lynchehaun's conviction the state had provided her with permanent police protection; ironically the police on guard duty made a temporary residence of Lynchehaun's house and shop, doubtless paying the Landlady rent for their use.

On 24 September 1921, she made a will leaving everything she possessed to her son, Leslie Elliot, and the instrument was witnessed by F. Harrison, engineer, and Lucy Harrison, married woman, both of 63 Bryanston Street, London, W.1.

Death came to her suddenly on 28 May 1923. Though never given to self-indulgence the 'Yellow Lady' or '*Cailleach a Valley*' (the Old Woman of the Valley) as she had come to be called, is said to have died alone with a glass of wine in her hand that her maid had just brought to her. The

---

[2] Young lad.

shattered glass lay beside her where she fell. The total value of her estate was a little over £5000.

In 1917 Brother Paul made his last comment on Mrs MacDonnell, at first deceptively sympathetic, but (typical of all his references to her) with a sting in the tail. Following the false report of Lynchehaun's death in Cleveland he says:

The victim of his vengeance, Mrs MacDonnell, lives after him, although a wreck of his brutality for the last twenty-three years. She had her tenants processed for non-payment of rent in October 1917.

Edmund Carroll was part of Mrs MacDonnell's police guard for six months at some time after his arrest of Lynchehaun in 1918; however, during this period he never set eyes on her.

Brother Paul died, aged eighty-four, in 1928.

From 1918 onwards, James Lynchehaun is a wraith-like, insubstantial figure. His first meeting with the Irish authorities after the Treaty with Great Britain was auspicious.

Benedict Kiely, the Irish novelist, was a friend of Austin MacDonnell of Louisburg, Co. Mayo, a member of the Volunteers, who was sentenced to death in 1920, but had the sentence commuted. MacDonnell was a friend of Sean Moylan, the well-known pre-Truce IRA figure who, in the 1940's, filled successively the posts of Minister for Lands and Minister for Education under de Valera in the government of the Republic. At the time of the British withdrawal, as Moylan told Benedict Kiely, he was in command of the Irish forces who took over the barracks at Athlone. The Irish troops were doing police-duty when a drunken man was brought in, a half dozen soldiers holding him. Something clicked in Moylan's mind as he listened to the man's rantings, and he went over to him and said 'Are you Lynchehaun of Achill?' At attention right away the man said 'Yes, sir'. They shook hands, Moylan offered him a drink and peace was restored.

In December 1936, Lynchehaun was admitted to the Workhouse in Castlebar, but after thirty-two days residence there he was discharged and went to live with his brother, Tom.

According to McHugh, Lynchehaun died in or about 1937 in Girvan in Scotland and would, at that time, have been about seventy-seven. Another local account says that he died in Girvan shortly after the end of the second World War, which would leave him in his mid-eighties.

Whichever way it be *go ndéana Dia trócaire ar a anam*, may God have mercy on his soul.